# ICE COUNTRY

A Dwellers Saga Sister Novel

Book Two of

The Country Saga

David Estes

This book is dedicated to my incredible team of beta readers. Your kindness, selflessness, and gently honest feedback has helped craft this series more than you may realize.

# One

It all starts with a girl. Nay, more like a witch. An evil witch, disguised as a young seventeen-year-old princess, complete with a cute button nose, full red lips, long dark eyelashes, and deep, mesmerizing baby blues. Not a real, magic-wielding witch, but a witch just the same.

Oh yah, and a really good throwing arm. "Get out!" she screams, flinging yet another ceramic vase in my general direction.

I duck and it rebounds off the wall, not shattering until it hits the shiny marble floor. Thousands of vase-crumbles crunch under my feet as I scramble for the door. I fling it open and slip through, slamming it hard behind me. Just in time, too, as I hear the thud of something heavy on the other side. Evidently she's taken to throwing something new, maybe boots or perhaps herself.

Luckily, her father's not home, or he'd probably be throwing things too. After all, he warned his daughter about Brown District boys.

Taking a deep breath, I cringe as a spout of obscenities shrieks through the painted-red door and whirls around my head, stinging me in a dozen places. You'd think *I* was the one who ran around with a four-toed eighteen-year-old womanizer named LaRoy. (That's LaRoy with a "La", as he likes to say.) As it turns out, I think *La*Roy has softer hands than she does.

As I slink away from the witch's upscale residence licking my wounds, I try to figure out where the chill I went wrong. Despite her constant insults, narrow-mindedness, and niggling reminders of how I am nothing more than a lazy, liquid-ice-drinking, no-good scoundrel, I think I managed to treat her pretty well. I was faithful, always there for her—not once was I employed while courting her—and known on occasion to show up at her door with gifts, like snowflake flowers or frosty delights from Gobbler's Bakery down the road. She said the flowers made her feel inadequate, on account of them being too beautiful—as if there was such a thing—and the frosty's, well, she said I gave them to her to make her fat.

She was my first ever girlfriend from the White District. I should've listened to my best friend, Buff, when he said it would end in disaster.

Now I wish I hadn't wasted my gambling winnings on the likes of her.

In fact, it was just yesterday morning when I last stopped by to deliver some sweet treats, only to hear the obvious sounds of giggling and flirting wafting through the red wood of her father's elegant front door. Needless to say, I was on the wrong side of things, and much to my frustration the door was barred by something heavy.

So I waited.

And waited.

After about three hours her father returned home, and soft-hands LaRoy emerged looking more pleased with himself than a young child taking its first step. In much less time than it took for the witch to put the smile on his face, I wiped it off, using a couple of handfuls of ever-present snow and my rougher-than-bark hands. I capped him off with matching black eyes and a slightly crooked, heavily bleeding nose. He screamed like a girl and ran away crying tears that froze on his cheeks well before they made it to his chin.

Hence the big-time breakup today.

Best of luck, witch, I hope crooked-nosed LaRoy makes you very happy.

Why do I always pick the wrong kinds of girls? Answer: because the wrong kinds of girls usually pick me.

Since my formal schooling ended when I was fourteen, I've had a total of three girlfriends, one each year. None ended well, as endings usually go.

Walking down the snow-covered street, I mumble curses at the beautiful stone houses on either side. The White District, full of the best and the richest people in ice country. And the witch, too, of course, the latest girl to add to my so-not-worth-the-time-and-effort list.

I pull my collar tight against the icy wind, and head for my other girlfriend's place, Fro-Yo's, a local pub with less atmosphere than booze, where a mug of liquid ice will cost you less than a minute's pay and the rest of your day. Okay, the pub's not really my girlfriend, but sometimes I wish it was. I've been drinking there since I turned sixteen and passed the "age of responsibility".

Although it's barely midmorning, Fro's is open and full of customers. But then again, the pub is always open and full of customers. We might not have jobs, but we'll support Yo, the pub owner, just the same.

Snow is piled up in drifts against the gray block-cut stone of the pubhouse, recently shoveled after last night's dumping. Yo's handiman, Grimes, is hunched against the wind with a shovel, clearing away the last of it along the side, leaving a slip-free path to the outhouse, which will be essential later on, when half the joint gets up at the same time to relieve themselves. There are two things that don't mix: liquid ice and real ice. I've seen more broken bones and near broken necks than I'd like around this place.

"Mornin', Grimes," I say as I pass.

Grimes doesn't look up, his matted gray hair a dangling mess of moisture and grease, but mumbles something that sounds a lot like, "Icin' neverendin' colder'n chill night storms..." I think there's more but I stop listening when he starts swearing. I've had enough of that for one day. And yet, I push through the door of the obscenity capital of ice country.

"Dazz! I was wondering when you'd freezin' show up," my best friend says when I enter. Following protocol, I stamp the snow off my boots on the mat that says *Stamp Here*, and tromp across the liquid-ice-stained floorboards. Buff kicks out a stool at the bar as I approach. He's grinning like an icin' fool.

For a moment the place goes silent, as half the patrons stare at me, but as soon as they recognize me as one of the regulars, the dull drone of conversation continues, mixing with the clink of tin jugs and gulps of amber liquid ice.

"Get a 'quiddy for Dazz," Buff shouts to Yo above the din. The grizzled pub owner and bartender sloshes the contents of a dirty, old pitcher into a tinny and slides it along the bar. Well-practiced bar sitters dodge the frothing jug as it skates to a stop directly in front of me. As always, Yo's aim is perfect.

"Thanks," I shout. Yo nods his pockmarked forehead in my direction and strokes his gray-streaked brown beard thoughtfully, as if I've just said something filled with wisdom, before heading off to refill another customer's jug. He doesn't get many thanks around this place.

"Out with it," Buff says, slapping me on the shoulder. His sharp green eyes reflect even the miniscule shreds of daylight that manage to sneak through the dirt-smudged windows.

"Out with what?"

Shaking his head, he runs a hand through his dirty-blonde hair. "Uh, the big breakup with her highness, Queen Witch-Bitch herself. It's all anyone's been talking about all morning. Where've you been? I've been dying to get all the details."

Elbows on the bar, I lean my head against my fist. "It just happened! How the chill do you know already?"

Buff laughs. "You know as well as anyone that word travels scary fast in this town."

I do. Normally, though, the gossip's about me getting broken up with after having done something freeze-brained, not the other way around. "What are they saying?" I ask, taking a sip of 'quiddy and relishing the warmth in my throat and chest.

Buff's excitement seems to wane. He stares at his half-empty mug. "You don't wanna know," he says, and then finishes off the last half of his tinny in a series of throat-bobbing gulps.

"Tell me," I push.

"Look, Dazz..." Buff lowers his voice, a deep rumble that only I can hear. "...the thing about girls is, when you want 'em they're scarcer than a ray of sunshine in ice country, and when you don't, they're on you like a double-wide fleece blanket." Now I'm the one looking at my unfinished drink, because, for once, one of Buff's snowballs of wisdom is spot on. I thought I wanted the witch—because of her looks—but as soon as I got to know her I wanted to toss her out with the mud on my boots.

Using my knuckles, I knock myself in the head three times, exactly like I rapped on the witch's door this morning before it all went down. *Don't ask, don't ask, don't ask,* I mentally command myself. "What are they saying?" I ask, repeating myself. Having not listened to my own internal advice, I feel like knocking my skull against the heavy, wooden bar a few dozen more times, but I manage to restrain myself as I wait for Buff's response.

"Well...some of them are saying good sticks for you, she got what she deserved, Brown District pride and all that bullshiver. You know the shiv I mean, right?"

All too well. I nod. "And the others?"

Buff chews on his lip, as if deciding how to break something to me lightly.

"Give it to me straight," I say.

He sighs. "You know tomorrow they'll move onto the next freezin' bit of juicy gossip, right?"

"Buff," I say, a warning in my voice. I know what's coming, so I tilt my tinny back, draining every last drop in a single burning gulp.

"If I tell you, promise me you won't start anything—I'm not in the mood."

Looking directly into his black pupils, I say, "I promise."

He rolls his eyes, knowing full well I just lied to him. Then he tells me anyway. "Coker's been saying the witch was too good for you, that she shoulda dumped your Mountain-fearin' arse a long time ag—"

I'm on my feet and breaking my false promise before Buff can even finish telling me. My stool clatters to the floor, but I barely notice it. I get a bead on Coker, who's between two of his stone cutting mates, laughing about something. Regardless of what it is, and even though they've probably moved on from discussing me and the witch already, I pretend it's about me. About how I'm not good enough for someone in the White District. About how I'm lazy and good for nothing.

My fists clench and my jaw hardens as heat rises in my chest. Always aware of what's happening in his pub, Yo says, "Now, Dazz, don't start nuthin', remember the last time…"

"Dazz, hold up," Buff says, his feet scuffling along behind me.

I ignore them both.

When I reach Coker he's already half-turned around, as if sensing me coming. I spin him the rest of the way and slam my fist right between his eyes. A two for one special, like down at the market. Two black eyes for the price of one. His head snaps back and thuds gruesomely off the bar, but, like any stonecutter, he's tougher than dried goat meat, and rebounds with a heavy punch of his own, which glances off my shoulder, sending vibrations through my arm.

And his friends aren't gonna sit back and watch things unfold either; they jump on me in less time than it took for the White District witch to cheat on me, swinging fists of iron at my head. One catches my chin and the other my cheek. I jerk backwards, seeing red, blue, and yellow stars against a black backdrop, and feel my tailbone slam into something hard and flat. The wooden table collapses, sending splinters and legs in every direction—both table legs and people legs. I'm still not seeing much, other than stars, but based on the tangle of limbs I'd say the table I crashed into was occupied by at least three Icers, maybe four.

I shake my head and furiously try to blink away the dark cloud obscuring my sight, feeling a dull ache spreading through the whole of my backside. When my vision returns, the first thing I see is Buff hammering rapid-fire rabbit punches into one of the stone cutter's, sending him sprawling. The area's clearing out, with patrons scampering for the door, which is a good thing, because Coker gets ahold of Buff and throws him into another table, which topples over and skids into the wall.

Me and Buff spring to our feet simultaneously, cocking our fists side by side like we've done so many times growing up in the rugged Brown District. Buff takes Coker's friend and I take Coker. We circle each other a few times and then all chill breaks loose, as the fists start flying. After taking a hit in the ribs, I land a solid blow to Coker's jaw that has him reeling, off balance and stunned. I follow it up with a hook that sends a jolt of pain through my hand, which is likely not even a quarter of the pain that I just sent through his face. He drops faster than a morning turd in the outhouse.

I whirl around to find Buff in a similar position, standing over his guy and shaking his hand like he's just punched a wall. The guy he was fighting was so thick it probably *was* like hitting a wall. We stand over our fallen foes, grinning like the seventeen-year-old unemployed idiots that we are, enjoying the aliveness that always comes with winning a good, old-fashioned fair fight.

Yo's glaring at us, one hand on his hip and the other holding an empty pitcher. I shrug just as his eyes flick to the side, looking past us. The last thing I hear is a well-muffled scuff.

Everything goes black when the wooden stool slams into the back of my head.

# Two

I wake up to a slap in the face. Not a loving, caring slap when the doc smacks a newborn baby in the butt to get it to cry, but a stinging, full handed palm across the face that snaps my head to the side and will likely leave a fierce red handprint on my cheek. I'd be lying if I told you it didn't conjure up memories of at least one ex-girlfriend.

"Yow!" I yelp. "What the chill?"

As I blink away the wave of dizziness that spins my vision in blurry swirls, I hear the sharp crack of palm flesh on cheek flesh. For a moment I'm left wondering whether it's an echo from me getting slapped, but then I hear a similar outburst from someone close by.

I close my eyes, fighting back the urge to vomit as the spinning room gradually slows. "Buff, is that you?" I slur.

"Dazz?"

"Yah."

"You breathin'?"

"Nay," I say.

"What the freeze happened?" Buff asks.

Before I can answer, a third voice chimes in. "You two and your icin' prideful stupidity tore up my pub, is what happened," Yo bellows. Yo. The slapper. I've never seen a day when his hands were clean. I'll have to wash my face a half-dozen times…just as soon as I can figure out the difference between up and down.

"Sorry, Yo," Buff says diplomatically. "It won't happen again."

"That's two fights last week and three this 'un. Nay, it freezin' won't happen again, 'cause you ain't welcome back."

My eyes snap open and I see three Yo's standing over me, looking angrier than a skinned bear in a snowstorm. His thick mess of beard is right over my face and I clamp my mouth shut for fear of getting a hairy appetizer before lunch.

"But, Yo, you can't do that—we've *always* come here." Buff's words come out as a plea, which is exactly what it is. I expect if he was physically able to, he'd be on his knees with his hands clasped tight, praying to the Heart of the Mountain for Yo to reconsider.

The red hot anger leeches from Yo's face, leaving him paler than one of the Pasties from the Glass City out in fire country. "You think I don't know that?" he says, dropping his voice to a whisper. "Chill, I practically raised you boys." Wellll, I wouldn't go that far. I respect Yo and how well he runs his business, but honestly, I'd rather be raised by wolves, and not the tame, gentle kind who pull our sleds; the sharp-fanged vicious ones who are known to drag children into the forest.

But at the same time, there's a degree of truth to his words. Most of what we've learned about life has come from our time spent in Fro-Yo's. First, when we were just kids, brought by my father after school to "learn how to be men," and then, after he caught the Cold and passed on, we kept going back. Yo could've turned us away, because we were too young without having a parent there, but he didn't. Knowing full well from the gossip that my mother would probably never be motherly again, he served us wafers and goat's cheese and gumberry juice, never charging us a thing. And we learned how to be men, or at least the ice-country-tavern version of men, drinking hard and fighting harder.

Look where it's got us.

I don't say a thing, because the memories are caught in my throat.

"C'mon, Yo, we were provoked," Buff says, less nostalgic than me. Really what he means is that *Dazz* was provoked, and even that's a lie. There's a chilluva difference between saying a few nasty words in someone's general direction and throwing a full-force punch between the eyes, although sometimes the nuances of good behavior and manners are completely lost on me.

"No 'scuses, boys," Yo says. "Look, the best I can do is that I'll consider lettin' you back if you can prove you've changed your fightin' ways."

"And how are we supposed to do that?" I ask, finally dislodging the memories from my windpipe.

"Get a job. Pay for all the damages. And if I don't hear about you startin'"—he cocks his head to the side thoughtfully—"or endin' any fights, I'll let you come back."

I groan, but not from the pounding headache that I suddenly feel in the back of my head. From where I'm lying, his requirements seem impossible. Bye, bye girlfriend number two.

"Sure, Yo, whatever you say," Buff says, but I can hear the dismay in his voice. "We'll prove it to you."

"Now you best run home and put some ice on those heads of yours. My oak stools pack a wallop, all right."

He helps Buff to his feet, and then me. We stand side by side, two fierce warriors, swaying and unsteady on our feet like we might topple over at any moment. Some warriors.

Buff flops a heavy arm around my shoulders, nearly knocking me over. I cling to him just as tightly. We stagger for the door like drunks, open it awkwardly. Before we leave, I look back and ask a final question. "Who hit us from behind?"

Yo shakes his head. "You'll just go and start a fight if I tell you."

"Naw, Yo, I just wanna know how we lost. We don't usually lose." Never, really.

Yo closes one eye, as if he's got a bit of dirt in it. "One of those stonecutters," he says. "The third one, who you both thought was out of the picture."

We close the door, welcoming the cold.

~~~

"Yah, she was pretty icy," Buff says, "but there are plenny of fish in the ice streams." The thing about that is, I've gone ice

17

fishing twenny times this winter and I ain't never caught a freezin' thing.

"Yah," I say, not really agreeing. It's just a bit of bad luck, I tell myself, referring to the three broken and mangled "relationships" I've left in my wake. If bad luck's got two-mile-long legs, a deadly white smile, and more curves than a snowman, then that's exactly what I got.

"You'll bounce back. We both will," Buff says, scraping a boot in the snow. We're sitting in a snowdrift, having never made it home. Neither of us has much to go home to anyway, and there's plenny of snow and ice to treat our throbbing heads.

"How?" I say, adding another clump of snow to the snow helmet I'm wearing. "How in the chill are we supposed to get enough silver to pay for everything we broke?"

"There's always boulders-'n-avalanches," Buff says, referring to our favorite card game of the gambling variety, another vice we picked up the moment we turned sixteen and were permitted into the Chance Holes.

I feel a zing of energy through my bruised body. It's a longshot, but...

"How much silver do you have to put on the line?" I ask.

Buff shrugs, removes the snowball he's holding against his skull, chucks it at a tree, missing badly. "Twenny sickles," he says.

I frown, scrape the snow away from my own head, doing the math. Combined we have maybe fitty, give or take a sickle. Probably a quarter of what we need to pay Yo back. We'd have to get awfully lucky at b-'n-a to win that kind of silver. I pack the snow into a tight ball, launch it at the same tree Buff aimed for, missing by twice as much.

I look up at the gray-blanketed sky, striped with streaks of red, like bloody claw marks, where the crimson sky manages to peek through the dense cloud cover. When I look down again, I know:

We have no other choice—we've gotta try.

Luckily, cards have nothing to do with throwing snowballs.

~ ~ ~

The bland gray of the daytime is long past, giving way to a heavy night. I end up stopping at home to get my last bundle of silver coins. When I pry it from behind the bearskin insulation we've got pressed against the stacked-tree-trunk walls, it feels lighter than it should. Turns out I've got even less than I thought, only twenny sickles. The missing sickles are probably because Mother found my stash and stole what she needed to buy enough ice powder to keep her in a sufficient stupor to forget about me and my older brother, who she says, "Reminds me of your father more than anything."

Wouldn't want to do that.

Not that it matters. If she didn't find some of my silver, she'd have found another way. She always does. That's one thing I've learned about addicts: they'll get what they need one way or another. Sell a piece of furniture, steal it, trade something. Whatever it takes.

I don't confront her about it, because it wouldn't do any good anyway. She barely knows I'm there, sitting blank-eyed and cross-legged in front of the dry, charred fireplace logs, holding her hands out as if to warm them on the invisible flames. "Oooh," she murmurs softly to herself.

I sigh. If we do win anything tonight, I'll have to find a better place to hide whatever's left over after paying Yo back. Like somewhere in another country, fire country perhaps.

Shaking my head, I light a small fire so my mother doesn't freeze to death.

My brother, Wes, isn't around, because unlike me, he has a job doing the nightshift in the mines. Ain't much of a job if you ask me, but without his dirt-blackened face we'd have died of starvation months ago. He's only two years older than me, but if you asked him, he'd tell you he's ten years my senior in maturity. Not that I'm arguing.

Given our situation, I should've gotten a job a long time ago, when I turned fourteen and school ended. Or at least at age sixteen, when most guys do, after they've had their two years of fun. So why am I seventeen and wasting my life away? I wish I knew.

My little sister, Jolie, is staying with a neighbor down the street until my mother can pull it together. The way things are going, she might be there forever. Although I've had a pretty shivvy day, not seeing Jolie's smiling face at home is the worst part. She's only twelve, and yet, I swear she's one of the only people who really gets me. Her and Buff, that is.

I leave my mother babbling to herself about how the Cold is growing wings and flying above the clouds, or some rubbish like that. The warmth of the fire I made chases me out the door.

It's colder than my ex-girlfriend's personality outside. Even with my slightly-too-small double-layered bearskin coat that I won playing boulders when I was fifteen, and the three thick shirts underneath it, I'm instantly frozen from head to toe. When the wind blows it goes right through me, like I'm naked and made of brittle parchment, and I find myself running just to keep warm. My bruised skull aches with each step.

Before heading to meet Buff, I stop at our neighbor's place to see Jolie. Although not rich by any stretch of the imagination, Clint and his wife, Looza, are better off than us, which I'm glad for. It means Jolie gets a decent place to stay, three warm meals a day, and a taste for what it's like to be part of a real family. Selfishly, I want my mother to get cleaned up so my sister can come home, but I know that might not be the best thing for her. Either way, I'm glad she's close by.

I rap firmly on the door, feeling every thud echo in my head. On the third knock the door opens and Jolie pokes her head out. "Dazz!" she exclaims, breaking into a huge smile that instantly warms my frozen body and soul. Her dark brown hair is in a long, tight braid down her back, almost to her waist. It's not done exactly like how I would do it, but it's close enough. When my dad died and my mother lost herself, I had to learn how to braid real quick, because Jolie wouldn't have it any other way.

She rushes out into my arms and the cold. As always, she stands on the tops of my snow-capped boots, her socks getting soaked through. She's getting so big that my toes get crushed under her weight, but I can't bring myself to tell her. "You'll catch the Cold," I say, walking us both inside where I can feel the tempting heat from a crackling fire.

Face smashed against my chest, she says, "Are you staying for a while tonight?"

I can hear the memory in her voice, a desperate longing for another time, when life was simpler and nights were spent listening to Father's stories by the fire, or playing sticks and rocks on the big bearskin rug between our beds.

But those days are long spent. "I'm sorry, Joles, there's something I have to do."

She steps off my feet and looks up at me all pouty mouthed. She calls it her sad sled dog face. "Fro-Yo's," she says, accusation in her voice.

"Uhhhh…" I wish? I can't tell her the truth—about my fighting and getting banned from the pub. I hate lying to her, but I can't let her down, not now when she needs a big brother to be proud of. "Nay, nothing like that. Actually, I have a job." As if. The words just pop into my head, like my heart wished them into existence. But even just saying the words makes me feel a little lighter, like even pretending to be respectable in front of my sister makes me a better person.

Jolie's eyes widen and her smile returns like a flint spark. "Really?"

I nod uncertainly, on an angle, like I'm not sure whether I'm saying yah or nay. She takes it as a yah. "That's wonderful, Dazz! Does that mean I can come home soon?" Her hopeful words are like ice daggers shoved between my ribs and I find myself breathless.

She senses my hesitation. "Mom?" she says.

"She's still pretty bad," I admit. "But maybe soon," I say, unable to resist giving her a small measure of happiness, even if it's as false as the so-called job I have to do tonight.

"What's the job?" Jolie asks, which is the natural question that I'm totally unprepared for. I've got to come up with something, and fast, because she's looking at me with that cocked-head snowbird expression that usually makes me laugh.

"Master of Chance," I say, once more going with the first thing that flashes to mind. Technically I won't be *the* Master of

Chance tonight, but I will be a master of chance of sorts as I participate in a few rounds of boulders-'n-avalanches.

"Congratulations," she says, giving me another hug. Hopefully her congratulations will still be appropriate tomorrow, when I've quadrupled my tiny pouch of silver.

"Thanks, Joles," I say, giving her a final squeeze. "See you tomorrow?"

"Promise?"

"Yah, Joles, I promise." This one I'll keep.

"Will you at least stay for supper, young man?" Clint says from across the room. I didn't even notice the thin sandy-haired carpenter and his wife, silently preparing dinner and listening to us.

"Evenin' sir and ma'am. Sorry, I didn't see you there. I'd love to, but I really must be on my way. First day and all." More like *last night*. If I'm not lucky, that is.

"Are you sure, sweetie?" Looza says, chiming in, her wide waist swinging from side to side as she mixes something in a big pot. "There's plenny of soup." As if to illustrate, she scoops up a ladleful of hearty stew, letting it slowly drip back into the mixture. My stomach rumbles as the delicious aroma of tender bear meat and winter vegetables fills my nostrils.

"I'll take it with me, if that's all right with you," I say.

She sighs, but nods and begins filling a largish pouch.

"Bye, kid," I say, kissing Jolie lightly on the forehead.

She steps back up onto my boots and I lean down so she can kiss my cheek. "Bye, Dazz. I'll miss you."

"I'll miss you, too, Joles," I say, clenching my stomach around the empty pit that's forming. I take the pouch from Looza and open the door. "Thank—" I start to say, but she muscles me outside, still holding onto her half of the pouch. She pulls the door shut on my sister.

I look at her face, which has formed a question mark out of her eyes, nose and mouth. "Don't do anything to hurt that little girl," she says, her eyes as iron grey as the clouds were earlier.

"I won't, ma'am," I say, unsure of what she's getting at.

"Well, then you might want to turn around and go right back home," she says, firmly but not unkindly.

"But my job," I say, knowing how weak it sounds.

"Yah. Your job," she says.

Easing the stew pouch from her grip, I say, "Thank you, ma'am. For the stew and…well, for everything."

# Three

I take the trail to the lower Brown District, where Buff lives. The further you go down the mountain, the less silver people have and the shivvier their jobs are—if they have work at all. Buff's father's a treejacker, earning a sickle a day from backbreaking work that supplies all the timber to the White District and the palace. There's not much new construction in the Brown District, so little of the wood is sent our way. By the time Buff's father gets home he's so bone-weary that it's all he can do to take dinner in bed and go right to sleep.

Buff's younger sister, Darce, is a pretty little thing of all of twelve years old, like Joles. After their mother died of the Cold three years ago, she took over the motherly duties of raising all six of Buff's other little brothers and sisters, as well as feeding

Buff and his father. She's a woman trapped in a girl's body. The exact opposite of what my mother has become.

I pause on the edge of a large, snow-covered rock before I make the final descent, breathing in the crisp, pine-scented air and gazing down the mountainside. The first part is covered in a winter blanket of white, smooth and unmarked except for the handful of trails where the snowshoes of treejackers and miners have trod a deep path in the high crests of powdery snow. But eventually, beyond the snowy slopes, the mountain turns brown, dotted with heavy boulders and spindly, leafless trees. Further down still, heavy oaks rise tall and majestic, all the way to the edge of ice country, where it seems to collide with fire country. The desert, they call it, bare and lifeless. Even the sky seems to recognize the difference, as the moment the forest gives way to sand and dirt, the clouds stop, as if running up against an invisible barrier that ends their unceasing march across the night sky.

For a moment, as I have many times before, I wonder what's out there, in fire country, beyond the borders. From what the men at Fro-Yo's say, there are the Heaters, a peaceful tribe of desert-dwellers. Then there are the Glassies, who I like to call the Pasties, on account of how eerily white their skin is, even whiter than most of ours. No one really knows where they came from, but they're our friends, too, apparently. According to King Goff's shouters, who come down from the palace a few times a year to present us with news from the crown, we have trade agreements with both the Heaters and the Pasties. We give them wood, bear meat, and a few other odds and ends, and the Heaters give us what they call tug and 'zard meat, which have become something of a delicacy. I don't know what either a tug or a 'zard is, but the few times I've been lucky enough to eat their meat, I've been impressed—it's much better than bear or rabbit. The Heaters also help guard our borders, although I'm not sure who they're guarding against. The Pasties, on the other hand, are something of an enigma. No one seems to know what we get from them in exchange for the provisions we provide them with.

I've never seen a Heater before, but the men at the pub say they have brown skin and are scared of being cold, whatever that means. That's why they never come up the mountain. The Pasties, however, appear from time to time in the White District, on their way to the palace. They never stop at any of the local businesses, nor do they speak to anyone but each other. After disappearing through the palace gates, they reappear a few hours later and march right back down the mountain and toward fire country and their Glass City, which I've also never seen, other than in the paintings you can buy in Chiller's Market. But as far as I'm concerned, the drawings are pure fiction—no one could build a glass structure big enough to enclose an entire town.

In fire country, there's also the Fire, which we call the Cold, an airborne plague that kills many each year, both in fire and ice country. Only, down there, on the flatlands, it's much worse, or so they say, killing many of them before their thirtieth year. I shudder as a burst of ice runs down my spine. If I lived in fire country, I'd be more than halfway through my life. At least up here where it snows almost every day of the year, the Cold is slowed, allowing us to live into our forties. It certainly puts things into perspective.

It's forbidden to go to fire country, on account of the disease.

I turn to look up at the monster-like peaks rising above me to the north. Sometimes during the day, when a rare ray of sunlight manages to squeeze through the towers of clouds, one of the peaks looks like the head of a wolf, with caves for eyes and a gaping crevice with fang-like rock formations protruding from its craggy lips. But at night it just looks like a superior being, sturdy and unchanging, even when the whole world around it seems to be constantly moving in a million directions.

Under my breath I whisper a silent prayer to the Heart of the Mountain for luck tonight, and continue down the trail.

Buff's family's place is a dilapidated wooden structure that's half the size of our sturdy house. Unlike our thick, full-trunked walls, their walls are constructed of thin planks with chunks of mud frozen solid between them. It does well enough to keep the cold air out, but only when there's a fire going in a pit in the center and you're wearing three layers of clothing. For Buff, going to Fro-Yo's means a bit of real warmth he can't get at home. I want to help him recover that right more than anything.

My hands are too cold to pound on another door, so I just open it.

Inside, there's chaos.

One of Buff's little sisters is shoveling spoons of soup into her mouth so fast that it's dripping from her chin, while he tries to get her to eat slower. One of his younger brothers, who's practically a clone of Buff, is running around naked as Darce tries to corral him into a melted-snow bath. Yet another little-person is painting streaks of brown on the wall with his hands. Only it's not paint. It's mud, which he's collecting from a mushy pit on the dirt floor. The unmatched assortment of beds against one wall are scattered with a few more dozing children. Buff's father isn't there—another late night at the lumber yards.

When Buff sees me, he shoots me a thank-the-Heart-of-the-Mountain look, grabs his heaviest coat, and pushes me out the door, shouting, "Darce, I'm going out—be back late." He slams the door behind him. "What took you so freezin' long," he snaps, his eyes darting around as if more of his maniac siblings might be hiding outside somewhere.

Smirking, I lay down my trump card. "Joles," I say, not admitting to the five minutes of peace I spent on the mountainside.

His face softens and his eyes focus on me for the first time. "Alright, alright, you got me. C'mon."

We make our way through his neighborhood, catching a few glances from the lucky few who happen to have windows in their huts, giving us looks and shaking their heads as if we're no more than common hooligans. Don't they know we have an almost perfect pub-fighting record? I stare right back at them, give them a growl, and a few of them shrink back and out of sight. I laugh.

"Do you have to do that?" Buff says.

"Yah," I say. "What's eating you, man? You're acting all uptight tonight."

Buff's steps are more like stomps beside my easy footfalls. "I am not uptight!" he snaps, proving my point. He realizes it, shakes his head, and says, "I don't know, I'm just nervous and frustrated about..." His voice fades into the night breeze.

"About Fro-Yo's?"

Stomp, stomp, stomp. I stop him, put both hands on his shoulders. "It'll be fine, all right? We'll get the money, get our pub rights back, maybe even get real jobs afterwards. Then we'll start our climb to the top, where it'll be full of White District ladies dying to take us home to meet their parents. But we'll reject every last one of them."

Buff snorts. Finally my easygoing best friend is back. He slaps my arms away. "You can reject them all you want, but that doesn't mean I have to."

"Whatever pulls your sled," I say.

We trudge along in silence for a few minutes. "Hey," I say, remembering Looza's pouch. "Want to share my stew?"

Buff flashes me a do-you-really-have-to-ask look, so I hand him the pouch. He slurps at it, groaning in delight. "You made this?" he says between his slurp-chews.

"Naw. It's Looza's." I grab it back after he sucks in another mouthful. "Leave me some, man." I ease some of the chunky liquid past my lips, relishing the perfectly balanced combination of flavors. Looza may not trust me to do the right thing by my sister, but she sure can whip up a good stew. I finish it off, wishing I'd asked for two servings, and then tuck the empty pouch in my pocket to return to her tomorrow.

We fight our way back up the same hill I just descended, and with each slipping, sliding step I wish we'd agreed to meet at my place. After a lot of heavy breathing and near falls, we reach the path to the Red District. It's not really the kind of place most people would want to go at night, but we know our way around better than most.

As we pass a two-storied wooden structure on our left, a dark-eyed, silky-haired head pops out of a doorway, spilling soft reddish-orange light on the snow. "Hi, boys," a lustrous voice drawls.

"Evenin', Lola," Buff says. "It's a cold 'un. Better keep that door shut to keep the warmth in."

31

With a full-lipped smile that says she lives for contradicting people, Lola takes two strutting steps outside into the snow. Her feet are bare and she's wearing a sheer, lacy dress that lets through more than its fair share of light. Underneath she wears only the barest of essentials, something lacy up top and down below, leaving little to imagination. She's got to be freaking freezing her perfectly sculpted buttocks off, but if she is, she doesn't show it.

"Sure you won't reconsider my previous offers?" she says in a seductive, lilting tone, swaying her hips side to side, in a way that's *completely* different to how Looza was earlier when she was mixing the stew.

"Uh, well, I think, we have to..." Buff is a tangle of words.

"Sorry, Lola. Not tonight," I say. Not ever. When I find the right girl and the time is right, I certainly won't be looking to pay for it.

"Another time, perhaps," she says with a wink.

"Uh, yah, you too," Buff says nonsensically as we walk away. He looks back several times.

"By the Heart of the Mountain, you're pathetic sometimes," I say.

"Says the King of Bad Breakups," he retorts, magically finding order to his words again.

"At least I'm the king of something."

"Hopefully we're both the kings of boulders tonight," he says. "Did you get the silver?"

I screw up my mouth. "Yah, but it's only twenny."

"Iceballs! It turned out I only had ten."

"Son of a no-good, snow blowin'..." I spout off a few more choice words. With only thirty sickles we'll be lucky if they even let us in the Chance Hole.

32

"Sorry. Darce had to use the rest of it to fix a hole in the wall."

That brings me back to reality pretty quick. "Buff, I'm sorry. This is my fault. I never shoulda started something with Coker."

"Icin' right it's your fault," he says, but he's grinning. "But he did have it coming to him. And it was kinda fun, at least until that freezin' stoner dropped that stool on our heads.

I grin back. "It was fun, wasn't it?"

Buff claps me on the back. "Like you said, Dazzo, we'll fix things, just like we always do."

~~~

We know we've reached our destination when the pipe smoke starts curling around our heads.

Against the stark white of the winter scenery, the gray smoke almost seems to take on a life of its own, with fingers that grab and clutch without ever actually touching you. The smoke wafts out from a stone staircase that descends cellar-like beneath a two story building that, based on the sign on the door, claims to specialize in *Custom Doors*. Other than in the White District, there's not much demand for that sort of thing these days—most of us are just happy to have any type of door—so I suspect it's just a front for the gambling operation.

Heavy voices rumble from below like distant thunder from some fire country storm. Moments later, a short man emerges from the cellar, looking distraught, glancing behind him with wary eyes, as if he's likely to get knifed in the back. Which, coming out of a place like that, he just might.

He's heading right for us, but not looking where he's going. We just stand there, watching him, waiting for him to notice, but he keeps on coming. When he finally looks up, he's so close he barely stops before running smack into my chest. "Oh," he exclaims, twitching so hard that his knitted cap flops off his head and into the snow, revealing a head as bald as the day he was born. Buff reaches down and picks it up.

"Uh, sorry…and thanks…and, uh, sorry," the man says, taking the cap and sort of bowing with his hands clasped together around the edges. He's jerking every which way and can't seem to keep his eyes focused on us for more than a few seconds. Each time they dart away, it's toward the cellar steps.

"Are you waiting for someone?" I ask, nodding toward the steps.

"Oh, nay…nay, nay, nay, nay, nay! Most definitely not. But I really don't know how I'll…never mind, it's not your concern." The odd little man scurries off, his feet sinking into the snow up to his knees. "Not enough sickles in the world…ever pay them back?…What'll Marta say?" he mumbles to himself as he plods away, trying to replace the hat on his head. But his hands are so jittery he can't get it right, and eventually gives up, settling for cold ears until he gets to wherever his destination is.

"He lost big time," Buff says. I nod, wishing it wasn't true. Although perhaps if other patrons of the Chance Hole are losing, that means there's plenny of room for us to win.

I hang onto that thought as we descend the steps. There's no smoke or voices now, as the thick door at the bottom is closed again. A man as big as a boulder with legs like tree trunks stands in front of the door, thick arms crossed over his chest.

"I ain't seen you two before," he says in a voice that suggests his father is a bear. Given the thickness of his beard, his mother might be a bear too.

Buff lets me do the talking after his unfortunate tongue tie up when he spoke to Lola. "You haven't. Usually we play small time, but we're looking to up the ante tonight." Yah, with the all of thirty sickles we have to play with.

He looks me up and down with a crooked smile, as if he doesn't believe for a second that we've got the stones to play with the high rollers. My nerve falters under his gaze, but I don't let it show on my face. When his heavy brown eyes return to mine, he says, "Buy-in's twenny sickles, five-sickle ante per hand, betting starts immediately."

When he opens the door the smoke and noise hit us like a morning fog.

# Four

Inside is full of snakes. Not the slivery brown rattlers you'll find in the woods sometimes in the heart of summer, but the greasy, venom-eyed, hustling kind who work the Red District underground. There are a dozen tables and all appear to be full. The slap of cards, jingle of coins, and groans of loss or shouts of victory muddle into one stream of sound that represents one thing and one thing alone: greed.

Here is where fortunes are made and bigger fortunes are lost. Just by stepping through this door we've proved that we belong, certainly more than the bald-headed man with the unsteady hands who left earlier.

Through the pipe smog, I scan the crowd, laughing when a chubby guy with a lopsided smile scrapes a pile of coins from the center of a table while a hooded man slams his cards down. For every winner there's a loser.

"Advance?" a nasally voice says from beside us.

A pointy-nosed woman sits at a desk, stacks of coins in front of her.

"Excuse me?" I say, being as polite as possible.

She lifts a hand to her curly red hair, shakes her head, rolls her eyes. Maybe we don't belong here after all. Even she knows we're new to this scene. Slowing her pace, she says, "Would. You. Like. An. Advance?" She motions to the coins.

Forget trying to act the part. This woman appears to be offering us money—which we desperately need—so I need to understand. Keeping my voice low, I say, "Look, you know as well as us that we're new to...all of this." I wave my hand across the room. "We've played cards plenny of times, but never in a joint like this—for high stakes. So can you please explain how it works. The advance, I mean."

She sighs, seems to resign herself to the fact that I'm not going away without some information. "Most of our...*customers*...are high rollers. They play for big stakes and they don't back down. You think they carry hundreds of sickles in their pockets? Forget about it. They come here empty handed, and we keep a tally of their balance. We can also advance you silver so long as you're good for it. We can do up to a thousand sickles the first time, until you've proven you'll pay it back. Then we can go as high as ten thousand."

A thousand sickles? Ten thousand? I haven't ever seen that kind of wealth in my life. "You'll give me silver?" I say slowly.

She laughs, which comes out as nasally as her voice. "Not give—loan. Each day you don't pay it back, the balance goes up by ten-hundredths of the amount you owe."

Buff and I look at each other. The green of his eyes almost looks silver, as if he's been staring so hard at the piles of coins that they've gotten stuck there. "What do we do?" he asks.

I shrug, trying to think. If we keep doubling our thirty sickles each time we play, we won't really need anything else. But we could also lose it all in the first round.

I lean in, so only she'll be able to hear me. "How far will thirty sickles get us?"

"Thirty sickles each?" she says, tapping her chin with a long, white finger.

"Uh. Thirty sickles total," I admit.

Her nostril-heightened laugh is back. "You're joking, right? Didn't Ham tell you the buy-in's twenny? You won't both be able to play if you've only got thirty sicks."

Decision time. Take the money now, or one of us has to walk out the door. Or we could both leave. But then where will we be? No money, no jobs, no pub. I steel myself and go for it. "We'll take thirty sickles," I say.

"Minimum advance is one hundred," she says flatly.

"Make it two hundred," I blurt out before I can stop myself.

Buff nudges me, his eyes wide and green again. I shrug. *Just go with it*, I mouth.

Nostril-voice counts out the coins and hands them to me. "Welcome to the Hole. May you have bad luck," she says, smirking. I hope she says that to all the customers, but I have a feeling she brought it out special just for us.

I lead the way, skating between the tables like I belong, even though inside of me Looza's stew is sloshing and churning, like even it knows we're doing something we shouldn't. The slap of cards is like a hammer to the back of my head, which starts to ache again.

Every table appears to be full, except one, which has two chairs pulled out at an angle, as if whoever vacated them left in a hurry. One of them was probably the nervous-looking bald guy's. They're still playing, but the game almost seems friendly, as if they're just having a bit of fun, without care as to whether they win or lose. Seems like our kind of table.

I approach, ducking my head to draw one of the gambler's eyes. A round-faced guy with double-pierced ears looks up at me with a smile broader than Looza's hips. His eyes are blue and twinkling with red flecks under the lantern light. "Hey, kid. You want in?" His tone is light and friendly. We're just here to enjoy each other's company, it seems to say.

"Sure, thanks," I say, feeling more and more at ease. It almost feels like the cards we normally play back in the Brown District. Only we've got a hundred sickles each that aren't ours to play with. "Mind if my buddy joins, too?" I ask, motioning to Buff.

"The more the merrier," he says.

I give Buff a hundred sickles from the advance, and keep the same for myself. That should be plenny to get us started. Sliding into a seat, I watch Buff do the same. He looks less pale than before, as if he's settling into things, too. We watch as the players finish out their hand, tossing in bets of a few sickles each, and laughing when the merry-eyed guy with the big smile wins a nice pot of perhaps forty sickles when he shows double boulders.

A friendly game amongst friends. The others at the table appear equally easygoing. On my left is the guy who invited us to play, and on my right is a thin, clean-shaven guy with a long face that almost touches the table. He's got at least two hundred sickles piled up in front of him, perhaps double what

I've got. On either side of Buff are twins, each with jet-black hair and knit caps that they've kept on despite the relative heat of the crowded cellar. They're all quick to smile and don't seem to mind parting with their silver if it means one of their buddies wins.

"Ante's five sickles," Pierced-Ears announces.

Buff and I grab a five-sickle piece each and toss it in the center of the table. The other four do the same. Excitement builds in my chest at the prospect of winning even the ante, which is five times the normal one-sickle ante I'm used to. Twin-Number-One deals, two cards each, facedown. I'm feeling more and more at home. This is my element. I've been playing boulders-'n-avalanches since I was old enough to understand the rules. I've always been good at it. This is just like any other game.

I peek at my cards. Twin boulders! *What are the chances?* I think. I do my best to hide my excitement behind a blank stare, but my heart's beating so hard I swear the others can hear it. Pierced-Ears takes a look at his cards and rolls his eyes, tosses them in the middle. "I'm out," he says. A small stone and a minor tree branch. He was smart to fold. No chance of winning with cards like that.

Twin-Number-One dealt, so it's Buff's turn to bet. He glances at me but I can't read him. Glances back at his cards. "Five sickles," he says, tossing in another coin. There's no way he's got my hand beat, but it doesn't really matter. Me taking his money is as good as him keeping it. We'll split all the winnings anyway. Twin-Number-Two nods and tosses in some silver. Long-Face chews on his lip and then does the same.

My bet. I've got to play this one slow, or they'll know right away I've got something good. I toss in the minimum required to stay in the hand, five sickles. We skip Pierced-Ears since he's out. Twin-Number-One throws his cards in the middle, facedown. Another one out.

It's time to show the first of the draw cards. An arrow. No impact on my hand, which is already very strong. Unless someone else has twin arrows, I'm probably still winning.

Back to Buff. He passes, lets the bet go to the twin on his left. The twin places his cards on the table, stretches his arms over his head, and then throws in two large coins. Twenny sickles. Already the pot is heating up and I'm starting to worry the remaining twin does have something good, like two arrows, which would leave him with a triplet, automatically beating my twins. Across the table, Buff's eyes widen.

Without even a sideways glance, Long-Face throws in the required coins, along with two more, both ten sickle pieces! The bet for this round alone is up to forty sicks, more than we came with. If I keep playing and lose this hand, I'll already be broke *and* owe Nasal-Voice silver. Sweat begins beading under my arms and below my knees. Feeling somewhat faint, I wriggle out of my heavy coat and drape it over the chair behind me. It helps, but my mind is still spinning. If I fold now, I'll be throwing away the best hand I might get all night. Plus, maybe in a high stakes game every pot will be this big. If I'm going to take a chance, now is the time to do it.

I throw in forty, trying to breathe evenly.

Buff stares at me like I'm crazy. He's gotta throw in forty to stay in it. He throws his cards in instead, face up. Twin medium stones. Not a bad hand, but not good enough considering how fast the pot's growing. It's all up to me now.

Twin-Two throws his cards as well, unwilling to match Long-Face's raise. Down to me and Long. Twin-One flips over another draw card. A boulder! *Chill freezin' yah!* I scream silently. I think the edge of my lip twitches, but that's as much celebration as I'll allow myself outwardly. There's still money to be made, and there's no doubt I've got the best hand now.

Buff stares at me—now he's trying to read me. I can see it in his eyes: he knows what I've got. After playing a whole lot of cards with him, he knows me too well. I hope Long's still in the dark.

The bet's over to Long, who burns a hole through the two draw cards—the arrow and boulder—with his eyes, as if he hates what he sees. Either he's an icin' good actor, or he knows that last card wasn't good for him. He passes to me.

A tough call. I know I've got the better hand, but if I bet big then Long will suspect it, too, unless he thinks I'm bluffing. He might fold, which of course means I'll take a pretty nice pot. But on the other hand, if I can get him to keep betting, I can make it an even bigger take. I toss in a modest thirty sickle bet, beginning to feel like a real high roller, if only because I now consider thirty sickles to be modest. As if it's nothing at all, Long slides the required coins across, smiling. He won't be smiling in a minute.

Another card is flipped. Another boulder. *Un-freezin'-believable!*

Four of anything will win you a hand almost every time. Four boulders, well, that's a lock. Long taps the table, signaling he's passing to me again. Finally able to show my emotion, I smile, big enough to make him think I've got a good hand, which I do, but small enough to hopefully convince him I'm bluffing. The math's gotten too convoluted for me to have any clue as to how much is already in the pot, but I know it's more silver than I've ever had in my life, enough to pay back our

42

advance, fix the stuff we broke at Yo's, and buy something nice for Jolie.

I push every last one of my remaining coins into the pile in the center.

Long scrunches up his nose and folds, leaving his cards hidden. I'll never know what he had, but I don't give two shivers about that, because my hands are curled around a mound of silver, raking it in front of me, trying not to tremble with excitement.

There are smiles all around the table, except from Long. "Nice hand," Pierced-Ears says.

"Thanks," I say, standing up and starting to shovel the coins into my pouch, "for the game." Buff's already on his feet.

Pierced's smile fades quicker than visibility in a snowstorm. "Whoa there, pretty boy. Didn't they tell you at the door? It's a five hand minimum for a seat at a table. No winning and running."

I feel the color drain from my face. "No one told us that," I say.

"Must've slipped Ham's mind. He can be a bit of a snowflake sometimes. All brawn and no brains. You know the type, right?"

"Well, he didn't tell us, so…" I push in my chair.

"Sit down, boy!" Pierced screams, his face red and snaked with popping veins. All activity in the Hole ceases abruptly. Someone drops a coin and we can all hear it rolling across the floor, not stopping until it runs into the wall.

Silence.

I stare at Pierced, who now looks nothing like the kind, fun-loving card player from before. Despite the fact that he didn't lose anything but his five sickle ante in the last hand, he's dead set on us playing at least four more hands. A hostile environment is nothing new to me, except normally I'm the one bringing the hostility. As I look around, I see more than a few faces that look like they'll die before letting us leave.

My eyes meet Buff's and he shakes his head. The odds are against us—not the right time to pick a fight. I pull my chair out and sit down, scattering my silver on the table. Buff does the same, although his pile is much smaller than mine.

Gone are the smiles around the table, replaced by narrowed eyes and glares. This is not a friendly card game anymore, if it ever was to begin with.

"Deal," Pierced-Ears commands Buff. Buff scoops up the used cards and blends them back into the main deck. Hands them to Twin-Two, who does a bit of blending of his own before passing them back. Buff deals and I take a deep breath.

Four hands. We can just play it easy, fold out each hand, losing only the ante. It'll take a chunk out of the winnings, but not so much that we won't be able to take care of what we owe Yo.

I look at my cards, if only for show. A crown and small stone. Not the worst hand, but not the best either. I'll be careful with it. Buff doesn't even look at his, just tosses them into the center facedown. He's got the right idea. Twin-Two bets twenny sickles and I add my cards to the center before the betting even makes it around. Pierced's eyes never leave mine as he throws in the required silver. The betting goes around and around as they play out the hand, but still Pierced's eyes are glued to me. I look down, look away, count and recount my coins, but I can feel him on my face, as if he's physically touching me.

Pierced wins a sizeable pot and then it starts over again, with Twin-Two dealing. Three more hands and then we're outta here, no big deal.

I lift just the corner of my cards to have a peek, and then toss them in the center immediately, just a second behind Buff's even speedier fold. I had twin small stones. A playable hand, but not worth losing any more silver over.

The hand plays out quickly and one of the twins goes away with a pretty weak pot. Two to go. Fold and fold and we're done.

Mimicking Buff's technique, I fold the next hand without looking at my cards, but I can't resist sliding them in face up, where the twin crowns stare back at me, almost gleaming brighter than the silver ante coins in the middle. A really strong hand. I grit my teeth, trying to bite back the regret that tightens in my throat. Regardless of whether playing the hand was a smart move, showing my cards is high on the list of stupidest things I could've done. Pierced smiles at me, but not kindly like he did before, but with icicle teeth, cold and sharp, knowing full well that I'm not playing for real anymore.

"Hmmm," he muses. "I don't think it counts if you fold all five hands, isn't that right Mobe?"

Long-Face has a name. Mobe straightens up, drums his fingers on the table. "I'd have to check the rulebook, but I think that's right."

"You said five hands," I say between clenched teeth. Fighting's suddenly feeling like something I'd really like to do.

"Rules are rules," Pierced says.

"What do we have to do?" Buff says, trying to placate Pierced. He can probably see the violence all over my face. I got him in hot water with my temper once today—he won't let me do it again.

Pierced flicks a look at Buff. "Wise choice, kid. If one of you bets in the next hand, then you'll have fulfilled your obligation to the table."

I look at Buff—he looks back at me. It'll be more winnings lost, but worth it to avoid a fight. "Deal," I say.

The hand plays out with us waiting on the sidelines. Long-Face wins a small pot; it's almost as if no one was really trying. Last hand. Ante plus one of us betting and it's over. My deal. I blend the cards, slide them to Pierced to blend some more, and then hand them out facedown, two to each player.

When I look at my cards I feel a swirl of exhilaration in my chest. Impossible. The chances of what's just happened have to be close to zero. For the second time in five hands I've come up with twin boulders.

# Five

I stare at my cards, half-expecting them to morph into something more normal, like a bear claw and a stick, or a medium stone and a crown. Anything but what I've got. But the boulders remain, two big old rough eyes staring right back at me. Maybe my prayer to the Heart of the Mountain worked more than I thought.

"Your bet," Pierced says.

My head snaps up, where everyone's watching me. I dealt, so I should be betting last, not first. But then I notice: there's a heaping pile of silver already in the center. Everyone's already bet, and by the looks of it, they've bet big. "Sorry, I missed the bets," I say, feeling stupid and amateurish.

Pierced shakes his head like his child's just painted mud on the walls. Luckily, Buff helps me out. "Initial bet was twenny.

That was matched by everyone but me." So Buff's out already, which means I have to bet. He's left his cards face up as if to prove to me that he had no choice. A stick and a small boulder. One of the worst hands you can get.

"Thanks," I mumble. So all I gotta do is throw in twenny sickles and it's over. We leave with whatever we've got left. I do some quick math in my head. The one-oh-five I won in the first hand is down to eighty five with the four antes. Take away Buff's four antes and we're left with sixty five in winnings, before I ever even bet this hand. If I throw in twenny now…well, an extra forty five sickles will be nice, but they might not even cover the repairs to Yo's tables and chairs.

But I have no choice—I have to play. So if I've got to play with twin boulders in my hand, I might as well play big.

I shove forty sickles into the middle.

"Whoa, we've got a player," Pierced exclaims, rubbing his hands together. Like everyone else, me and Buff included, I think he expected me to just throw away my twenny sickles and run out with my tail between my legs. Not tonight.

He flips two more coins in and I watch as everyone else except Buff does the same. It's the biggest pot of the night and not even a single draw card has been turned. I flip the first card. A boulder! Excitement buzzes through me as I realize I'm about to make both Buff and I rich. But amongst the shower of silver coins that are floating through my mind, I see only one face. Jolie's. She's smiling the biggest, happiest smile I've ever seen as she comes home. Although I thought we started this because of what happened at Yo's, I realize now that subconsciously I was always doing it for her—to bring our family back together.

Although my butt's glued to the very chair I desperately wanted to leave not too long ago, I feel like I'm flying way up high where the summer songbirds cut lazy circles across the gray clouds. Nay, higher than that, above the clouds, where the sky's redder than blood and the sun's hotter than chill. Nothing can bring down my mood, not even a thirty sickle bet by one of the twins. Everyone, including me, matches it, but I run a few more coins through my fingers, trying to decide whether to add a bet on top.

Anticipation of adding silver to the pot zips up my spine. Everything feels so light, like I could fly right out of here with all the silver on the table and a new life.

Somehow I manage to bet small, flattening my face like a stone wall. Twenny more sickles. I expect a few folds, but everyone matches. I meet Buff's eyes, which are unblinking and wider than the palace grounds.

I flip the second card. A medium stone. I'm still way ahead with my triple boulders. No bets this time around, so I throw in another twenny, which everyone matches. We're all in too deep to back down now, but what none of them knows is that I've got them right where I want them.

Last card. A small stone, nothing against my trifecta of boulders.

The final round of betting begins with a surprise. Pierced-Ears raises an eyebrow and then pushes his entire pile into the pot. My mouth drops open, and so does Buff's, but everyone else looks like it's the most natural thing in the world for him to do at this point, even though they have to all know I've got a huge hand.

Then the folding begins. Both twins chuck their cards into the mountain-sized pile of coins with gusto. A couple of them flip over, a crown and an arrow, nothing that could've stacked up against mine anyway. Long-Face shakes his head and then flips his cards over to show us before folding. Twin crowns. A good hand, but not good enough.

It's down to me and Pierced and I can't for the life of me see how he could have me beat, and it doesn't matter anyway. I've already got so much riding on this hand that I was always going to see it through to the end. I push whatever coins I've got left into the pot.

"Maybe you've got stones after all, kid," Pierced says with a nod.

I smile, basking in the unexpected bit of respect from a guy who looked ready to take my head off four hands ago. And now I'm going to take all his silver.

"But you ain't got no brains," he adds, which wipes the smile right off my face. Huh? What does he know? "Show 'em."

He doesn't have to ask me twice. I snap one boulder over, then the other, slide them toward the draw cards to make it obvious what I've got.

He glares at the cards like he's going to grab them and rip them to shreds. But then his expression changes: his lips turn up, his eyebrows arch, and he laughs. Of all things, he laughs.

With a short twist of his wrist, he reveals his cards, the final boulder and a medium stone. I gawk at them, try to figure out what they mean, think back to how in the chill those cards could be better than my three boulders. The name of the very game we're playing springs to mind. Boulders-'n-*avalanches*. His two cards, when combined with the draw cards: two boulders, two medium stones, and one small stone—an avalanche. The best hand in the game, and a nail in my coffin.

I stare at him, unable to breathe, unable to speak, feeling every prick of his continued laughter in my skin, drawing blood. Final blood.

I drop my head in my hands as he rakes at the pile with greedy fingers.

Time passes painfully slow. Chairs scrape the floor. There are voices, pats on the back, but I barely hear them, barely feel them. Eventually, the voices die down and I'm left in silence. I feel a presence nearby and finally raise my head.

Buff sits next to me, staring off into space. "I—I—" I start to say, but my throat's too dry and it just comes out as a rasp.

"You had a good hand," Buff says, turning to look at me. "You did the right thing."

His words are no comfort. "I lost everything. Silver that wasn't even ours to lose." What's my sister going to think of me now that I'm broker than a lumberjack's leg trapped under a fallen tree?

"Not everything," Buff says, pointing to what's left of his pile of silver. Maybe a hundred sickle. He was the smart one. He played it safe, didn't take any big risks. "And you still got me as a friend."

His words only make the loss hurt more. I don't deserve him as a friend. I don't deserve anyone. All I'm doing is bringing down pain on everyone I touch. "You should stay away from me," I say.

Buff shakes his head. "You can't get rid of me that easily," he says. "We're gonna get through this together. We'll pay back every sickle."

I feel numb. "How?"

A nasally voice chimes in. "You will pay back every sickle," the redhead says. "And you'll do it our way."

"What the freeze is that supposed to—" I start to say.

"My boss has a job for you. Two months of it and we'll call things square."

"What kind of a job?" Buff asks.

"Now you're working for the king," she says.

~~~

"I got a job," I announce proudly. I don't mention that half of my pay will go to the Chance Hole, at least until I've paid off my debts. The funny thing is, I don't even mind that part of it. I was two seconds away from being broke and jobless—now I'm just broke.

"I thought you already had a job," Jolie says, cocking her head quizzically. It's nice having my sister at home, even if she's only allowed to stay until Wes and I leave. She can't be alone with my mother.

"Ha! Dazz, having a job—you must be thinking of someone else, Joles," Wes says with a laugh. My older brother stirs a mug of steaming tea for mother, who's curled up on our bearskin rug.

I give Joles a look, hoping she'll get the message to forget about what I said before. "Uh, that didn't work out. But this one's different."

"Did Yo finally convince you to work behind the bar?" Wes says. He always tells me I spend so much time at the pub that I might as well get paid while I'm there. He helps mother to a sitting position and folds her hands around the mug.

I smile, anticipating the look on his face when I tell him who I'll be working for. "Naw, nothing like that," I say.

"Tell us," Jolie says, resting her head on my shoulder.

"I don't think Wes is interested, but I'll tell you." Jolie giggles, sticks her ear close to my mouth so I can tell just her.

"I'm. Working. For. The. King," I whisper.

Joles pulls back, an awed expression flashing across her face. "Are you joking?" she asks. A fair question, considering how much I joke with her.

I tickle her, drawing a fresh set of giggles. "Stop, stop," she cries, but I don't listen, focusing on her stomach, which is her most ticklish spot. She's squirming and laughing and yelling for me to stop. Finally, I relent and we both gasp for air.

"Are you really working for the king?" she asks, grabbing my hand.

I nod.

"What?" Wes says, suddenly interested in what we're doing. He finishes wrapping Mother in a blanket and turns to face me. He has a rare day off from the mines today and it's weird to see him without even a smudge of dirt on his face. Without the dirt, he's the spitting image of my father, even more so than me. His dark hair is even cropped short with a slight curl at the top, just like Father used to wear it. His strong jawline, freshly shaved cheeks and chin, and tree-bark brown eyes complete the picture. Me, I've got two days' worth of dark stubble and too-long hair that puts the *un* in unruly. Feeling self-conscious all of a sudden next to my well-groomed brother, I run a hand through my hair like a comb, trying to straighten it.

"I got a job," I repeat.

"Nay, I got that part. The part about the king."

"The job's working for the king," I say with a shrug, as if it's no big deal.

Wes scoffs. "C'mon, Dazz. Where are you really working?"

"He's working for the king," Joles says, her hands on her hips, looking more like a mother than a sister. I laugh and put an arm around her. She's always given me more credit than I deserve. But for once, it's not misplaced.

"But how…?" Wes's expression alone is worth all the bad things that happened yesterday. Was it really just yesterday that I broke up with the witch? So much has happened that it seems like last year.

"What can I say, the king has an uncanny ability to recognize talent," I say, grinning. This is great.

Wes shakes his head, still coming to terms with the possibility that I'm not lying. He fills his own mug with boiling water, takes a sip.

"Buff's working with me too," I blurt out.

Wes spews a mouthful of tea across the room, causing Joles to erupt into a fit of laughter. I can't help cracking up, too. Everything about this morning is turning out to be perfect. While Wes is wiping his mouth and trying to compose himself, I add, "We start tomorrow, under a two month contract. If things work out, who knows? It could become permanent."

Wes uses a cloth to wipe up the mess on the floor. Then he stands, looks me in the eyes, says, "Well done, Dazz. I'm really—really proud of you." I swear there's melted snow in his eyes, but then it's gone. "So what kind of work will you be doing?"

It's not something that should be hard to answer, but Nasal-Talker wasn't very forthcoming with details before we left the Hole last night. As we repaid as much of the loan as we could with Buff's silver, she told us where to show up and when, and that was it. She wouldn't tell us anything else, except that the job wasn't difficult, paid well, and was of the utmost importance to the king. Who were we to argue? Under the circumstances, the job was a gift.

"Uhhh…stuff," I say. Well said.

"What sort of stuff?" Wes pushes.

"Tell him, Dazz," Joles urges, as if she knows exactly what I'll be doing. I wish she did so she could tell me.

"Important stuff," I add, winking. "Yah, uh, really important stuff that's top-secret and I can't really talk about it."

"Like spy stuff?" Jolie asks, excitement building in her eyes.

"That's all I can say."

"Are you for real?" Wes asks, frowning.

"I wish I could say more, but I'd lose my job."

Wes gives me a hard look, but then his face lightens. "Well, whatever you'll be doing, it's a big step. You're becoming a man." I ignore the implication of his last comment—that I'm not already a man—because I'm just happy that he's not asking anymore questions.

Wes slaps me on the back, ruffles Jolie's hair, gives Mother a kiss on the cheek, and then says, "I'm heading out to grab a few things. See you later?"

Jolie and I nod. Mother says, "Tell your father to bring in another load of firewood." Her hands are still cupped around her full mug of tea. The tea's cold.

# Six

We're right where we're supposed to be. The only problem: there's no one else here.

"She did say Skeleton Rock, didn't she?" Buff asks.

I gaze up at the large rock formation that protrudes from the mountainside. As its name suggests, the rocks are arranged in such a way that it looks like the decomposed remains of a large beast. The biggest rock is the skull and is shaped almost like a human's head. The story goes that there was a tribe of ogre-like creatures, called Yags, that once roamed the mountainside, eating everything in sight, from rabbits to bears to humans. But when the Star Rock crashed into earth, and our ancestors hid in the Heart of the Mountain, the Yags disappeared, either killed or having found somewhere else to hide. Some of the older Icers still believe there are a few of them left, and they get the blame whenever something unusual happens, like when a kid gets mysteriously killed, or a dead bear is found in the forest with no sign of how it died. *The Yags musta done it!* people say. I think it's all a load of shiver.

"Definitely Skeleton Rock," I say, scraping away a bit of the freshly fallen snow from the rocks with my toe. "And arsecrack of dawn, right?"

As if remembering how early it is, Buff yawns, rubs his eyes. "That's what she said, only without the arse…or the crack."

"Maybe we just misheard on account of the extreme nasalness of her voice."

Buff laughs, rips the pastry we bought in town in half, hands me a chunk. Wes gave me two sickles so I could buy it, as a sort of congratulations on the new job. A day's pay. For a second we both chew, relishing the warmth of the fresh bread.

The black of the clouds begins to lighten to a dark gray. It's snowing, but not heavily, which is the same as a clear sky for this time of year.

I sit down in a snow bank. "Do you think the king will show up personally?"

"Yah," Buff says. "And he'll personally tell us how proud he is that we were able to lose so badly in b-'n-a."

I grunt. "So badly and pathetically that he'd want to offer us a job." I pack a snowball, but don't throw it, just let it sit at my feet, start on another. "Must be a pretty shivvy job," I say, "if he'd pick two of the biggest losers around to do it."

"Hey, speak for yourself," Buff says, throwing a handful of snow in my face. I return the favor with my two snowballs, one in the chest, one in the kisser. For a minute we both wipe the cold off our faces and just laugh. Being frozen solider than an ice block will make you a little crazy sometimes, like wild-eyed

Jarp down in the Brown District. Sitting on the corner, he'll laugh at most everything. A bird flying overhead, a misshapen cloud, a normal-shapen cloud, a person walking by: he'll laugh so hard he has to hold his sides, as if his skin might tear open and let his insides out.

I start packing another snowball while we wait for…whatever it is we're waiting for. We wait and wait, wondering when Nasal-Talker is going to come by and tell us it was all a joke and that we better find a real job to pay back our debts before she gets someone to break our legs.

Right when I'm considering avoiding all that and heading back to the village, the mountain starts shaking beneath us, like it's awakening from a long sleep, ready to buck us off. It's a surreal feeling I've felt many times before, but it still leaves me breathless and clutching at the ground. "Are we in trouble?" Buff shouts above the earthy thunder.

We're both wondering the same thing, but slowly coming to the same conclusion. We shake our heads at the same time. "Nay," I say, voicing Buff's thoughts. "The avalanche must be a good two miles away. The west side of the mountain maybe?"

Buff nods. "It's a good guess."

As the tremors subside, I breathe easier in our consensus that whatever massive load of boulders and snow and ice is plummeting down the mountainside won't come anywhere near us. We typically get at least one nasty rockslide each winter, which might take out a handful of houses and maybe kill someone who's even unluckier than me, but we haven't had a "Village Killer" avalanche since before I was born. Since before my mother was born even. The last VK was more than fitty years ago and wiped out most of the Brown District and a good chunk of the Red too. The middle-class Blue District was hit less severely, and the castle and the White District were well above the melee, avoiding it completely. Big shocker. Even nature bows down to the rich.

"Will we get hit this year?" Buff asks. It's a question that gets asked dozens of times at Yo's each year.

I shrug. "You can only control what you can control," I say.

"Like how much you gamble and lose?" Buff says, smirking.

"Shut the chill—" I start to say, but then stop when I hear a whoop.

We scramble to our feet, spin around, gaze up the snowy mountainside. Plumes of snow burst from the ground like low-flying clouds. Blurs of black snowsuits flash down the incline, cutting side to side, carving up the slope. A line of sliders, chasing each other playfully, head right toward us.

"Look out!" Buff shouts, but I'm not sure if he's talking to me or the sliders bearing down on us. I don't have time to clarify as I jump to one side, narrowly avoiding getting chopped down like a poorly placed snowman.

When I look up there's snow in the scruff of my thin beard and flecks of ice on my eyelashes. "What the chill?" I say, pushing to my feet, warmth flooding through my limbs. I'm not warm, but something inside me wants me to be.

Three sliders are stopped just past us, having turned their slides at sharp angles to brake suddenly. It's almost like they were aiming right for us. We can't see their faces, because they're wearing thick masks to keep the snow and cold away, but their eyes are alight with adrenaline and blinking away coldness-induced moisture.

"You Daisy and Barf?" one of them says, his alert eyes flicking between us.

"What?" I say, taking a step forward. "I oughta beat you senseless for a move like that."

The guy laughs. "The king calls the shots here. You touch me and you'll be off the job quicker than you got on it. And trust me, you don't want that."

"What?" I say. "You mean, you're the ones meeting us?"

"Get wit' it, kid," another of the guys says. "You must be Daisy, the big gambler who lost enough silver to land you wit' us."

"It's Dazz," I say, taking another step forward. "Call me that one more time and you can slide the rest of the way down the mountain with a broken arm."

"And I'm Buff," Buff says, stepping beside me, his fists knotted. He's all riled up, too, which almost makes me grin. Nothing like a good scrap to start our first day on the job.

"Calm the freeze down," the first guy says, shaking his head. "Heart of the Mountain, you'd think we actually hit you guys."

"Near enough," Buff says, not giving an inch.

"Look, we're on the same side. Consider it a bit of friendly first day initiation. Now do you want to get to work or swing those antsy fists of yers?"

The honest answer is that I want to swing my fists, but this new job is supposed to be part of a fresh start, so I flex my hands, trying to coax the fight out of them. But I'm also not about to back off without some form of retribution. Weakness like that can haunt a guy. I pick up one of my snowballs and launch it hard enough to do some serious damage. *Crunch!* Although it was headed right for the main speaker's head, the ball slams into the open hand of one of the other guys, the biggest of the lot. Good reflexes. He grunts, squeezes the ball into mush in his fist, lets it crumble to the ground.

The main guy laughs. "Nice arm," he says. "That's why we keep this guy around. We call him Hightower, on account of…well, I think it's obvious."

*Obvious as a wolf in a sled dog team*, I think, staring at the big, brown eyes of the gargantuan who's at eye level despite being a good foot further down the hill than me.

"I'm Abe," the guy continues. "This fella is Brock." He motions to the other one who spoke to us. His eyes glare back, sort of cross-eyed. "And this little guy is…" Abe looks around, scanning at waist level, like he's trying to find a missing child. There's no one else around. "Where the freeze is Nebo?"

Brock gazes up the mountain. "'E was right 'ere a minute ago…Musta gotten lost at the hairpin." Something about his tone tells me he knows exactly what happened to the one they call Nebo.

Hightower grunts and points, so we all follow his gesture until we spot another slider coming down slowly, barely spraying any snow at all. We track his progress all the way to us, although it takes so long I swear another inch of fresh snow has fallen by the time he gets down. His every movement is uncertain, awkward, unbalanced, and when he tries to stop, his slider gets all tangled up with his feet and he goes down face first.

The others are laughing—even Buff is sniggering—and normally I'd probably join in, but something about the guy seems so helpless, so pathetic, that I don't feel like getting pleasure at his expense. After all, I've been pretty pathetic lately myself.

"Shut it," I say, punching Buff and shooting icicles at the others. I help the guy, who really is quite small, to his feet, using the back of my hand to brush some of the snow off.

Right away he pulls at his mask, which is caked with snow, until it pops off his head.

He's bald...and short...and jittery.

It's the man who came out of the Chance Hole last night.

"You!" I say, loud enough that the small man takes a step back, concern flashing across his red face.

"Do I know you?" he asks, saying it in such a way that it sounds like he thinks he probably should.

"We saw you leaving the Hole last night," I say.

He screws up his face. "Last night. Not a good night," he says.

"Ah, I wouldn't say that, Neebs," Abe says. "Your new losses pretty much guarantee you'll be working with us for the rest of time." Abe chuckles, takes a few steps over to smack Nebo on the back. Nebo cringes and puts a hand to his mouth as if the weak blow knocked a few of his teeth loose. "You're late. Where you been?"

"Uh, sir, I'm sorry, but uh, Brock here, he, well, he..."

"Spit it out!" Abe says, glancing at Brock. "What did Brock do?"

Behind Abe's back I see Brock use his thumb to make a slashing motion across his throat. "I, uh, well, Brock didn't do anything actually. I just, well, sort of fell going around a bend, sir. I'm sorry, it won't happen again," Nebo finishes lamely, ducking his head like he expects to be hit.

Clearly there's more to the story, and if I had to guess, it was probably Brock who caused the fall in the first place.

I chew on my lip, which is suddenly feeling numb. "So this is his first day, too?" I ask, wondering why he didn't meet them at the same place as us.

"Ha ha ha!" Brock laughs boisterously. "First day—that's funny. Despite Neeb's awful display of sliding, 'e's actually been runnin' with us for comin' on a year now."

"Then why…" I start to ask, but then figure out exactly what happened. Why would Nebo be playing high stakes boulders-'n-avalanches if he's already got a job and debts to pay? Simple. Because he wanted out. One lucky night and he could pay his way back to whatever normal job he might've had before he first lost big at the Chance Hole. But why would he want out of a job working for the king?

"Why what?" Abe says, staring at me strangely, as if he can see the tail end of the question hanging off the tip of my tongue.

"Nothing," I say.

"Good," he says, ripping off his mask. His face is pale white with a nose so flat it looks like someone uses it for a punching bag on daily basis. His ears stick out and sort of up, like maybe he can hear as well as an animal, like a rabbit. He's older than us, but only by a few years. "First, some instruction."

Beside me, Buff mumbles, "I thought school was long over."

Abe ignores him. "Brock. Wanna start with the rules?"

Brock nods and pull off his mask, revealing a face that only a mother could love, and even that would be stretch. It's so bruised and scarred that it looks like he mighta had a pet dog and offered his cheeks as a chew toy. Either that or this guy's been in a lot of fights, and not just of the fists and brawn variety. A long, six-inch scar runs from the edge of his right eye to his lips, like a curved scythe. It reeks of knife wound.

Maybe it's a good thing we didn't start something with these guys. Between grunting Hightower and Brock, whose eyes are looking crazier by the second, we mighta had our hands full.

Brock says, "We ain't got many rules, but if you break one, we'll break you." He sniggers, but I don't think he's joking. "One. Do as yer told. Abe gets 'is instructions straight from the crown, so take what 'e says as if King Goff's the one sayin' it. And don't ask questions. If we don't tell you somethin', it's cuz we don't want you to know. Got it?"

He pauses, as if testing us to see if we'll ask any questions right after him telling us not to. We both just nod.

"Number two. Don't tell anyone about what you do while on the job. You work fer the king, helpin' wit' the fire country trade routes. That's it."

"Well done," Abe says, which draws a grotesque smile from Brock's pock- and scar-marked face. "Maybe you got more than just rocks fer brains after all." Brock's smile fades and he looks like he wants to add a few scars to Abe's mostly smooth face.

"It's forbidden to go to fire country," I say, taking care to craft my question as a statement.

"Not for us," Abe growls.

"And you're the ones in charge of all the fire country trade," I say. Another statement.

"We're not the only group," he says cryptically. "But we're the most important ones."

I look at Buff, who shrugs. "Let's do this," he says, cracking his knuckles beneath his thick gloves.

Whatever *this* is.

# Seven

The job is freezin' easy.

First off, Abe gives us our own sliders. Beautifully carved, sanded, and polished planks of wood that are smoother than my arse was the day I was born. "Straight from the king's stores," Abe said when Hightower removes them from where they're strapped to his back and hands them to us. Compared to the homemade sliders we used to make as kids, these are perfection. And somehow they fit our feet perfectly, as if someone came and measured our feet while we were sleeping. Stepping onto them, we put one foot in front of the other, tying the ropes tight around our ankles.

On they feel even better than they looked off. Buff's smile says he's thinking the same thing.

With a couple of whoops and a few hollers (and at least one grunt from Hightower), we push off from the mountain, and all the hours I logged sliding as a kid seem to surround me as I feel every bump, slide into every turn, and dodge every obstacle. Buff's never been as good at sliding as me, but he has no trouble either. Compared to Nebo we're both sliding geniuses, and compared to the others, well, we pretty much fit right in. I've got no idea where we're going or what we're doing, but if I'm getting paid for sliding down the mountain then I figure not asking questions should be no problem at all.

We carve up the mountain for almost an hour, feeling the icy wind whipping around us, pushing life into our limbs and hope into our hearts. Maybe, just maybe, by our own stupidity we've stumbled upon the perfect job for us.

With every passing minute my body temperature warms, both from the athletic exertion and because some of the sting seems to drain from the air, as if our very motion is siphoning the cold away. Eventually, the thick, powdery snow thins, giving way to hard packed ice that propels us forward at speeds that are beyond anything I've ever imagined, sending bolts of excitement up my spine and whirling around my chest.

It's easy. Abe leads, and we follow, matching his every turn, cut, and angle, until the ice turns to slush, like it does sometimes in the Brown District in the very heart of the summer when it hasn't snowed for a few days and the sun sneaks a peak between the clouds.

Except this slush seems permanent, like it never really gets solid again, not even after a good snowfall. Like maybe it's not cold enough to sustain it.

A minute later my eyes widen and something lurches in my stomach when I see what lies ahead. Armies of trees, as spindly

66

and free of leaves as the ones that surround the village, but different somehow. It takes me a moment to realize what it is. They're not covered in snow. We're in the thick of winter, the coldest time of year, and they're as brown and snow-free as if it's the least cold summer day of the year.

As I'm thinking all this, Abe pulls up, sending up splashes of brown muck that seem as much dirt as snow, and even then, *snow* is a loose term. In fact, it's almost more water than snow. We're sliding on water and dirt.

We stop in a line, staring out at the brown and gray forest before us, naked, as if its white blanket has been picked up by a giant and rolled away, leaving it bare and unprotected. And beyond the trees are flatlands, dotted with strange green and gray plants, with gnarled branches, protruding at strange angles. The land is so flat I can see for miles, all the way to the horizon, where the cloud-free sky starts its rise in a pool of red blood. From where we're standing, a full quarter of the sky is red, and it's the most beautiful thing I've ever seen.

"Welcome to the border," Abe says, grinning. I grin back just as Nebo slides past us, out of control until he loses his balance and crashes down the river of water melting off the mountainside.

~~~

When we reach the border, the barest glint of sunlight slices through the battalions of gray before the clouds are able to close ranks and block it again. The sun is high in the sky, at its peak: midday has arrived. A full half day of work spent sliding down the hill. Not too shabby.

To think, the border can be reached in only a half day. If it wasn't for the fear of catching the Cold, you'd think Icers would come down to see it all the time, regardless of whether the king forbids it.

Then I see them: the Heaters. People of fire country. My first ever glimpse.

Two brown-skinned men man a lonely wooden watchtower that rises above the trees at the very edge of ice country. I can't take my eyes off them as they hop over a railing and descend a planked ladder, wearing almost nothing. They must be colder than a baby who's lost its blanket!

But then I feel it. A sort of tingling that starts in my toes and stretches up my legs and through my torso. Eventually it reaches my fingers and even the tip of my nose, leaving everything feeling…warm. Nay, more than that. More than warm. Hot. Like I've just stepped into our fireplace back at home, letting the flames surround me. Sweat beads on my face and drips off my nose and chin.

I look around to see if anyone else is feeling the same sensation.

While I've been staring at the Heaters, everyone else's been stripping. Bearskin coats and gloves and hats are flying all over the place, discarded haphazardly. Buff's got his pants half off too, leaving the bottom half of his muscled legs looking exceedingly white and hairy in his black undergarments. The others are taking their pants off, too, but underneath they're wearing some kind of short pants, looser than undergarments, and much less embarrassing. Without any other choice, I follow Buff's lead and strip down to my skivvies, relishing the feel of the warm—not just *not cold*, but *warm!* like it's full of hot stew or warm tea—air. Although I feel out of place amongst the other

68

more appropriately clad Icers, once the Heaters approach I feel better. They've got next to nothing on—just a thin cloth covers their torsos, giving them an almost savage look. Their hair and eyes are dark, and their bodies lean and tight and firm, like their skin's been twice-stretched over their bones and muscles. They carry long spears and have wooden bows looped on their backs with leather straps.

Heaters. What a day. Maybe I should lose at cards more often.

One of them speaks, using language that's the same as ours, but sounds so different coming from his mouth, like every word's rounder and longer. "I don't recognize these two baggards," he says, motioning to Buff and me.

"They're new. Today," Abe says.

The Heater nods, says, "Got a full load of searin' tugmeat and at least ten bags o' 'zard niblets. The king's favorite."

"That it?" Abe asks.

"Yeah," the other Heater says. He's taller than the first, but every bit as strong-looking. "Might be a coupla more months 'fore we have any special cargo."

I look at Abe, wait for him to question what the brown guy means by *special cargo*, but he just shrugs. "Roan's paid up that long anyway," he says. "He'll get his herbs either way."

*Herbs?* What are these guys talking about? Tugmeat and 'zards I understand. Fire country delicacies. No big deal. The king probably gets them delivered all the time. But the other stuff—huh?

I glance at Buff, whose cheek is raised. He's as confused as I am.

~~~

I come home in the dark with half a day's pay and a stiff back. Although the trip to the border was fun and easy—what with the high-quality slider strapped to my feet—the jaunt back to the top of the mountain was long and grueling, especially because we were carrying huge packs of meat on our backs, along with our sliders. Hightower took about twice as much as everyone else though, so that helped quite a lot. Like Abe said, he's handy to have around.

We dropped it off to a guy with a cart, just outside the palace walls. Abe told us good work and that the next job wouldn't be for three days, so we should rest up and meet him back at the same place at dawn. And that was that. On account of being so icin' exhausted, Buff and I barely said a word to each other as we walked back to the Brown District. Chill, I don't even think I'd be in the mood to fight anyone, even if such an opportunity arose.

But still, I can't complain. As far as I'm concerned, I've got the best job in the world.

Pausing a moment in front of our door, I stomp the snow off my boots and scrape the ice and muck off my shiny new slider. When I push through the door and duck inside, I feel a warm blast of heat from a healthy fire. Although it reminds me of the heat of the sun down at the border, it's not the same. Nothing will ever be the same.

"Welcome back, Brother." Wes is home already, having worked the dayshift, a smile plastered on his face as if he's been like that all evening, just waiting for me. It's a bigger smile than a new job warrants...

"What?" I say, somewhat rudely.

Wes strides over, claps me on the back. I flinch, suddenly feeling hot in my multi-layered getup. "Take a look," he says.

"Take a look at wha—"

He cuts me off with a hand in the air, pointing.

I look at him strangely, then follow his gesture over to where—

I gasp. This has to be a joke. For weeks and weeks, months and months, when I came home from wherever I'd been, Wes would usually be out working, and Mother, well, she'd be in the same ice-powder-induced stupor, usually rocking on the floor, babbling about how the things in the walls were creeping in on her, or some such rot.

But not tonight.

Tonight she sits upright, in a chair. She's still gazing into the fire, as if it might have beautiful pictures within the folds of its flames, but she's not babbling. In fact, the sound coming out of her mouth brings back memories of some of the best times of my life, back when we were a family—me and Wes and Joles and Mother and Father. None of us staying with neighbors. None of us addicted to ice. None of us dead. A real family.

She's humming.

It's a tune she used to hum to us before sleep, when our eyelids were so heavy I swore there were boulders tied onto and hanging from them. Countless nights my last memory was of her smiling face, just hum-hum-humming us to sleep.

I can feel the smile that lights up my face, every bit as big as Wes's, every bit as heartfelt. "What happened?" I whisper, as if raising my voice might break the spell, melt her back into the addict she became after my father died.

Wes shakes his head, claps me on the back again. "I'm not sure exactly. I was fixing to head for the mines, you know, shortly after you left. Joles had already scampered back on down the street. Mother was talking, mumbling, what sounded like her usual rubbish. But when I went to kiss her on the forehead, she looked at me."

"She looked *at* you?" My words are unbelieving.

Wes raises his eyebrows. "I know what you're getting at, and I swear it's true. She looked *at* me, not *through* me. Not like I wasn't even there. We made eye contact, and then her mumbles were reasonably coherent—weak sounding, yah—but real words and phrases. Of this world."

"What'd she say?" I can't help but to sneak another peek at her, my mother, who looks and sounds like a different person, what with her sitting in a chair and humming an old memory.

"She said she was sorry. She said she needed help. She said she loved us."

"And that was it?"

"Not exactly. She said if you—meaning *you*, Dazz—could do it, then she could too. I think you getting a job inspired her."

Now it's my turn to raise my eyebrows. If they only knew. If Mother only knew. How my gambling losses led to a job that I'd swear was a gift from the Heart of the Mountain. If she knew that, would she still have been inspired? Doesn't matter. Not one bit. What matters is she's clean for the first time in a long time. But there's a long way to go.

"Any signs of the need?" I ask Wes, who's back to smiling. His lips curl opposite and he frowns. It's almost like he was avoiding the topic. The few times we've been able to get Mother clean haven't worked out so well. The need always comes back, and with it the shakes and the sweats and the cursing and the scratching. And then she gets her hands on some ice, almost magically, and we're right back where we started.

This is life after Father.

"Not yet," Wes says. "I skipped work today to watch her, but I can't miss again."

"I've got it covered for the next two days," I say.

"Don't tell me," Wes says, and I can see what he thinks in his narrowed eyes.

"I still got a job," I say, not getting angry at Wes's assumption. It was probably a fair one anyway.

Wes frowns. "Then how do you got it covered?"

"We've got two days off," I say, shrugging. "It's different than most jobs."

"I'll say," Wes says. "But they're paying you?"

He wouldn't believe me if I told him how much. But they took half of it to repay my debts, so what's left over seems more reasonable. I show him the silver.

He whistles, high and loud. "That's for a day?"

I shrug again, give him half. "For food and such," I say.

He grins. "My brother, the working man."

~~~

Wes thinks five to six days should do the trick. So I'll watch her for the next two, then he'll try to get off work again for the third, and hopefully I'll get another couple of days off to cover the end of her needing period.

But I can't wait that long to tell Jolie, even if I'm getting her hopes up more than I should.

I'm too excited to even take the time to get washed up before heading down the road. Neither do I eat anything before I leave. Truth be told, I'm secretly hoping for more of Looza's famous stew. Talk about a perfect ending to a perfect day. I never knew having a job could be like this; if I did, I'd have gotten one as soon as I was done with school, when I was fourteen.

I find myself whistling the same tune Mother was humming as I stroll along, stepping in deep footprints made by someone a lot bigger than me. Not a care in the world.

I almost pass the house, which I never do. Because the lights are out, which they never are. Not this late anyway.

I stop, look along the row of squat, stone houses. Every last one's got the orange glow of firelight coming from them. But not Clint and Looza's place. Are they out? Do they ever go out? And if they did, wouldn't they tell me? They know I come by to visit every night, without fail, even if it's only for a minute before I traipse on down to Fro-Yo's.

My heart's beating faster and I don't know why. There's no cause for concern just because the lights are out. It is rather late—perhaps they turned in early. But still…

I peek in the window, see only darkness. And then—

I'm blinded by the flash of something bright and sharp in my eyes. A beam of light through the window. I cry out, look away, blinking at the spots as if they're something I can crush between my eyelids.

Something's not right, but I can't see well enough yet. I keep blinking, furiously, rubbing at my eyes with the backs of my hands. When I open my eyes again I can still see the ghost of the light flaring up before my vision each time I blink, clouding it, but not enough that I can't see at all.

As I grope for the door, there's a scream, high-pitched and small and almost animalistic, desperate, but it's cut off only halfway through.

Jolie.

My tainted vision is nothing. My aching muscles and bones are nothing. A surge of energy rips through me and I find the door, thrust it open, right away spotting the beam of light dancing away from me with scuffles and scrapes and muffled cries.

I'm a mountain lion and Jolie's my cub. And whoever's got her will face my wrath. With reckless abandon I barge through the house, trying to guide my feet by memory. Quick step to the left, avoid the table. Quick step to the right, avoid the—

CRASH! I bash into something soft, toppling it over and getting my legs all knotted up, bringing me down on top of it. There's a muffled cry, but I'm already rolling off, because I don't need even a shred of moonlight to know that it's Looza, wide and soft and rough with ropes, tied up. Either Clint's the culprit, gone off-his-mind crazy, or he's around here somewhere, tied up too.

I move on, barely catching a glimpse of the bouncing light as it exits out the back door, taking my sister with it.

An odd numbness buzzes through my legs, but I force them forward, charging for the door, meeting it just as it's slammed in my face. I don't feel the impact—because it's my sister they've got—just bounce off, rock on my heels, push off, tear open the door, leap out into the frozen night.

The light's there, stopped, as if waiting for me. I can't see past it, because it's like a shield, glowing round and bright, blocking my vision as effectively as a stone wall. I'm unsure for a second, because up until this point, the light's been running, so of course I had to try to catch it. But now that I've caught up, my bear-in-an-ice-sculpture-museum routine may not be the most effective method of getting Joles back.

Fists clenched at my sides, I take a step forward. "Give her bac—"

Just like during the fight at the pub, something wallops me in the back of the head. The light and Jolie's muffled cries and my perfect day...all go black.

# Eight

A bad dream. I know that's what it was as soon as I open my eyes. Almost like a trick, it had good parts, like getting a job and my mother being clean and Jolie being able to come home to live with us again, before turning nightmarish with a bright light and a rock to the back of the head.

I quiver, trying to separate dream from reality. Why am I so cold?

Heavy swirls of gray and black shift overhead, spitting bits of white. Some of it lands on my face and I wipe it away.

A voice echoes hollowly from somewhere. A dream voice?

A dream inside a dream, maybe. When I wake up I won't remember, because I never remember my dreams.

The voice again. Wes. Dream Wes. Probably just as responsible and stick-in-the-mud as the real Wes. I don't really want to see him now, because I'm too cold, too filled with heaviness after nightmare number one. Even though I know it's not real, it hurts like it is.

"Dazz? What the...? Mountain Heart, Dazz! There's blood!"

"Just a dream," I say. "Go away." Everything's blurry, but not because of spots from a bright light or the white wetness what floats above me. Just real blurry.

I close my eyes.

"Where's Jolie?" Wes says.

~~~

The next time I awake it's not dream number three.

But dream number one and dream number two are still alive in my memory, which is unusual for me. I keep my eyes closed, waiting for them to fade away so I can be happy again.

Murmurs caress the air around me. Saying something...I don't know what. Don't care much either, as long as the memories of the dreams are trapped in my head. "Go away," I say, both to the murmurs and the nightmare-memories. My voice is crackly, like dry leaves.

"Dazz?" my brother's voice says.

"Nay, it's the King of the Yags," I say. "All who stand before me shall tremble in fear."

"Dazz, you need to tell us what happened," Wes says, as if what happened is real. Perhaps he's talking about what happened at the pub. Maybe I'm just waking up from the hit I took and everything's been a head-injury-created dream. That would make more sense than me actually working for the king.

"Dazz." A different voice this time. Buff. "Where's Jolie?"

The bad dreams scream through my head, throbbing, throbbing, pounding, chucking a massive tantrum, ripping my skull apart. Buff's two words change everything, tell me everything I already knew.

Not a dream. Jolie's been taken.

"They took her," I whisper. I won't open my eyes. Can't. Not with them looking at me. Not when I failed her.

"Who?" Wes again.

"The light," I say, making no sense at all.

"There was a light?" Wes asks, understanding me like only a brother can.

I nod. "Didn't see them. Heard Jolie. Someone hit me." They probably figured that much out while I was sleeping. Some help I am. Although I feel like there's something invisible holding me to the bed, I push up with all my might, try to get to my feet, ripping at something soft that's tight against my head, fighting the double sets of hands that push me back down, swing at them, hit one of them, but my punch is so weak I don't think either of us feels it.

Everything rushes past and I start to fade.

"Jolieeeeeeee…" I say.

~~~

Jolie's gone and Mother's back on the ice. Mountain Heart only knows where she got the money. I've been in bed for two solid days. Not by choice. If it was up to me I'd be out there looking for Joles, but the doctor said my head's pretty bad, and walking's out of the question for at least a week.

I questioned it though, even when they strapped me to the bed with ropes. I pulled them away, squirmed my way out, ran for the door, feeling like I was floating the whole time. Perfectly fine.

But Wes and Buff cut me off before I got too far, fought me back into bed, tied the ropes even tighter. I cursed them out, said some things I should probably regret, but don't. After all, they're stopping me from finding her.

A Brown District search party's already out there looking. The District lawkeeper's been out to Clint and Looza's house, inspected the footprints and the bloody mess I left, and supposedly he's confident they'll find her.

I'm not holding my breath.

Clint and Looza are shaken up, but fine. They came by to talk to me. Like me, they saw nothing, were surprised by men in masks at the door who forced their way in and tied them up. After smothering the fire, the men started to wrestle Joles out the door. That's when I showed up.

I've got work tomorrow, but Buff says he talked to Abe and it's okay, given the circumstances. I'll still get paid just the same, as if I worked. Why would he be so generous? Not that I give a shiver about any of that right now. Silver and sickles and debts and boulders-'n-avalanches seem like meaningless things now that Jolie's gone. I guess they always were pretty meaningless in the scheme of things.

Wes is out looking for Jolie. He got time off from work too, but he won't get paid anything while he's gone. I guess the mines aren't as generous as the king.

Buff's here, mostly to watch me, although I can barely move to scratch an itch, much less work my way outta the complex web of ropes they've strung up to keep me still. My head's pounding something fierce, but I can't sleep for one second longer, so I hold my eyes open.

"We'll find her," Buff says, sitting nearby. Mother's beyond him, waving her hands at the fireplace, like she's coaxing dead spirits out of it. Wes hasn't got a clue where she got the ice from, but it's almost a relief that she's back on it so we don't have to deal with her needing time while we're trying to find my sister.

"I'll find her," I say.

"Not until your head's on the mend," Buff says.

"It's fine now," I retort.

"You're so weak I could kick your arse with one arm and a leg tied behind my back," he says.

"One, that's physically impossible, and two, I'd eat yellow snow before I'd ever let you beat me in a fight," I say, almost managing a smile.

Buff curls half a lip. Smiles are luxuries right now. "Just give it a couple more days and then we'll go looking for her together."

"Like I have a choice," I say, straining against the ropes to show him just how helpless I am.

"You want something to eat?" Buff says.

"Like I want you spooning soup in my mouth. It's bad enough when Wes does it." Just the same, I know it's a rare thing to have a friend like Buff.

Buff shrugs. "I could find you a nurse. A real icy one, even icier than the White District witch."

"The witch wasn't icy. And I'll pass. I'm on a break from girls. Maybe permanently."

We're both quiet for a minute, tired of the type of banter we used to both love. Questions hang in the air like drying shirts on a clothesline.

"Why'd they take her?" I ask the air.

"Only the Heart of the Mountain knows," Buff says, thinking the question was for him.

Why her? Why anyone? Who took her? Where'd they take her? Are they going to hurt her? Is she—is she—is she............?

The questions are dropping from the air like falling stars, bashing me from all sides—and the last question keeps hitting me, rebounding, hitting me again, never quite finishing, because to finish it will make it true.

(Is she dead?)

"We're going to find her," I say, clinging to the statement with every bit of false hope I can muster.

# Nine

Life marches on.

Bad shiv happens, people cry—not me, but some people—and then everyone forgets about it, keeps on keeping on as if nothing bad happened in the first place.

Wes lost his job after three weeks of not showing up. I've gained more respect for him than ever before, because he put Joles before his job, before Mother, before everything. Not that it helped.

Buff's been great too, spending all his days off with me, scouring the town, peeking in windows, asking people itchy questions, like "Where were you on the night..." and "Have you seen a little girl..." We even romped through the Red District one night, sneaking down alleys that aren't safe even during the day, picking fights with guys we had no business picking fights with. The two black eyes would've been worth it if we'd found out anything at all about where Jolie might've been taken, and by whom. But nobody knew an icin' thing, or if they did, they weren't talking, other than with their fists.

Abe told Buff I have to go back to work tonight or he'll stop paying me, by order of the king, which I think is a bunch of bearshiv, because the king don't know me from a three-legged goat. I could be dead in a cold grave and King Goff would go on nibbling on his fire country delicacies as if nothing had changed.

But I'm going back to work anyway, not because Abe says I have to, but because I need a distraction, and our family needs a bit of that meaningless silver, so we can keep eating.

Buff's pretty much kept me up to date on the job, what he's seen, what he's done. It hasn't been that much different than the first day. He and the others slide down the snowy part of the mountain, hike through the unsnowy bits, and then either deliver trade items—like bear meat and furs—or pick up fire country goods. Then they climb back to the top. Easy breezy.

Just like life, Buff and I march on, too, out of the Brown District, through the Blue District, and around the White District, even though that's the long way. I'm in no mood to see any witches today.

As high and formidable as they are, the greystone palace walls do little to hide the grandeur of the king's royal castle. Surrounded by the turreted wall, the heavy stone blocks of the castle rise up in five different places. Four thin towers that nearly reach the clouds can be seen from almost anywhere in ice country. And the fifth tower, in the center of the four thin ones, is the marvel of the Icers, rising higher than the others, splitting the clouds in half. It is said that from the uppermost lofts of that tower, the king can see direct sunlight, no different than in fire country.

With the teeth-chattering cold of night already fallen, we're stuck waiting on the outside, as winter whips the snow-filled air around us. Neither of us have the faintest clue as to why we have to do this job at night, but it doesn't really matter because we'll do it either way. It's too cold to talk, so we pull our slider masks over our heads.

It's the clearest night we've had all winter, and the dim light of a few stars pokes through the intermittent cloud cover. The brighter light of the moon glows overhead, casting a surreal sheen on everything. If we have to work at night, tonight's as good a night as any.

When the palace gates open and Abe ambles out from inside, everything I thought about him changes in an instant. *He was actually...inside?* Maybe he does get his orders directly from the king. Maybe he does have as much power as he says he does.

He seems to recognize how impressed I am. Icin' eyes. Always giving my thoughts away for free. "Welcome back," he says, directly to me. "I just had a chat with Goff"—he says the king's name casually, like they're old friends—"and we got special cargo arrivin' in a few days, so we hafta deliver some extra goods today." He's speaking words I understand, but when you put them all together like he does, they make no sense. Questions pop up in my mind, but I swallow them away, because questions are against the rules.

Nebo arrives next, looking as skittish as a pup that's lost its mother. I try to greet him, but his eyes never leave the ground, darting around like he's trying to locate his lost marbles.

Brock and Hightower arrive last and together, which makes me wonder whether they're friends, whether they talk at all. Well, not talk talk, but something like conversation, with Brock saying something and Tower grunting a response, maybe adding an extra grunt that Brock can then respond to.

They nod a greeting, which we return, but no one says anything about my sister, for which I'm glad. I haven't given up on her, not by a longshot, but that don't mean I want to talk about her all day and night.

"New guy," Abe says, and both Buff and I look at him. He laughs, not in a nice way, but like he enjoys making us look foolish. "You," he says, pointing at me. "Daisy."

Something in me snaps. Or maybe was already snapped from the night Joles was taken from me. Whatever the case, I can't control my fists, which start swinging at Abe like I'm taking on a whole gang of Red District rowdies. The first punch is a gut shot and bends him at the waist—the second takes his head off. He spins from the impact, torqueing around in an awkward, twisting way, and then goes down in a heap.

Brock's on me like a beggar on a bear steak, while Hightower holds Buff away from the fray. "You didn't just do that," Brock says, half-laughing, like he's been hoping I'd do something crazy. "Nice punch," he adds, which surprises me. What's the plan? Compliment me to death?

I grit my teeth and wait for him to pull a knife. He doesn't.

Although I hit Abe with everything I had and my hand is stinging, he's pulling himself to his feet, massaging his jaw, one eye closed and the other one all bugged out and angry as chill.

"I'll leave," I say. "I'll find another way to pay the Hole back." Even as I say it I wish there was another way, wish I could take back those two punches thrown only out of frustration and anger and sorrow about my sister. Not because Abe called me Daisy, a stupid lowbrow insult. That was just removing the lid covering what's been boiling up in me for days.

Abe laughs again and it sounds slightly maniacal. Okay, *a lot* maniacal, which I suspect is the only way a laugh can sound when it comes right after taking a haymaker uppercut to the jaw.

"That's not the way things work around here," he laughs. He cracks his jaw, sighing, like it was out of place and is now as good as new. "You'll take your punishment and then we'll get on with the job. Other than that, your only other option is a shallow grave."

I'll pass, thanks. "Whatever," I say, secretly thankful for whatever's coming. Whatever it is, it'll be better than losing the best—and only—job I've ever had.

Brock moves forward, his arms out like I might bite him. "I gotta 'old you," he explains. I don't want crazy-eyes holding me, but I don't have much of a choice, do I? So I relax and let him pull my arms behind my back, clamping them tight so I can't defend myself.

"Now wait just one minute," Buff says, struggling against Tower's iron grip.

"It's okay," I say. "I earned this one."

Abe saunters up, cracking his knuckles, impressing me further at how well he took my best punch. He's not a big guy, but not small either, and clearly there's a toughness in him that's beyond flesh and bone.

I lick my lips, waiting for the first blow to come.

When it does it's like a wooden plank to the gut, taking every last bit of breath out of me. But that's not the end of it.

Oh nay, not by a mile. While I wheeze and try to get my breath back, Abe lays into me like an avalanche, pummeling my stomach, chest, and finally my face. No stranger to a good beating, I take every punch with dignity, never crying out, but wishing that each shot will be the last. There's blood running down my lips and I can feel things swelling all over, but still he continues the barrage.

The only strange thing about it all: Abe seems to start taking a little bit off his punches near the end. It's not like him—at least not like I'd expect. I'd expect him to beat on me full force from start to finish.

When he's finally done, I'm hanging limp from Brock's hold, all fight sapped out of me. Through watery, puffy eyes, I can see Buff's red face, his taut muscles, the last remnants of his fight to break free from Hightower to help me. In a weird way, I'm glad he didn't. I got what I deserved, and now I can hold my head high again.

I spit out a clump of blood. This morning I had black eyes; tomorrow I'll have black eyes on black eyes on swollen lips.

The price of a temper.

"We're even," Abe says, not looking at me, as if he might be trying to convince himself. He glances at the castle guards, who are laughing and watching. "You'll take a regular load plus the extra cargo."

~~~

With the moonlight guiding us, we make it down the mountain in record time. Or at least most of us do. Nebo's five or six minutes back, trying not to kill himself on one of the many dark, protruding boulders that we zigzag around.

Although Abe's beating left me hurting every place from the waist up, the exercise feels good, and the cold's left me numb. I'll pay for it tomorrow, but tonight I'm okay. Even the hefty load I'm carrying didn't bother me too much. I've got three bear skins, four sizeable jugs of melted snow water that are starting to freeze, and the "extra cargo", which basically looks like some big bags of some kind of herb. I want to ask about it, but at this point a question might get me killed.

My muscles start locking up during the hike to the border, but I bite back my grunts and soldier on, determined to bear it like a man. I don't know why, but I want Abe's respect now more than ever.

As the cloudbanks roll away overhead, the brilliant night sky looms above, full of more stars than I even knew existed. It's like the whole sky is stars. And the moon is a pale globe, bigger than I've ever seen it, fuller than full. An owl hoots softly somewhere in the forest, as if asking us our names.

We don't offer them.

The sound of axes tearing into wood clucks through the forest. *There are jackers working this late?* I wonder to myself. And this far down the mountain—all the way at the border? It doesn't make sense. There are trees aplenny around the Districts, and more are constantly being planted. We could never harvest them all. Then who?

Abe sticks two fingers in his mouth and whistles. The chopping stops and his whistle is returned. Clearly someone's expecting us.

We trod on, breaking out from the trees and stepping onto the hard-packed dirt that runs right up to the trees. Further on into the flatlands the landscape is powdery, what the Heaters call sand. I wonder what it'd feel like to walk on it, but I know now's not the time to find out. We have a job to do.

Out of the tangle of the forest, we walk faster, skirting the edge of our two countries. Ahead of us a group of Heaters emerge from the shadows, lugging axes and picks and shovels. The choppers. Not Icer lumberjacks after all, which makes more sense. But are the Heaters allowed to harvest ice country trees?

Abe doesn't seem bothered at all, just strides right up, dumps his cargo on the ground in front of them. "It's all here," he says. "Extra cargo, too, this time."

The rest of us catch up and unload everything we're carrying, save for our sliders. I straighten up, feeling instant relief in my back and bones, hoping there's no pick up tonight. Hiking back up the mountain will be hard enough without tugmeat strapped to our backs.

With coppery eyes and more black hair than a Yag, a short, barrel-chested man steps forward, hand extended as if ceremonially accepting the trade items. "Thank ye," he says, his voice scratchier than a gnarled thicket. "Load up, you tugs!" he bellows.

The Heaters behind him move forward and grab the packs and sling them over their backs, staggering under the weight. These men don't look like the two muscly border guards I saw before. They're tanned and lean, yah, but their leanness is over the border to skinny. The rags they wear around their midsections are tattered and dirty, like they've been wearing them for weeks, maybe months. Scars crisscross their backs, arms, and chests in a pattern that matches the leather, multi-tasseled whip hanging from the bushy-bearded spokesman's belt.

To me, they look like prisoners.

# Ten

We transfer goods to the fire country prisoners three more times that winter, always at night, always to different locations. The day trips are pretty stock standard, trading ice country goods for fire country goods, but the night trips always include the strange bags of mystery herbs.

"Do you think those herbs are some kind of drug?" I ask Buff as we walk through the Blue District. We've given up on the Red District. If someone took my sister there, she's well hidden, because we've scoped out every last shivhole in that shivvy District.

"Can't be," Buff says. We've talked about the herbs a dozen times, but always end up chasing ourselves in a circle. "The only drug I've ever heard of is ice powder. If there was some herb floating around, we'd know about it."

"Maybe it's the king's secret stash," I say.

"It's possible," Buff says. "You mean, kind of like a leader to leader exchange thing."

"Yah, with the fire country guy—what's his name?—uh, Roan." It's the only explanation I can come up with. Other than that, the herb is just an herb, and why would it require all the night work, secrecy, and smuggling in by Heater prisoners?

I know I shouldn't care about the herbs, or the trade with the Heaters, or anything other than getting Jolie back, but my theories are the only thing keeping me sane. Every day that passes without seeing Jolie is like a bruise on my soul, an ache in places that are impossible to reach and that don't heal, not with time, not with talk, not with sleep.

The lawkeeper stopped the search weeks ago, chalking it up to a mysterious disappearance, despite the fact that Clint, Looza and I all saw someone take her. But I won't stop searching, not now, not ever.

Now with winter waning and the throes of a frosty spring upon us, I know that if I don't figure out what happened to Jolie soon, it might be too late. It might already be too late. *Shut up!* I tell myself. If I think like that, I might as well curl up in a thick patch of snow and let the Cold take me.

Speaking of the Cold, incidents of the disease have been on the rise as of late. Some say it's because the winter was one of the coldest yet, and others believe the Heart of the Mountain is angry with us for all of the evils that take place in the Red District. Me, I don't care either way. If the Cold will come, it'll come. Who am I to question the why or the how?

I pause in front of an arched doorway. The Blue District isn't nearly as well off as the White District, but it beats the chill out of the Brown. The streets are clean and free of beggars, the houses are solid and well-maintained, and the people are smart enough to slam their doors in our faces as soon as they realize we're not from around these parts. I'm not saying I like it, but there are plenny of bad folk who might try to take advantage of them, so they're right to be cautious.

Another door to knock, this one painted bright green under its white archway. Recently touched up by the look of it. Smooth and bright. I rap on the door with my knuckles as Buff rubs his gloved hands together beside me, trying to generate some heat.

Someone hollers from behind the door, but I can't make it out. Unusual for this District. Usually the people are quiet and timid. The boisterousness of the cry reminds me of a good old Brown District welcome.

The door opens.

Nebo stands before us, bald and short and altogether the most unintimidating person you could ever meet. His mouth forms an O and he sucks in a gasping "Uhhh!" and then tries to slam the door.

I swing my foot out and wedge it between the door and the jamb. The heavy wood crunches my toes, but I'm already moving forward, lowering my shoulder, barging my way inside. Nebo's thrown backwards and into the house as the door rebounds off the wall with a solid thud.

He tries to scramble away from us on his arse, but runs right into a table leg, his eyes full of terror.

"Whoa there, Neebs. We're not going to hurt you," I say, feeling somewhat bad about the jittery man's response to our forced arrival.

"Like—like—chill you're not," he says. What is this man so afraid of?

94

"Nay, really, Neebs. We didn't even know you lived here. We were knocking on every door on this street," Buff says.

Neebs is shaking his head, his eyes closed. "Go—go away."

"We just want to ask you a few questions," I say. Although I'm pretty sure the nervous little man can't help us with Jolie, clearly he's scared of something and I want to know what. Plus, he's been working for Abe/King Goff much longer than us, so he might know more about the mystery herb.

"Nay, nay, nay, nay, nay," Neebs drones on.

"It'll only take a minute," Buff adds.

"Nay, nay, nay, nay, nay."

Ten "nays" and we haven't even asked a question yet. Nebo's as still as a statue, still on the floor, back against the table leg. He looks sort of like a child throwing a tantrum, his eyes all squinted shut, his mouth crunched in an overdone scowl.

I kneel in front of him and he twitches, like he can sense how close I am. "First question," I say, as soothingly as I can. To my ears my voice sounds like grated rocks.

"No questions," Neebs says.

I ignore him, say, "Why don't you want to work for the king anymore?"

"Rule one: no questions," Neebs says.

"We're not on the job," I say, "and you're not Abe, so I'll ask you any freezin' thing I want to." It comes out a little harsher than I'd planned, but I'm getting frustrated. I repeat the question.

"Bad man," Neebs says.

"Abe's a bad man?" Buff asks, sliding in beside me.

"Nay, nay, nay, nay, nay," Neebo hisses. His eyes are still closed and his mannerisms are so jerky I wonder if he's got more wrong with him than just silver problems. "The king." He clamps a hand over his mouth as if he just swore at his mother.

"The king is bad?"

"Not saying any more," he says, pouting out a lip like a child.

"What are those herbs?" I ask.

He shakes his head.

"Drugs?"

He shakes his head but I don't think it's an answer.

"Tea leaves?"

Another shake of the head.

"Spices?"

His eyes flash open and I'm surprised to find them clear and blue. "Not spices," he says.

It's like my mind is trying to climb a sheer rock face, and its fingers are scrabbling for something to grab on to, but they keep coming up empty, keep sliding down it, getting torn by the stone, slipping farther and farther toward a fall that will eventually kill it. Nothing makes any sense. That's usually when *everything* makes sense. It hits me.

"Is it some kind of medicine, like the concoctions the healers use?"

The look on his face tells me I've hit on something that's close to the truth. "Abe made me promise not to talk about all that," he says.

"All what?" Buff says with a growl, but I warn him off with my eyes. I don't want to scare him back into his shell.

"Nope," Neebo says, crossing his arms.

"What kind of medicine?" I ask. I soften my voice. "Please—it's important."

He bites his lip, as if he has to keep it from telling me everything.

"Please," I say again.

"Uh-uh."

"What's the special cargo we'll be picking up soon?" I ask.

His eyes close and he goes back to shaking his head.

"Do you know what happened to my sister?" I ask.

He stops shaking, but doesn't open his eyes, doesn't give an answer. Just sits there.

We leave, knowing more than we did when we arrived, and yet knowing nothing.

~~~

It's quiet on the home front. Mother's passed out on the floor in front of a dwindling fire, a blanket draped over her, clearly placed there by Wes, who's sitting in a wooden chair just watching the last few flames dissolve into hot embers.

He doesn't acknowledge my arrival. Not even when I slam the door much harder than is necessary. I hate going home these days.

"I knocked about a hundred doors in the Blue District," I announce. Wes flinches, as if I've pulled him out of a daze, but doesn't turn or say anything. "No one was really in the talking mood."

Wes just stares at the fire. He's beginning to scare me. He's always been the strong, responsible one—the replacement for my father. Mother could never cope, could never be the one to provide for us, but Wes was stalwart, unflappable. "Get on with what has to be done," he would always say, mimicking one of my father's favorite expressions and sounding a chill of a lot like him. But now, ever since Jolie…

Well, he's still out of work. And it's not like he's just been sitting at home staring at the fire. He's tried to find a job, but things are tight right now, and nothing's available. Nothing respectable anyway. Luckily I'm making enough to support us—barely. I think that's what hurts him the most, feeling like he's relying on someone else, like he can't stand on his own two feet.

I hate seeing him like this.

"You should get some sleep," I say. Wes nods. "Are you gonna be okay?" He nods again. "Goodnight."

My mother shifts in her sleep, murmurs, "Your hair is all a mess, Joles, let me braid it for you."

Wes's shoulders shake as he cries.

I go to bed, crying on the inside.

# Eleven

Today's the day. The special cargo delivery from fire country. Regardless of whether Nebo would answer our questions, we'll find out soon enough what we'll be collecting. As usual, it'll be a night job, so Buff and I have got the whole day to kill.

Neither of us can take another day of knocking doors and getting them slammed in our faces, so we decide to go sliding for fun. It feels like forever since we've felt the freedom of the mountain without Abe and his gang surrounding us as part of a job.

We tackle the west slopes, where the pines thin out and leave a relatively unobstructed path of fresh powder. It's not as cold as it was even yesterday, a clear sign that spring is here to stay. The snow might melt off in a few months, if it does at all, but today it's as thick as Looza's stew—perfect for sliding.

We trudge to the top of a steep hill, panting heavily by the time we reach the crest. Sitting next to each other, we grin like a couple of well-fed dogs as we strap our sliders to our feet. For a moment I feel like a child again, back when things were simpler, and my only responsibilities were having fun and getting in trouble. Although I still seem to have the trouble part down pat.

"Ready?" I say, as we push to our feet.

"Chill yah," Buff says, still grinning.

"Go!" I yell, and we slip over the edge, letting gravity do all the work, practically sucking us down the mountainside.

"Woohooo!" we cry, giddy as schoolboys.

The cold wind whips against my face, bright and fresh and alive, and I'm glad I didn't wear a slider's mask. A small patch of pines runs toward us, like they've got feet and they're the ones moving, not us. I cut hard to the right, carving a curving line in the snow, while Buff goes left.

We whip around the trees and then come together on the other side. I lean forward to gain speed, edging in front of Buff, and then angle across his path, switching sides. The game is on, cat and mouse we used to call it, and Buff passes me, swapping sides. Again and again we trade places, ripping a continuous zigzag down the slope.

The hill begins to flatten out, to a perfect landing area for this particular run, but I'm not ready to stop, not ready for the distraction from real life to end, so I lead Buff across a swatch of ice that gives us enough momentum to get to another slope, one that slices through the forest. It's not intended for sliding, but I feel invincible, like I could slide right through a tree or boulder or anything else that tries to get in my way.

With a whoop, I lift the tip of my slide up and over the edge of the next hill. I'm forced to half-skid/half-turn hard to the right when a sharp gray boulder rises up directly in our path. Powdery snow sprays all around me as I hit a soft patch, cutting back to the left to avoid the edge of the trees on the right hand side.

The challenging natural course doesn't get any easier from there. A couple of times I think I'm freezed when the slope narrows and trees and rocks close in on all sides and sometimes right in front of me, but I always barely manage to squeeze through even the tiniest gaps. I can still hear the scrape and *whoomp* of Buff's slider behind me, so I know he's managed to follow in my wake so far.

Invincible. That's what we are. Indestructible.

Such are my thoughts as I cross a trail that leads away to the east, back toward the village. That's when something grabs me from beneath the snow.

~~~

One second I'm invincible, a slider warrior, and the next I'm airborne, like some icin' snowbird, except with a broken wing, unable to fly, flipping and spinning and going so fast that there's only one thing to do.

*Crash!*

My right shoulder hits first and it feels like I've landed on sheer stone, except for the fact that it's white and my bones crunch through it—and I know for a fact that my shoulder isn't hard enough to break through rock. So it must be snow. Well, more like a mixture of snow and ice, hard packed and without much give to it.

Then I tumble end over end, arse over heels, shoulders to tailbone to knees to bones and parts I don't even know the names of. It hurts like I'm getting a beat down from Abe all over again.

Eventually though, the friction of my coat and slider against the snow pinches in enough to bring me to a stop, leaving my head spinning and my heart pounding. I stare at the gray-covered sky, which seems to be moving a chilluva lot more than usual. Or maybe it's me that's moving. Or something else entirely.

Buff skids to a graceful stop beside me. "Whoa, man, you all right?" he says.

I go to nod, but my neck feels stiffer than a wood plank. "Urrr," I say, which obviously means yah.

"What happened?" he asks

Even if I knew, I wouldn't be able to tell him. "Hurts," I manage. And then, "Urrr."

"Anything broken?"

More like *everything* broken. But I'm just being a baby. The wind's knocked outta me and I got a few bruises—nothing major. I've had worse. "Need…a second," I say, whistling in breaths between puckered lips.

"What the chill?" Buff says, but this time he's not speaking to me. He's looking back up the hill, back toward where I fell, where something—I swear to the Mountain Heart I'm not making this up—*grabbed* me. It was like it reached up from beneath the snow and clamped down on the front of my slider.

"Urrr, what?" I say, trying to twist my sore neck to see where he's looking.

"I think…" Buff trails off. *I think what?* I want to ask but it seems I've spent all my words. He unclasps his slider and starts walking away, back up the hill. I groan, meaning "wait".

But he's already off. Whatever's up there, I want to see it too, want to know what caused my fall. Burning holes in the clouds with my eyes, I lean forward and rip off my slider, feeling sharp pain hitting me everywhere, in places I didn't even know I had. I laugh because it hurts so badly and I wonder if I'm becoming like Abe, laughing at pain.

"Holy shiverbones," I hear Buff say as I crawl on hands and knees to where he's standing, looking at something stumpy and dark, like a section of tree trunk, blotched against the snow. I could swear it wasn't there a minute ago.

"What is it?" I rasp as I approach him one hand and knee at a time.

"Not *what*," he says, not making any sense.

The thing comes into view and I gasp.

"Who," Buff says.

It's Nebo. Frozen harder than a snowman and deader than a fallen tree.

~~~

"Nebo's dead," I say to Abe that night.

"What?" he says, brows curled. He looks surprised. There's something else in his expression too, but I can't place it, or maybe he's just hiding it too well.

"We found him in the woods. Looked he was bludgeoned to death, his head all mashed up."

Buff's staring at his hands. We didn't know what to do, so we pulled him into the woods, dug a hole in the snow, and stuck him in it. Neither of us really liked the idea, but if we'd brought him in, the lawkeepers would've had questions— questions we might not be able to answer. Like why we were in the Blue District knocking on Nebo's door not a day earlier, just before he showed up dead.

"Mountain Heart," Abe says. There's a twinge of something in his voice—something not normal for how you should sound just after hearing about someone you know having died. He's shocked, yah, but not as much as I'd expect him to be.

"Do you know something about this?" I say sharply, stepping toward him.

Brock and Hightower move forward at the same time, penning me in.

He looks at me absently, like he's not seeing me. "Heart, I never thought they'd…" He trails off.

"Never thought who would what?" I ask, bumping Brock.

Abe's murky expression clears and the fire returns to his dark eyes. Whatever surprise or confusion is gone. "Here's the deal," he says. "You're asking too many questions, which as you well know, is against the rules. But we'll let it slide this one time, just like the last time you did something stupid by hitting me. This is it. Your last chance."

"And Nebo?" I say, glancing at Brock's fingers, which are twitching wildly, like he's hoping I go for Abe again so he can go for me.

"He was out of chances," Abe says, his words cold, but his tone not. Something doesn't make sense. Abe's saying all the things he's supposed to, but there's nothing behind them.

He knows something.

The cold soup I ate for dinner rolls in my gut. Nebo's frozen, bashed-in face flashes through my mind. Everything in me is saying "Fight! Attack! Punch! Hit!" but for once in my life, I ignore my temper. These guys are serious. Either they killed a man or they knew someone might kill a man. At least one that we know of. Probably more. All in the service of the king. *Bad man*, Nebo had said. I think he was referring to the king, but his words seem to apply to everyone standing in front of me.

"What's the medicine for?" I say, breaking another rule. A challenge.

"They're just tea leaves," Abe says, his face blank, not reacting to my guess as to the nature of the herbs.

"It's medicine," I say, pushing my luck.

"Don't do this," Abe says.

I grin at him, filling my smile with as much hate as I can muster. I raise a fist, flash it toward him and he flinches back. When Brock and Tower inch forward, I laugh. "A bit jumpy, aren't you?" I say.

I lean down and strap on my slider, ignoring the glares Abe's firing in my direction. As much as I'd love to take on all three of them, it'd be suicide, for Buff too; plus, even though the two months are up and our debts are paid off, I need to keep this job so I can find out what in Heart's name is going on.

I'll bide my time.

I won't forget what they did to Nebo. And I surely won't forgive it.

~~~

The Heaters are waiting for us when we reach the bottom, at a place on the border we've never been before. The prisoners aren't there to meet us this time. It's a big man, alone, wearing more clothes than the other Heaters I've seen, full length pants and a loose-fitting, V-necked shirt.

"King Goff sends his regards," Abe says.

"And pass along mine to him," the Heater says.

"Where's the cargo, Roan?" Abe's looking all around, like it might be scampering across fire country. *Roan!* So this is the Heater leader—they call him the Head Greynote.

"We've had a slight problem," Roan says, his eyes darker than the night.

Abe's eyes narrow. "What sort of problem?"

"You have to understand, we're under attack from all sides. The Killers are attacking again. The Glassies seem to want us wiped off the face of fire country. The Wildes steal more and more of our women every year."

"But you still have your alliance with the Marked?" Abe says. I'm trying to keep up with the conversation, but most of it's going in one ear and out the other. Killers? Wildes? Marked? At least I understand the Glassies, but why would they want to wipe out the Heaters?

"I'd hardly call it an alliance," Roan says. "More like an understanding. But yes, we trade wood and food for their services."

"So what's the problem?" Abe persists.

"We couldn't get any cargo this season," Roan says. I want to scream out "What is the freezin' cargo?" but I know if I do I might end up in a snowy grave next to Nebo.

Abe shakes his head, a look of wonder crossing his face. "You couldn't, or you *wouldn't?*"

Roan's jaw goes tight and I see his hands curl into fists. His face turns a darker shade of brown. I know those signs. This is a man with a temper. A bad one, maybe worse than mine, which would be saying something. And his dark expression isn't saying punch and wrestle and fight…it's saying kill.

"Couldn't," he says through gritted teeth. "We'll have cargo for you at the end of spring."

"Ha!" Abe laughs. "You expect to get your precious herbs for a full season based on the promise of cargo in three months' time? Is that really what you want me to tell the king?"

Roan steps forward, his face speckled with starlight and mottled with anger. "You will do what I tell you to do, and let Goff make the decisions. You're nothing but a filthy messenger."

I almost laugh, but manage to hold it in, passing it off as a cough. The tension is so tight that no one even looks my way. Abe's trying to hold it together, to keep a brave face, but I can see he's intimidated by Roan, his lip quivering, his cheeks sagging. "Okay," he says. "I'll tell the king what you said. But no promises."

"Good," Roan says. "When he agrees to the new terms, which I'm confident he will, bring the Cure here in three days' time."

As we turn and walk away, one word thumps through my head: Cure.

# Twelve

"Cure for what?" I say, already knowing the answer.

"There's only one thing that needs a cure," Buff says.

"The Cold," I say.

"They call it the Fire," Buff says.

"The Fire…" I murmur, as if it's something sacred, like the Heart of the Mountain. "But Goff can't have a cure for the Cold—the Fire. People are dying of it more than ever. Almost every day." I know the answer to that too, but I want Buff to confirm it.

"He's keeping it from us," Buff says.

"And giving it to the Heaters." Ice him! Freeze him! How can he have a cure and not share it with his own people? But wait…

"But the Heaters are still dying of the Fire. I hear them talking about it all the time when we go to the border," I say, frowning. It clicks and this time I don't wait for Buff to say it first. "Roan's keeping it from his people too, because he's only getting enough for himself and maybe the other leaders."

"Icin' straight," Buff says.

It's all coming together. The secrecy. Why the king had to have Nebo killed off. Not because he knew, but because he might talk about it. If we were able to draw a bit of information out of him, then maybe someone else could get the whole story. And the king couldn't have that. There would be mutiny, rebellion. The Icers would string him up from a tree branch.

*We killed Nebo.*

The realization hits me like a winter wind, chilling me to my bones. If we hadn't questioned him, hadn't got him riled up enough to tell us about the medicine, he might still be alive. But how would the king have known what Nebo told us? One of his men must've been spying. "Ice it!" I say.

"What do we do?" Buff says.

"Nothing," I say. "There's more to this story, and we need to know everything before we make a move." Starting with what the special cargo is that Roan failed to deliver. Unfortunately, that means we'll have to wait until the end of spring to find out.

~~~

We play the game, show up for work every few days, deliver blah blah blah to the border, collect some other blah blah blah and lug it back to the castle. Evidently King Goff buckled to Roan's new terms, because every few weeks we deliver bags of the Cure. Keeping the Heater leader alive and free of the Fire, while Icers and Heaters continue to die from the Cold.

Something about that just doesn't seem fair.

Summer arrives and the snow starts to melt, but not completely, because it's unusually cold for this time of year. The special cargo still hasn't arrived and Abe's getting grumpier by the day, probably because Goff's getting even grumpier from behind his palace walls. He's paying for the cargo with the Cure, but he's not getting anything in return. That'd make even the most happy-go-lucky king grumpy. And I have a feeling Goff isn't the happy-go-lucky kind.

Finally, however, one night when we show up for a delivery, Abe's usual angriness has melted away to a muted melancholy. "We've got special cargo tonight," he says.

What does that even mean? I want to say, but as usual, I hold my question inside. I'm getting pretty good at it considering how many unanswerable questions I've got.

Buff and I just nod as if we understand.

Brock and Hightower show up a few minutes later and Abe says the same thing to them, and they don similarly gloomy expressions. Why do they look so miserable? Isn't the special cargo what we've all been waiting for? On a night like this, I'd expect them to be smiling wolfishly, grinning like banshees, all excitement and energy. Not so...somber.

The five of us take the usual route to the borderlands, except we have to dismount our sliders earlier than usual, on account of the less than usual snow as we approach the bottom. It may be a cold summer, but down the mountain it's much warmer this time of year. We trudge the rest of the way through the forest, which is teeming with fresh, green life, thicker than Yo's beard.

There's a commotion when we reach fire country. I stand stock still for a moment, taking it all in, wondering what and where and when and *huh?* Then I think, *What the freezin' son of a goat herder?* There's no cargo, just five adult Heaters, standing tall and brown around a cluster of children. Heater children. None of them look older than—

—I can barely even think it but—

—older than my sister. In fact, all of them are much younger.

The thought sits in my brain like a dull ache. "What's going on?" I say aloud, finally letting one of my questions slip out and away.

"Just stay cool," Abe says, warning me off with his eyes. "There's no going back from this point, so I'll answer your questions after it's over."

I want to grab him by the shirt, lift him up, shake him till he spills it, tells me everything he knows. But, as usual, I don't. Can't. It's not the right time—not the right way. I have to be patient.

We approach the Heaters.

One of them steps forward. These men are dressed like Roan was, more covered, less wild-looking. They are clearly Roan's fellow leaders. The Greynotes. "Will seven units cover us through the summer?" the Heater asks.

Abe walks around the children, who cower in the middle, lashed together, just a splash of brown with arms and legs sticking out every which way. He eyes them up, from head to toe, as if inspecting a prize sled dog. "They strong?" he asks.

"Always are," the Heater replies.

Abe nods. "That should do it. You'll get the herbs till autumn, then we'll have to talk to Roan again, agree on new terms."

*What the chill?* I think, tired of thinking that same question over and over, as if I can't even formulate a more intelligent thought.

"They're all yours," the Heater says, waving his hand in a circle. In a pack, the Heaters stride off, back into fire country, the desert moon beating a shimmering path across the sand.

The children look at us with scared, unblinking eyes.

"Round 'em up," Abe says.

Right away, Brock and Tower step toward the Heater children, cracking their knuckles and almost daring them to run. Without thinking, I step in front of them, blocking their path. Buff does the same, shoulder to shoulder.

"Git outta our way," Brock says. Tower grunts his own complaint.

"Not till you tell us what this is all about," I say. "These are kids—not cargo."

Abe sighs, as if he's been through this conversation too many times before. I wonder just how many times—for how many kids. "I told you I'll tell you and I will," he says, "but not until we get 'em back to the palace."

"Nay," I say.

"Excuse me?" Abe's voice is incredulous. He's not used to being denied. "Are you forgetting rule number one?"

"You can take rule number one and shove it up your—"

"Dazz!" Buff says sharply. He's thinking with his brain, and I'm thinking with my heart. If we start a fight here, we'll lose. We've been in plenny of scraps, and we know how to fight, especially together, but these guys are no less experienced, and they've got Hightower, which is like having three guys in one body.

I take a deep breath. "Look," I say. "I didn't sign up for kidnapping." *Kidnapping.* That's what it is. Taking kids from their homes. Just like…

I don't need to finish the thought. I don't want to finish the thought.

Because I already know.

If there's a King who'll take kids from another country, then he'll take kids from his own country too.

"It's just business," Abe says, but there's no conviction in his voice. "They give us kids, we give them the Cure. It's not our job to think." I might not know Abe that well, but I know enough to realize he's more than just hired muscle. He's got a brain. So why does he refuse to use it?

Brock moves to step around me, but I shift to block him. "What does the king do with them?" I ask, my sister's face dancing around the question. I don't want to know, but I have to know. If Jolie's behind those palace walls, I need to know if she's in any immediate danger.

Abe says, "Not my busin—"

"Tell me!" I explode, feeling veins popping out all over my forehead. Jolie. Jolie. Where are you?

Abe steps away, taken aback by my outburst. The kids huddle together even tighter.

"For the love of the Mountain, kid. Can you get a grip on yer temper?" Abe says. "Honestly, I don't have a freezin' clue what he does with 'em, and I don't ask. He'd kil…" He leaves the thought hanging, unfinished. Instead says, "He pays me too well for that. And he'd kill me if I ever asked. Do you really not understand who yer dealin' with? It's the Heart-icin' King for

Heart's sake! He's got a whole freezin' army of men just waitin' to crush anyone who gets in his way. Do you think we're the ones who killed Nebo? Do you really think we're so heartless to not feel bad about what happened to him, too? He was strange, yah, but we liked him. I even shed a few tears for the stumpy little man. Ice, kid! Are you really so clueless? He's got spies watchin' us all, just waitin' for us to make a wrong move, to cross him in any way. After all yer icin' questions, I had to stick my neck out for you so he wouldn't kill you, too!"

I raise a hand to my aching head, massage my temples. Abe stood up for me? The king's watching us? The king trades the Cure for little kids—little kids just like my sister? Everything's so tangled, like the forest, all knotted and growing and twisting together, vine-covered and spiky and windblown. I turn to look at the kids, who are hanging onto each other, whispering something that sounds like a prayer, to the Heart of the Mountain, or whoever it is that they pray to.

Turning back, I say, "They're watching us right now?"

"Yah," Abe says. "You try anything stupid and you'll be bird-feathered with arrows before you get more than two steps."

"Where?" I say, looking around.

"For Heart's sake, kid, don't look around. Ice!"

I bring my gaze back to Abe, repeat the question. He says, "They're good at hiding. Even when you know they're there, you rarely ever see 'em. They're in the trees and in the brambles and under the leaves. They just watch…and wait."

"Ice it!" I say. "We don't have a choice here, do we?"

"No," Abe says, his single word filled with regret.

~~~

Every step up the mountain is like an arrow in my heart.

Before we leave, we wrap the kids in heavy, full-length coats that Abe has in his pack, so at least they'll be warm.

But everything else is awful. The brown children whimper and cast fearful glances around them as if everything in the forest is new to them, scary. Maybe it is. Do they have trees in fire country? Probably not, as they send their prisoners to ice country to chop wood.

Even though the kids are clearly scared, they're like little soldiers, never complaining or crying. They just march on, taking sips of water when we offer them, clinging to the rope that tethers them together like it's the only thing holding them up.

*How can I be doing this?* I ask myself at least a dozen times, swishing around a taste so bitter it's worse than yellow snow. *For Jolie,* I keep saying in my mind. Getting myself killed now will ensure everything I know is lost, and then she'll have no chance at all. My only option is to continue to play along, wait for the right moment. Be smart. I feel bad about the kids I'm taking from their families, but I can't help that either, can only hope that later I'll be able to help them, along with Jolie.

When we reach the start of the snow-covered slopes, which are shimmering under the pale moonlight, the kids' eyes light up, and I see the first indication that there's still some measure of childlike joy in them. They even reach down and pick some up, giggling and dropping it when they feel the cold. Abe gives them a look and I get the feeling that if I wasn't around, he would scold them and tell them to get a move on.

After a few more hours of trudging through the snow, the kids start to falter, tripping under their own weight, slipping on patches of ice. They're exhausted. Who knows how far they had to walk across fire country before we met them.

Just before we reach the final stretch to the palace gates, Abe veers off to the right. "Where are you going?" I say, breaking the no-question rule and floating the very last sliver of my luck across the night sky.

"Gotta go the long way. Safer." Safer for who? Not for the dead-on-their-feet kids. Not for anyone but the king, who's worried about the general public finding out about his secrets. The Cure. His penchant for stealing children in the dark of the night.

"These kids have to rest soon," I say.

Abe stops, glances at the kids, as if he's forgotten they're here, that they're people, capable of weariness. Perhaps that's the only way he can manage his guilt. Then, to my surprise, he shrugs. "I'll probably catch it from the king, but I'm ready for bed too."

He heads straight for the palace gate and we follow. Before the gate, he says, "I'll take it from here."

"I'll help you get them to bed," I say.

"Not a chance," Abe says. "They won't let anyone in but me. Take a hike."

Going home is the last thing I want to do. Thoughts of charging through the gates, fighting off sword- and bow-wielding guards with my bare fists, barging my way into the king's quarters, knocking him senseless, and taking my sister back cycle through my head.

Then I turn and walk away, Buff by my side.

Over my shoulder, Abe's voice carries on the wind. "Remember, don't tell anyone what you saw tonight. Yer bein' watched. Always."

# Thirteen

Knowing and not being able to do anything is almost worse than not knowing at all.

Every day Buff and I think up a dozen hare-brained plans to infiltrate the palace and rescue Joles and all the other kids, Heaters and Icers alike, but every day we shoot so many holes in our ideas that they cross the line from impossible to no-way-in-chill-buddy.

At night I literally pull my hair out trying to bully my brain into being smarter. In the morning I find strands of black on my pillow. I want to tell Wes everything, but I'm afraid they'll know if I do, and then I'll end up like Nebo. And because Wes'll know, he'll have to be taken out too.

It's a problem without a solution. The only thing I have going for me is the job, which at least allows me to see what's going on at the border, what the king is up to. But then, one day, the Heaters don't show up.

"Whaddya make of it?" Brock says, cracking his knuckles and staring off into fire country. It's a question, but I guess not one that's against the rules.

Abe scratches his chin. "They were s'posed to have supplies for us today. Something musta happened."

"Like what?" Buff says.

"Who knows?" Abe says, grabbing a handful of sand and letting it drift through his fingertips. It's hotter down here than I've ever felt before in my life, like sitting in a roaring fire. Even the light breeze is full of heat. Not even a wisp of a yellow cloud mars the great red sky. And the sun? Chill! It feels so close and big I have to shield my eyes with my hand.

I remember everything Roan said the night he failed to deliver the next batch of children. Shiv about being attacked from all sides, by something called Killers, and the pasty-skinned Glassies, and something about the Wildes stealing their girls, or some such rot. When all the time he's been giving away his children to King Goff anyway, so who is he to complain? Whatever the case, though, something's gone wrong, which means we have no choice but to trudge back up the mountain empty handed.

At the palace gates, I say, "I want to be the one to deliver the news to Goff."

"Forget it," Abe says.

Feeling restless and tired, I say, "Try to stop me," and march right for the gates, which start to open to let Abe in.

Abe grabs at my arm, but I shrug it off. He makes another grab, so I turn and push him, hard enough to get him to back off, but not as hard as the last time. To my surprise, he raises his hands in peace and lets me go.

"Don't do anything stupid, kid," he says.

Surprisingly, Brock and Hightower just watch me go, as if I'm their entertainment for the day. I reach the gates, which stretch higher than ten men on each other's shoulders, an arched entranceway that's normally barred by a heavy metal gate that's cranked open from below. The gate's more than halfway up now.

Two burly guards block my path, heavy battleaxes in their hands, crisscrossed between them. "I'm here to see the king in place of Abe," I say, hard-like, as if I really belong there.

"Those are not our orders," Burly Guard A says.

"Turn around and keep on walking," says Burly Guard B.

An important decision. To fight or not to fight? Why is it that I constantly have to make this decision over and over again? My standard answer used to be to fight, which I preferred, but now it's like my brain's taken over everything, and I don't know up from down. If I fight a couple of palace guards, maybe I break through, get as far as the next group of guards, but eventually I get stopped. Lose my job if I'm lucky; get dead or chucked in prison if I'm not.

But Jolie's in there! Argh! I know where my sister is—or at least I'm pretty icin' sure—and yet I can't do a freezin' thing about it.

"I said, move on," Burly Guard B says. Or is it A? I can't remember, but all I know is I've been standing there for way too long, drawing all kinds of attention from the wall guards, who are peeking over the edge at me, bows steady, arrow nocked and ready to fly.

Not fight.

The decision burns me up inside like I ate something rancy. It's not a natural decision for me, but I know it's the right one.

I walk away, expecting the guards to grab me and pull me inside at any second, to do to me what they did to Nebo.

But they don't, leaving me wondering why I seem to be able to get away with so much more than everyone else.

~~~

Something's gone down in fire country. Rumors are flying around like snowflakes in a winter's snowstorm. Or even like a summer snowstorm, like the one we've got now.

It's the warmest part of the year, but you wouldn't know by looking out your window at the blanket of cold white coating everything, and the blurry, snowflake-filled air.

Buff and I are camped out at my place, riding out the storm, drinking warm 'quiddy and speaking in hushed tones. I don't know why we're whispering, because Wes has gone out, still looking for a job, even in a snowstorm, and Mother, well, she's even more gone, although she's sitting not two steps away.

"People are saying the Heaters have been destroyed," Buff says.

I shake my head. "There's no way…" I say, although I know anything's possible around here. Like selling kids for cures.

"It would mean…"

"No job," I finish.

"We were so close," Buff says, groaning.

"Who gives a shiv about that," I say. "Yo'll probably let the last two payments go anyway." From what we were able to save, we handed a whole bundle of silver over to Yo, nearly paying for the damage we caused in the fight.

"You think?" Buff says optimistically.

"Yah, but like I said, who cares?" I regret saying it right away, because I see the hurt in Buff's eyes. "Look, I know Fro-Yo's is like home to you—it is to me too—but I'm just worried about how I'll ever get Jolie back without that job. It was my only connection to the palace."

"We'll find a way," Buff says.

I shake my head. "I don't see how."

"We'll start by going to the border."

~~~

So that's what we do. Every day, we wake up, grab our nice, shiny King-provided sliders, and slide/hike our way down to the borderlands, hoping to see something, to get some news of the Heaters. Why? Because if we can be the ones to bring news of what's happened in fire country to Goff, maybe he'll agree to see us.

And if I can just get behind those palace walls...

Then what? I break out dozens, maybe hundreds of children?

That's the plan.

The first few days we see nothing at the border. Just empty flatlands, hotter than chill, stretching off in the distance farther than the human eye can see. So we venture a little further in. Each day, we go a little farther. We strip off clothes as we go, until we're down to nothing but our skivvies.

And yet it's still hot. Amazing! I still don't get how it can be so cold and full of snow up the mountain, and fire-hot down here, in the desert. To my smallish brain, it don't make no logical sense.

One day, when we're trudging back into ice country after a long morning in the desert, I see something. A flash of movement in the trees. There and then gone. A bird maybe? Or a rabbit? I don't know why, but it felt bigger than that. Not bear-size, but much bigger than some woodland critter.

I stick a hand out to stop Buff. We're both wearing just our skivvies, having left our clothes hanging on a tree branch a little further into the woods. He raises an eyebrow questioningly, opens his lips to speak, but I raise a finger to my mouth, quieting him. I point in the direction I saw the movement.

There it is again, something creeping amongst the creepers. But whatever it is, it's almost blending in with the brown of the tree trunks, the earthy colors of the forest. Barely discernible, unless you happen to be looking right at it.

A twig snaps.

I charge toward the sound, feeling Buff right behind me. If it's a Heater, I gotta catch him, make him talk to me about what's going on in fire country. This might be my only chance.

I barge through a tangled thicket, getting scraped and poked by a half-dozen jaggedy branches, barely noticing the flashes of red on my skin.

More twigs are snapping in front of me, as my quarry realizes he's being chased, and has chosen haste over stealth. I follow the sound, grabbing tree trunks and swinging around them to increase my momentum. I can see him now, definitely a Heater, wearing brown skins that cover his arms and legs, as if he's expecting it to get cold real soon. He's fast too, cutting amongst the trees and bushes like a deer.

But he don't got nothing on me. I grew up in the forest, I know how it moves, how it breathes, where to expect the roots to jump out at you.

I close in.

His head bobs, his short dark hair ducking around trees, picking a path through the forest.

Almost close enough to grab.

I'm about to dive when—

He whirls around, stopping so quickly I almost bash into him. Except…

The him's a *her*.

I look the Heater woman over from head to toe in an instant, and I can't stop my eyes from stopping on her chest, which pushes her coat outward in a feminine curve. "You've got…but those are…I thought you were…" I say eloquently.

She looks at me with dark, mesmerizing eyes, her lips turned up in a fierce grin. "Yeah, and I got one of these too." Before I have a chance to even think about ducking, she decks me in the head with a fist that I swear is made of stone.

My last thought before my vision goes black: *she hits harder than me.*

# Fourteen

I wake up beaten by a girl. But she was a Heater, so I don't mind so much. I don't even mind the headache, which pounds like an angry drummer on my skull.

A leaf rests on my lips, which I blow off.

*Wow!* I think. Who was that? A Heater, obviously. But ice, was she ever—

"Urrr," someone moans nearby.

"Buff?" I say.

"Yah."

"You breathin'?" I ask, sitting up, holding my head to stop the forest from spinning.

"Nay," Buff says, lying flat on his back next to a large tree.

"What happened to you?" I ask, wondering if the Heater girl took him down too. I'm kind of hoping she did, because that would be even more impressive. I mean, we're not the best fighters in the world or anything, but I like to think we're better than most. Although that might just be my pride talking.

"Not sure," Buff says, trying to lift his head up, but thinking better of it and resting it back on the ground. He looks funny wearing just his underwear.

"Was it the girl?" I ask.

"Girl?" Buff says. "What girl?" He's speaking to the tops of the trees.

I drag myself over to him, so I can see his face. There's dried blood in a line from his split lip to his chin, and one of his eyes is purple and puffy. I wonder how it compares to my face.

"You look like chill," I say.

"What girl?" Buff repeats.

"The one I was chasing. I thought she was a guy, but then she turned, all short-haired and fierce. That's when she hit me."

"You got hit by a girl?" Buff says incredulously.

"Not hit, Buff. Knocked out. She hits harder than you do!"

Buff looks at me with the one eye he's able to open. Then he starts to laugh. "You got beat up by *a girl?*"

I shake my head. "She's probably the one who got you, too. She's crazy-tough. Unlike any Icer woman, that much I can tell you."

"She's not the one who got me," Buff says, squinting his one eye, like he's trying to remember something. "I was right on your tail, doing my iciest to keep up with the manic pace you were plowing through the woods, when something dark dropped from over my head, leaping from the trees. This wasn't no girl, Dazz, no one so easy to beat as that."

"She wasn't *easy to beat*," I interrupt.

125

He shakes his head again. "Anyway, this was definitely a guy, but not like the Heaters we've seen. He was cut like stone, brown-skinned, but covered in dark markings, like some kind of wild man. He was shirtless, but had a mess of skins over his shoulder. And he hit harder than some sissy-eyed Heater girl. He knocked me flat into tomorrow with a left and a right."

"Two hits?" I say. "Like I said, the sissy-eyed Heater girl knocked me out with one punch."

"I guess I can just take a hit better than you," Buff says, laughing. But then he grabs his head like he just got hit by an iceball.

I sigh. "We can argue about it later. What do you think they're doing here in ice country?"

"How the chill should I know? They're supposed to be destroyed."

"Maybe most of them are," I say. "Maybe they're coming here looking for help, someone to take them in."

"Funny way of asking for it," Buff grumbles.

"Well, we were chasing them."

Buff's eyes narrow. "Hey, describe this Heater girl again, will ya? You know, the *girl* who beat you up."

I punch him on the shoulder, but then I describe her.

"The short hair thing's kinda weird, isn't it?"

I shrug. "I guess so, but it sort of worked for her. She wasn't bad looking."

Buff says, "You know, I felt like there were more of them, too."

"More of who?"

"The Heaters, or Marked, or whoever they are. Although I only saw the guy with the markings, it felt like there were others watching the whole thing."

"How many?" I ask.

"I dunno. Like I said, it's just a feeling I had."

We both stare off into the forest for a few minutes, thinking about everything. Finally, Buff says, "What are we going to do?"

"Find them," I say.

~~~

It's dark by the time we get back to the Brown District. We agree to meet in the morning, to start looking for the mysterious invaders who gave us the quickest beating of our lives.

When I push through the door, I can't help the smile on my face. It quickly fades though when reality sets in. Mother's in front of the fire, rocking slightly, using her hands to drum out an uneven rhythm on the floor. Wes is off to the side on the floor too, back against the wall, hand against his head, a half-eaten bowl of soup beside him. And, of course, there's no Jolie. It's like losing her sucked all the life out of our already lifeless family. We may have only gotten to see her once or twice a day, but that was enough to make things different, to fill in a bit of the emptiness.

I can't. As hard as I try to think of the Heaters in ice country, I can't. Images of my broken family flood my mind and my lips stay flatter than the floor.

"Wes," I say.

He doesn't move.

"This has to stop," I say.

No response.

"I know where Jolie is."

His head snaps up and a pair of red-veined eyes stares at me. His face is moist. He's been crying. "That's not funny," he says.

"She's in the palace somewhere," I say.

"Cut it out."

"I'm being serious. I've got a lot to tell you. I should've told you sooner."

Over two fresh bowls of soup, both for me, and to the erratic sound of my mother's ceaseless drumming, I tell him everything. What the job really was, about the Cure, how we found Nebo dead and frozen, about the "special cargo", how I felt ill being a part of it. I wrap things up with our trips to fire country and "meeting" the Heaters.

Wes's eyes widen at parts, narrow at others, but mostly just pay rapt attention to every word I speak in between slurps of soup. When I finish, his eyes finally leave mine, drifting to watch Mother and her incessant drumming.

"You don't know for sure Jolie's in there," he says.

"I know," I say.

He nods, like he understands. It's a brother-sister thing. He knows, too.

"Why didn't you tell me sooner? I've been dying more and more every day." The way he says it sounds so weary-like, as if he might die right here, right now, on the spot, if he doesn't like my answer.

"Like I told you, they're watching me. Or at least they were when I worked for the king. I expect they're still watching, on account of what I know, although maybe they're not being quite as attentive now that the trade agreement seems to be on hold, or over, or whatever. I thought if they knew I told you, they'd kill us both." It's the honest to Mountain Heart truth.

Wes nods, sighs. "You did the right thing."

I close my eyes. My brother's back. The one who decides what's right and wrong, who always knows what to do, whose approval I've been desperately seeking even though maybe I didn't realize it until right now. His words seem to wash over me like cold water, cleansing me. Every decision I've made over the last few months has seemed so wrong, mostly because Jolie's still gone, but hearing Wes say those words seems to validate it all. I shouldn't need validation, but I do.

"Thanks," I say.

"What now?" he asks.

"I need your help."

Light flows into his eyes as he turns toward me, as if someone's just lit a fire, although the fireplace has been crackling since I entered the room. A purpose. Perhaps he can't get a job, can't provide for his family, but he can help me bring Jolie back, and that's a greater purpose than anything.

~~~

We don't know where to start looking, so we begin where it started, where Buff and I got our arse's handed to us by a girl and marked man.

"The trail's cold," Wes says, "but it's still here." I smile, both because of the words he's saying and because it's him that's saying them. I haven't heard him speak like that, with such confidence and directness, since Joles was taken.

"How many do you think there are?" I ask.

Wes chews his lip. "Can't tell just yet, but at least two. Maybe more."

"Good," I say. "Let's see where it takes us."

Wes leads, because he's the best tracker, and Buff brings up the rear, because, well, "You're the biggest arse I've ever met," I say.

He makes a gesture that borders on rude, but slips in behind me, stepping on the back of my boots every few minutes.

We're warm when we start, on account of our heavy clothing, but soon the trail leads us high enough up the mountain that it's downright chilly. "The Heaters we always met at the border were dressed for hot weather, wearing only thin skins," I say. "These ones had skins and looked ready to face the cold."

"Do you want to be the one to warm her up?" Buff says from behind.

"Shut it," I say. "Just because I was impressed with how she could throw a punch doesn't mean I'm looking to hug her."

Wes stops, looks at us both like we're slightly crazy, says, "The trail keeps leading up, so they'd be getting good use out of those skins right about now."

Wes keeps marching on and we follow. He stops every once in a while to inspect a broken tree branch or a shallow footprint.

When we reach the snowfields, there are dozens of prints, all clustered together, and then deep gouges in the snow where it looks like they laid down. "I can see five distinct sets of prints," Wes says.

"They'd have frozen their stones off lying in the snow like that," Buff says. Then, grinning, adds, "At least the Marked guy would've, but the girl wouldn't have any stones to freeze off, would she?"

"Oh, she had stones all right," I say, "just not the kind you're talking about."

"Don't they know snow is cold?" Wes asks.

I shrug. "They've probably never seen it. You should've seen the look on the Heater children's faces when we came through these parts. They were in awe of the white stuff."

"Don't see what the allure is," Buff says. "I've had enough of it to last me for ten lifetimes."

I bend down to touch the impressions in the snow, imagining the Heater girl in the snow, knee bent, smiling at the white ground around her. What is she doing so far from home?

"Well, whatever the case, even with their warm clothing they'd be getting pretty cold at this point, searching for shelter. Let's see where their footsteps lead," Wes says.

Sure enough, the trail leads off to the side, away from the snowfields and back into the forest, where the snow is thinner and there's more protection from the frosty wind. *Ahh, summer in ice country*, I think to myself. Not what the Heaters would be used to.

The prints run right up to a gigantic tree, with a trunk thicker than a Yag's chest and a huge hole in it, big enough to sleep five people, if everyone crammed together. And, according to Wes, they had to sleep five, so they were really crammed.

Inside are the remnants of a small fire, all ash and charred twigs left over, which is impressive. Fires aren't easy to make in ice country, especially when you're not used to doing it.

"They slept here," Buff says.

"Thanks for the input," I say.

"My pleasure."

The trail continues up the mountain, aiming right for the eastern edge of the village, the White District, and eventually the palace.

"They were heading for us," Wes says, meaning the Icers in general.

"Well, we could've led them," Buff says. "If they hadn't beaten the shiver out of us."

"Maybe they wanted to surprise the king," I say.

"Why?" Wes says.

"Because maybe Roan is dead," I say, feeling my brain working double time, spinning a few impossible theories into one possible one. "What if something did happen to the Heaters and the Marked? Something really big, really bad—devastating even. What if the Head Greynote, Roan, was killed? What if a bunch of the Greynotes were killed and there was a big shakeup in their leadership? You've all heard the rumors. People are saying the Heaters were destroyed, but maybe they were just attacked and they survived, but Roan and the other Greynotes were killed. If they have new leaders they'd want to check things out with their neighbors, make contact with Goff, figure out how things work with the trade agreement. Wouldn't they?"

The questions float for a moment, settling over us like the quiet before a winter storm.

"It's possible," Wes admits. "It would certainly explain them showing up out of nowhere. But we've never seen a Heater in ice country, not this far up the mountain anyway. I don't think the king would take too kindly to them appearing unannounced at the palace gates."

"Nay. He wouldn't. You're right about that," I say.

~~~

And the Heater's footprints do lead toward the palace gates, at least for a while, but then they veer off away from civilization again, taking us back into the thick woods.

"They're going around back," I say. It's still crazy that they're making for the palace at all, but at least they had enough brains to skip the knock-on-the-front-gates approach.

"There's an entrance in the back, isn't there?" Wes says.

"Yah," Buff and I say at the exact same time. We've talked about finding a way through the back door many a time. But like every other way in, it's well-guarded and impossible to breach.

We pick a path through the forest, easily following the mess of snapped twigs the Heaters left in their wake. When we reach a clearing, the path suddenly opens up in a wide swathe all the way to the palace walls. A guard stands atop the wall and I swear he's looking right at us.

"Shiv!" I hiss, ducking back behind the trees and pulling Wes and Buff with me.

"Did he see us?" Wes asks.

"I dunno. I don't see how he couldn't've," I say.

"Maybe he was looking past us, over the forest," Buff says.

"Maybe," I say wanting to believe it.

We wait for a long ten minutes, expecting a parade of palace guardsmen to come charging down the track at any moment. But they don't, and the forest stays quiet, save for the occasional song of a snowbird.

Ever so slowly, I stand up, conscious of keeping myself behind the army of trees that separate us from the palace. When I look at the tracks in the clearing I gasp.

Footprints trample every which way, but not just six sets. Twenny, maybe more, cut deep from heavy steps and packing

133

the snow down to a hard skin. But that's not what caused my sudden intake of air. There's blood, too, bright and wet on the snow. Mostly droplets, perfect little crimson circles burnt into the snow, but a few rivers too, crisscrossing and zigzagging around the middle of the clearing.

"What is it?" Wes says, hearing my gasp and standing up next to me. "Holy shiverbones!" he says.

"Not good," Buff says, taking it all in along with us. "The guards got 'em."

"You think they're…" I say.

"Nay," Buff says. "Goff woulda wanted to talk to them. But after what they did to us, I expect they'da fought like mountain lions. The blood might not even be theirs."

I think about that, hoping my friend's right. "Then they're prisoners," I say.

"Probably," Wes says. "I doubt they're guests, especially not the way they snuck in and put up a fight."

Prisoners. The word hangs heavy between my ears.

Prisoners. Just like Jolie.

# Fifteen

"We gotta get in there," I say. "Not just for Jolie, but for the Heaters too."

We're back at our place, discussing what to do next—me and Wes and Buff and my mother. Well, she's not discussing so much as scraping a rock in a circle, marking the floor. Every time she finishes another round, she cocks her head as if to say, "Huh?" like she can't figure out why the circle keeps on going. Then she draws another one.

"We've talked circles around infiltrating the palace," Buff says, motioning to my mother's drawing. I smirk, even though it's a bad joke. "It's impossible."

"Nothing's impossible," I say.

"Nay. Some things are," Buff says. "Like us getting rich. Like you getting the time of day from a White District girl."

I stand up, clenching my fists. "I got more than the time of day, you freezin' son of a snowblo—"

"Knock it off, you two," Wes says.

Glaring at Buff, I take a deep breath, slowly unfurl my fingers.

"I agree with Dazz," my brother says. "There has to be a way. We just have to think outside the snow globe."

"Buff won't be much help then," I mutter.

"Dazz!" Wes says sharply. "Focus."

I try, I really try, but Buff and I have thought about this question for a whole lot longer than Wes has. I feel like my mind's more fried than deer bacon on a cold winter's morning.

*Jolie. Are you okay? Has Goff hurt you? Are you a slave, carrying around buckets of soap water, scrubbing the palace floors, brown-skinned Heater children doing the same beside you? Have you made friends with them?*

Right when I stop thinking about the question and focus on who I'm asking it for, an idea hits me. And not a bad one either.

"We've got to talk to Abe," I say.

~~~

"Not in a million years," Abe says. "I'd just as soon be skinned and boiled by a Yag than cross the king."

I'm alone with Abe, a good ways down the mountain—he wouldn't talk to me any other way. Sleepy snowflakes flutter this way and that way in the wind, seeming to never reach the ground. "You owe me," I say.

"Ha!" Abe scoffs. "How do you figger? The last time I saw you, you disobeyed a direct order and shoved me."

"I did," I admit. "But I was desperate. Don't you get it? My sister's in there. Goff's got my sister. What am I supposed to do, just forget about it, let it go?" My voice rises over the last few words.

"That's exactly what yer s'posed to do," Abe says. "Just like me, you shouldn't cross the king, especially when he's got your loved one chained up somewhere."

What does he mean by *Just like me*? I shake off the thought, continue to work on him.

"I'm not asking you to cross him," I say. "Just help him make a hiring decision. He won't hire me or Buff, not with our shoddy records, not for any jobs inside the palace anyway, but Wes, he's a golden child, been nothing but a good worker everywhere he's been."

"Ferget it," Abe says, folding his arms defiantly.

"What if it were your sister?" I say, changing tactics.

"I don't have a sister," Abe says smugly.

"A brother?"

His face changes, softens somewhat. "I'd do anything for Hightower," he says.

Huh? "Tower's your brother?"

"Yah. So?"

"Uh, nothing. That's great." I try to keep my face expressionless even though I want to ask him what in Heart's name is wrong with his brother. "Okay. So if Tower was a prisoner somewhere, what would you do?"

"I'd freezin' bust him out and mangle the face of whoever put him there in the first place." He stops, wrinkles his face. "Oh," he says, seeing my point.

"Please," I say. "Just do this one thing and I'll never bother you again."

Abe cringes, looks like he's screaming but no sound comes out, punches his fist into his palm. "Heart-ice it! Why'd I ever hafta meet an ice-sucker like you?"

I don't think he means for me to answer him, but I do anyway. "Because this ice-sucker sucks royal ice at high stakes boulders-'n-avalanches," I say. "So you'll do it?"

"Yah. And then you'll never talk to me again."

"Deal," I say, grinning.

~~~

We're conspiring at Fro-Yo's. Like we suspected he might eventually, Yo bent a little and let us back in the pub with the promise we'd pay him the last few sickles we owe him as soon as we can. He even cleared the place out so we could hold our secret meeting here. He said he'd add the lost business to our tab.

Four tinnys sit on a round wooden table, similar to the one we broke the last time we were here. They're empty so Yo clears them away and replaces them with fresh ones, amber liquid frothing over the sides.

Abe leads the first part of the meeting. "Yer not Wes anymore," he says to Wes. "Yer Buck, son of Huck."

"Can I choose a different name?" Wes says.

"Nay," Abe says, settling the matter.

"You already got him the job?" I ask, surprised.

Abe lifts the edge of his lip, the closest thing to a smile we'll get from him tonight. "Course. I told you a million times, I got power in the palace. But I didn't know what he could do, so they couldn't place him. All you gotta do is tell me what yer good at."

"Uh," Wes says.

"He's good at digging up rocks," I joke, earning a sharp look from my brother.

"There ain't much rock-diggin' in the palace," Abe says seriously, not getting the joke. "But there's plenny of other stuff. Has he got any other skills?" He directs the question at me, as if I've suddenly become the authority on Wes's abilities.

"I can cook," Wes says, pulling Abe's gaze back to him.

"Perfect," Abe says. "The king's near always lookin' for kitchen workers, on account of him killin' most of 'em off when his supper doesn't agree with him."

The three of us just stare at Abe, shocked by his statement.

His lip curls again. "Jokin'," he says, smacking his leg. We all breathe out at the same time, like we've been collectively holding our breath. "Kitchen it is. You start tomorrow morning. Just go to the back gates and give them this." He hands Wes a type of gold coin I've never seen before. "Any questions?"

Wes shakes his head. "Good. Then it's been terrible knowin' you all. Try not to git yerselves killed doin' whatever it is yer doin'. An' don't ferget: yer name's Buck now." He grabs his tinny and chugs what's left of it, wiping his mouth with the back of his hand when he finishes.

"Yah, yah, son of Huck. I got it," Wes says.

"Thanks, Abe," I say, just before the door slams.

"I hope I never see the likes of him again," Buff says after he's gone.

"You and me both," I say, wondering whether I mean it as I take another sip of 'quiddy.

139

Wes slaps the gold coin on the table. "Right. I'm in. Now what's the rest of the plan, or am I supposed to get Joles out all by myself?"

"Yah. That's pretty much it," I say.

Wes stares at me. "What?"

"Jokin'," I say, imitating Abe's voice.

"Very funny," Wes says.

"Really? I thought it was an icin' dumb joke," Buff says.

"Right," I say. "The real plan. Me and Buff, we just have to do what we do best."

Buff cocks an eyebrow. "And what's that?" he says.

I grin. "Fight."

# Sixteen

We watch Wes from the morning shadows of the forest. He gets in without a hitch, the gold coin Abe gave him doing the trick.

So Wes is in. My mother's taken care of, with Clint and Looza looking after her. All that's left is us.

It's our turn to get in. And it's not the easy way.

We wait an hour before making our move, so that no one links us to Buck—I mean, Wes.

When we stomp into Yo's pub, every head in the place turns our way. The door slams off the inside wall.

It only takes a moment for us to locate our quarry. Coker and the other stonecutters sit at the end of the bar in their usual spot, sipping on 'quiddy.

*This will feel good,* I think, cracking my knuckles. Nothing like a good pub brawl to get the blood flowing. And with Yo's agreement to press charges, we'll surely end up in the dungeons.

When I take a step forward, the door thunders shut behind us. I look back, wondering why Buff closed it so hard. Five heavily armed castle guardsmen stand just inside the entrance.

"By the order of the king, you're under arrest," one of them says. I immediately recognize him as Burly Guard A.

Burly Guard B says, "Any resistance will be met with violence."

Then they grab us and bind our arms, leaving Buff and I staring at each other in wonderment as to what just happened. Did Abe turn us in? Or did my constant rule-breaking finally catch up with me? In either case, we're getting exactly what we wanted: imprisonment.

My only regret: I didn't get to break Coker's nose in the process.

~~~

The guards' took more than a few shots at us as they dragged us along, and now my whole body feels like I slid into a tree. Buff didn't fare much better than me. His face looks like he got mauled by a bear and he's all hunched over as he staggers along beside me, dragging chained feet.

But we're in, although I'm not sure what we're going to do now. The plan only went so far as getting us inside the palace and Wes figuring out a way to break us out of the dungeons. For all we know, he'll never make it down there and we'll be left to rot with the mice and creepy-crawlies.

"When will the king sentence us?" I slur to the guard who's prodding us along with some sharp instrument from behind. A raunchy joke comes to mind, but I swallow it down with a wad of spit.

"Consider yerself sentenced," the guard says.

I guess it was too much to hope that the king would personally attend to a couple of lowly tradesmen, but I figured it was worth a shot.

Through vision obscured by swollen eyes, I observe the palace. Despite his condition, I can tell Buff's doing the same. We'll compare notes later.

The guard marches us through a high archway, made of a kind of white stone that seems to glitter pink under the barest hint of summer sunlight infiltrating the cloud cover. The hallway beyond is grand, adorned with all manner of white and blue tapestries, which hang proudly along the walls, threaded with delicate scenes from ice country. Here a snowy slope, dotted with soft pines. There a mountain peak, blanketed with clouds. On my right a town teeming with people. Houses burning? People fleeing? Dark men on black horses chasing them, cutting them down with sharp swords. Men from bedtime stories.

I glance to the left and find a similar scene, except this one's not in ice country, it's in a land I've only heard tales about, a land far, far away, where they say the sun's bigger than here. A land of endless water and deserts that go all the way to the sea. In the tapestry there's a giant wooden vessel—they call them *ships* in the stories—bobbing on a wide splash of water, tied to a tree that looks curved and funny on the shore. Men are rushing from the ship, brandishing swords and torches, charging into an army of dark warriors on black horses, who are galloping toward them, legions of dark clouds and flashing lightning at their backs.

We trudge on and the tapestries are behind us, leaving only a burning memory.

I glance at Buff and he glances back, raising a bruised eyebrow.

(Yah, you can bruise your eyebrow, Buff proved it.)

He saw the depictions too. The violence. He remembers the stories told around warm hearths. Of the Stormers. A bloodthirsty people who conquer lands for one reason and one reason alone: to kill. To drink the blood of those who would oppose them. To ravage the women and enslave the children.

Riding crazed horses that live for the thrill of the battle, they've fought the water people, the Soakers, for many years, trying to destroy them and take control of the Big Waters.

But they're not real, right? Just stories. The king's walls are just an artist's depiction of the stories. Surely.

We pass under a smaller multi-colored stone archway, and into an even larger corridor, wider than ten men and taller than five. There's a voice booming from an open doorway on the right. "The *oldest* bottle I said!" the voice erupts. "This is the second oldest. Go back to the cellars! NOW!"

As we step by the opening, I look inside the room. It's like no room I've ever seen before. Constructed on white marble pillars, the room's so big it could fit a hundred of my houses. Two hundred of Buff's. A long blue carpet extends like a ribbon from the entranceway, all the way across the sparkling floor, where it reaches a seat. Nay, not a seat—a throne. With clawed paws like a bear, the granite throne looms upward, big enough to seat a family of Icers. But in it, basking in the exuberant daylight streaming through a dozen massive windows, is one man. Although I've never seen him before, he can be only one person: the king!

I stop, feeling the sharp prick of the guard's sword on my back.

Why would they take a common criminal past the throne room on the way to the dungeons? I ask myself. It makes no sense.

The king is a big man, old, maybe forty, maybe older, with a shaved bald head and a thin, neatly trimmed graying beard. He looks even bigger sitting on the raised throne.

A thin, white-clothed man scuttles down the blue carpet, away from the king and his booming voice, gone to fetch the oldest bottle of whatever drink the king desires. For a moment King Goff watches after him, almost amused, but then he looks past his servant, to where I stand. Our eyes meet and—

"Move along!" the guard barks, jabbing me harder. Unconsciously, my feet move forward, one after the other, like they have all my life, but my head is back in the throne room, facing Goff, the man who stole my sister. I'm so close.

Moments later, we descend into the dungeons. The air thickens and moistens and a nasty smell tickles my nose. Something's died down here. Or someone. Many maybe.

The guard plucks a torch from a wall fixture and waves it near my face, burning me. I flinch away but don't cry out. He laughs.

Sword at my back once more, he forces me forwards into an alcove. Seated on a squat wooden chair with a broken leg is a giant of a man, wearing a black mask with only mouth and eyeholes cut out. Across his lap rests a double-sided, double-edged battle axe. All four of its razor-sharp edges gleam under the firelight.

He stands, his girth filling half the small space. We're crammed in the other half with the guard. Wafting from his armpits is an odor that smells like what I imagine death would smell like. As I try to get a hold of my rebellious stomach, I consider yelling "I surrender!" and impaling myself on his axe, but I manage to close off my nostrils enough to regain control.

"Ain't you a couple of tasty morsels," he bellows, laughing before he's even finished saying it, a growling echoing chortle that spouts a stream of rotten breath, proving that this dungeon master is more than just a one-smell act.

He takes a step closer, which means his belly touches me— not his clothing, but his actual skin, because he's not wearing a shirt. Thankfully, I am, but the barrier seems so thin and insignificant I have to choke back another pulse of vomit.

"No funny business," he says, showing us all his teeth, which amount to half of what he would've started with as an adult, yellow and chipped.

"Nothing funny here," Buff says, and I agree wholeheartedly.

"All yers, Big," the sword-poking guard says.

As he turns to go, I say, "See you later," but he doesn't look back or return the sentiment. Probably because he doesn't expect he will.

"In," Big says, and I wonder whether he came out so large that his mother couldn't have possibly chosen any other name, or if the nickname was given later in life, when he quickly exceeded his peers in every physical way. Probably the former, if I had to guess.

When I forget to move, Big punches me forward, his fist like a battering ram, sending shudders through my bruised body. By the way Buff grunts behind me, I can tell he got the same treatment.

Torches line the walls of the dungeon, casting shadows in all the right places. Or the wrong places, if you're me and you can only imagine what's reaching out from the dark spots as you pass them.

I try to get a good look in the cells we pass, but their bars are thick and the shadows are deep, and if anyone's in them, then they're well hidden and quieter than a baby on its mother's teat.

"Get in," Big says, motioning with his axe to an open cell door on my left. I limp through, turn back to watch Buff do the same. "Not you," Big says, stopping Buff with an axe blade to his throat. He seems to use the axe for a lot of things. Like if he were to shave his back, which clearly, based on the thick tufts of fur growing back there, he doesn't, he would probably use his axe to do it.

He slams the cell door shut with a clang, twisting a big key in the lock in a practiced motion that I expect took him years to master given the sausage-like girth of his fingers, which clearly aren't made for dexterity. Clobbering, yah. Pummeling, most definitely. Turning keys in locks, not so much.

"Later, buddy," I say to Buff as Big pushes him forwards.

"Enjoy the food," he returns with a dried-blood smile.

I take a moment to study my surroundings, which only takes a moment, because the cell is tinier than Buff's house, and decorated with a miniscule assortment of gray stone walls, floor, and ceiling. A metal pail sits in one corner. I get the feeling I'll be holding the urge to use the bathroom as long as possible in this place.

As I settle in on a spot on the floor that looks slightly less dirty than anywhere else, I hear a clang, the rattle of a key in a lock, and then the thud of heavy footsteps as Big lumbers past. "No funny business," he hollers as he slams the dungeon door behind him.

I sigh. This is what I wanted. Right? Chill yah, I tell myself. It's better being locked up on the inside, where Jolie might be somewhere nearby, than free on the outside, always wondering what happened to my sister, whether she's alive, whether she's safe.

"Buff?" I say.

"Yah." His voice isn't particularly close, but it's not far either, maybe six or seven cells down the row.

"How you feeling?"

"Like a punching bag."

"You'll heal," I say with a smile.

"I know," he says.

"Buff."

"Yah."

"Thanks."

"You owe me," he says.

I'm about to respond when something scrapes the wall in the cell next to mine.

# Seventeen

I sit statue still for a few seconds, listening intently. Was it my imagination? Was it the scrape of a rat's tiny claws? Or was it something else entirely?

"Don't try and avoid me, Dazz," Buff says. "Just because we're locked up doesn't mean I won't come collecting one day. And it'll be something big, something mind-blowingly huge. You'll wish you'd never asked for my help in the first place."

But I'm not listening. Well, I'm listening, but not to Buff. I'm listening to the wall, because I hear the scrape again, only this time it's louder, and it almost sounds...*intentional*, like someone's trying to get my attention. Well, if so, it works, because I scoot across the stone floor, unconcerned about the dirt and whatever else has stained it so dark over the years. I shove my ear right up against the wall, willing Buff to shut his trap.

"You know, I might just ask for your firstborn at some point," he goes on. "If you can ever find a woman who'll tolerate you, that is."

"Shut up, shut up, shut up," I hiss.

"Or maybe you can just take my brothers and sisters off my hands for a while—or forever."

"Shut it, Buff," I finally say loud enough so he can hear.

"Heart of the Mountain, Dazz. No need to get testy. I was just kidding. Well, mostly."

The wall pinches me, right on the cheek.

I pull back, expecting to feel the wetness of blood, but it's dry. My skin stings slightly and I feel a tiny bump forming, but that's it. I reach out to touch the wall, to see if it'll sting me again. That's when it jumps out at me.

A stone clatters to the floor, leaving a gap in the wall.

When I peer through, dark brown eyes stare back.

"Who in the burnin' scorch are you?" the eyes say, as raspy as a punch to the face. "And why the scorch are you followin' me?"

"What the chill is scorch?" I say, feeling a warm blush on my cheeks. What the chill? I'm not a blusher. I don't blush.

"What the scorch is chill?" the icy voice says. Did I say icy? I meant raspy. Yah, just raspy.

"I'm Dazz," I say, memories of a strong, brown-skinned girl floating through my mind. A punch to the face.

"I don't give a burn whether yer King Goff," the Heater girl says, which confuses me for a second, because didn't she ask who I was? But she's speaking so different than what I'm used to, using words that make no sense and rounding them off, almost like the curve of her hips.

"Uhh," I say.

"Why're you followin' me?"

"I'm not," I say.

"Who're you talking to?" Buff calls.

"That Heater girl," I reply.

"I ain't no Heater girl," the Heater girl says sharply. "I'm a Wild One."

I grin. "I'm sure you are," I say, instantly pleased with my wit.

"You are?" Buff says.

"No, you 'zard-brained baggard. Not Wild—Wilde, like with an *e* on the end."

Roan's words come back to me. *The Wildes steal more and more of our women every year.*

"Yah, Buff, I am. Now can you please shut your icin' trap?" I shoot over my shoulder. I turn back to the hole in the wall and the set of mysterious brown eyes. "You're a Wilde?" I ask stupidly, considering that's what she just told me.

"Well, that settles it. I'm speakin' to a searin' fool. Sun goddess help us all."

Well, I don't know about the searin' part, but the fool bit's probably right, considering I'm in a dungeon on an impossible mission to rescue a sister who might not even be here. "Can we start over?" I say hopefully.

"Watcha mean?"

I take a deep breath. "I'm Dazz. I'm an Icer. I'm not following you."

"Oh-ho," the Wilde says.

"Okay, okay. I am, but not like you think. You see, my friend and me, his name's Buff. Say hi, Buff."

"Hi, Buff," Buff says. The Yag.

The set of deep brown eyes just look at me and I can see what they're thinking: *his friend's a searin' fool too.* Which is probably a fair thought to have at this point.

"Anywayyy," I say, "we were trying to get information on what happened to the Heaters, because there were rumors flying around about bad shiver, all kind of bad shiver, and then I saw you and I thought you were a Heater and so I chased you, not because I wanted to hurt you or anything like that, but because I wanted to talk to you, to ask a couple of questions about the Heaters and whether everything was okay and whether..." I stop. I'm rambling like a river of melting snow in the summer.

"What kinda questions?" the girl says, the rasp of her voice tickling my eardrums.

"I guess just, do you know what happened to the Heaters?" I ask.

"I was there," she says.

"But how? I thought the Wildes stole the Heaters' children."

"That's a burnin' lie," she says. "Give me back my brick." Because of my bumbling, arguably the most important conversation of my life is spiraling out of control.

"Wait, nay, I'm sorry, that was just what Roan told us."

Silence. Her eyes blink. Once. Twice. Three times. I feel the blush I never knew I had coming back. Something about being under this woman's scrutiny is like having my stones clamped in a vice.

(In a good way?)

"You know Roan?" she asks. There's something hard in her voice.

"Not really. I met him once at the border. As part of my job. He told us a lot of things, but maybe it wasn't all true. Do you know him?"

"Roan's my father," she says, pulling away from the hole.

~~~

I try for a few hours after that, trying to get her attention, to get her to come back to the hole, to talk to me, but she's not having any of it.

Buff interjects every once in a while, but mostly he's tossing jokes around, like the hits he took to the head have made him a little loopy.

Eventually, I get tired of speaking through the hole, so I shove the brick in, but only halfway, so I can pull it out again if I have to. I slump against the wall, force my eyes closed, try to sleep. I say one last thing before I drift off. "What's your name?"

"Buff," Buff says.

"Skye," the Wilde woman says, and then she's silent for good.

I sleep.

~~~

I'm awakened when the heavy dungeon door crashes open. For a moment I'm disoriented, scrabbling at the walls and reaching into the empty space in front of me, but then I remember where I am. In my cell, slumped against the wall, sleeping sitting up.

Big's voice is a deep rumble of thunder. "No funny…" Well, you know the rest.

Feet scuffle on the floor. More prisoners. I wonder if this is a busy day in the dungeons or if every day is like this, prisoners in, prisoners out. Do prisoners ever go *out*? Or is the sentence the same regardless of the crime: life in the dungeons. I wonder if they'll even feed us, or if we just wither away until we can't wither no more—and then we die.

The feet trod along, at least three sets, maybe four, in addition to Big's crashing footsteps, and I find myself shrinking into the shadows, like Skye—that's her name, isn't it? Or did I dream it?—musta done when we passed by her cell.

"What the scorch happened?" Skye says, her voice firm and echoing.

"Shut yer Heater pie hole!" Big roars.

"I ain't a Heater, you great big tub o' tug lard!" Skye retorts. I grin in the dark. She don't take nothing from nobody, and I've got the black eye to prove it.

"It's alright, Skye," another female voice says, its tone the exact opposite of Skye's husky timbre. Hers floats like a simple melody from a flute, calming everything and everyone that hears it.

Skye stays quiet.

Four people pass by my cell, their skin orangey-brown under the torchlight. They're wearing light-brown skins, exactly like Skye was wearing when I first met her. They look in at me but their eyes don't register any sort of recognition, because they can't see me in the shadows. A few hours ago I'd have said they

154

were Heaters, but now I have no clue, because no one except the men at the border seems to be Heaters.

Two are guys, two girls. I only get the barest glimpse, but one's got shortish black hair, longer than Skye's but only by a few months' growing, and could almost be her sister, if she wasn't so much skinnier. Still muscular, but with bones no bigger than the splinters I occasionally pull out of my feet. Next to her is a guy, lean, muscular, with a look of strength about him. Behind them is another woman, with long, black hair and a regal walk to her, almost like she's dancing. She looks strong as chill, too, but in a way that's more graceful than Skye. And bringing up the rear is the Marked man, every bit as full of muscle and hard edges as Buff described, covered with dark markings that shine a bit in the light, which, when combined with his dark eyes, give him an intimidating look.

Only I'm not intimidated. Not by him. Not by his posse.

The only one who might intimidate me is Skye, but I'm not admitting that just yet.

Then they're gone and I crawl back outta the shadows. Clinks and clanks and four more prisoners are locked in.

I return to the brick, waiting until Big passes and slams the door before pulling it out. "Skye," I hiss.

"Whaddya want, Icer?" And then her eyes are there and I'm blushing and my heart's beating just a little bit faster.

"Why weren't you with your friends?" I ask.

"Who're you talking to, sis?" a voice says from nearby. *Sis.* Must be the thin, splinter-boned one.

"Just that searin' Icy that tried to git us in the trees," she calls.

"Scram, Icy," another voice says, this one warm but full of pressure. The Marked guy. Gotta be.

"'S okay," Skye says. "He ain't causin' no problems, are you, Icy?"

I almost laugh at how they continue to refer to me as Icy. To me that means they think I'm attractive, but from their tone I know they mean it in an entirely different way. And not a friendly one. "Dazz," I say.

"What?" she says.

"My name. It's Dazz."

"Okay, Icy Dazz. Whaddya got to say fer yerself?" Skye says. I snort, unable to stop the laugh from escaping me.

"You laughin' at me?" Skye says.

"Sorry, nay. It's just…ah, never mind." I repeat my question from before.

Skye laughs, and it sends a beautiful tremor up my spine. "I mighta been causin' more trouble than they could handle," she says.

"You searin' nearly killed one of the guards," her sister says across my cell.

She closes her eyes and laughs again. "Siena's right," she says. "I mighta done just that."

"So they left you in the cell?" I ask.

"I'm here, ain't I?" I'm racking up some sort of a record for freeze-brained questions.

"Where'd they take the others?" I ask, moving on quickly.

"How the scorch should I know?" she says. "I been sittin' here havin' the most unfortunate conversation with you."

My face is becoming an unending pile of red blush.

"They took us to see the king," Siena says.

"King Goff?" I say.

"Is there more'n one King?" Siena says. "Anyway, he's more like King Goof if you ask me. Here we are, leaders of the new

156

fire country Tri-Tribes, and he's got us locked up tighter'n a hand up a tug's blazeshooter." Like her sister, Siena seems to have a way with words, although she has none of the grit in her voice that I admire so much about Skye.

Thankfully, Buff chimes in, because I've only got more stupid questions. "What happened in fire country?" he asks. "And what's this new Tri-Tribes you're talking about."

"You ask too many questions," the warm voice of the Marked guy says.

"It's okay, Feve," the song-like voice of the long-haired woman says. "Anyone we can tell our story to could help us." Although there's nothing special in her words, they seem to command attention, obedience, like she's used to people listening to what she has to say.

"Please," I say. "We've got as big a problem with Goff as anyone. Just tell us what happened."

"My father happened," Skye says.

# Eighteen

"It wasn't entirely his fault," Siena says.

"He didn't help matters though," Skye says.

"No, he didn't," says a fourth voice, one I haven't heard yet. The muscly, athletic-looking guy. I wonder what group he's affiliated with. "The Glassies attacked us," the guy explains.

"Who'd they attack?" I ask.

"The Heaters." So the other guy's a Heater. I'm still trying to figure out how everything fits together. "They've attacked us three times. The third time was just at the start of the summer. Siena and Skye's father...Roan...he was a bit of tyrant."

"A bit?" Skye says. "I still got scars from where he used his snapper on me. Siena too."

Sounds like a real good guy. "At least he was going out and getting the Cure for you," I point out.

"Ha!" Skye scoffs. "Whaddya you know about the Cure?"

Something in her tone tells me to tread carefully. "I, uh, I know we delivered it to Roan's men all the time."

"You don't know what he did with it?" the Heater guy says.

"We assumed he passed it out to the village," Buff says, even though we weren't really sure of that at all.

"He didn't." Siena again. "He kept it for himself and maybe a few of his baggard friends. There wasn't enough to go 'round, and no one knew 'bout it anyway."

I don't know what to say. Not only did Roan not share the Cure with the Heaters, but he kept it from his own children? It's not what I expected. "So back to the Glassies," I say. "They attacked the Heaters, but where do the rest of you fit in?"

"Me and Sie are Wildes," Skye says. "We ran away from home to join them. Wilde, well, she's the leader."

"Sorry, who's Wilde?" Buff asks.

"I am," says the musical voice.

"Yes you are," says Buff, like me, choosing the wrong time for a bad line. "I'm Buff. And my friend's Dazz."

"I'm Circ," says the other guy, the non-Marked one. Circ, Siena, Wilde, Feve, and Skye. Skye.

"Got it," I say. "So the ladies joined the Wildes. Then what?"

"My father tried to burnin' kill us," Skye says. "But we searin' near killed him and half his Hunters."

"I bet you did," I say, rubbing my bruised nose.

"Then when the Glassies attacked the Heaters, we went to help them. Not 'cause of my father. 'Cause of the rest of the Heaters. The good ones."

"We showed up to help, too," says Feve. "The Marked."

"Yeah, when the fight was mostly over," Siena says. There's a hint of something in her voice. Not hate necessarily, but something bordering on it, animosity maybe. She doesn't like Feve, and maybe not the Marked in general.

"The Heaters, Wildes, and Marked," I say. "The Tri-Tribes, right?"

"Right," Circ says. "Roan was killed, most of the—"

"Wait, Roan's dead?" Buff says.

"Searin' right," Skye says, not a speck of sadness for her father in her voice. "Glassies killed him deader'n two tons of tug meat."

Well, that explains why the trade stopped. Given the secrecy, I wonder if he didn't orchestrate the whole thing. He and Goff. Skye and the rest know about the Cure, but I wonder if they know about the "special cargo"…

Circ continues. "Most of the Greynotes were killed too. Given how small each tribe's numbers were, we declared a truce amongst us and formed the Tri-Tribes. At least until the danger from the Glassies passes."

"Why do the Glassies want to kill you?" I blurt out. There's silence for a minute, so I say, "They seem to like us just fine."

"You've seen them, Icy?" Feve says incredulously.

"Well, yah. Not that often, but they come up the mountain from time to time. Only to meet with the king though."

"What does the king have to do with the Glassies?" Feve's questions are filled with sharp edges, like jagged rocks and icicles.

"I dunno. I assume something trade related," I say. "It's all a bit secretive, and Goff doesn't really tell the Icers anything."

"Doesn't make any sense," Circ mutters.

"Doesn't make one burnin' lick of sense," Skye agrees.

I'm missing something. "What doesn't?" I look through the hole, but Skye's eyes aren't there. The back of her head rests against the wall.

Skye's not talking, so Circ says, "Goff's trading with Roan on one hand and then dealing with the Glassies on the other. Seems like he's straddling the middle, playing both sides. Or he's really on one side, and helping the other."

"But he'd be helping your side by giving you the Cure," I say.

"But my father didn't share it 'round," Siena interjects.

"But Goff doesn't know that," I reply.

"But you don't know what the scorch yer talkin' 'bout!" Skye suddenly yells, twisting her eyes around and pointing them back through the hole at me.

"Sorry," I say, feeling hot, although there's a cool chill in the dank dungeon air. "Look, I'm not trying to defend Goff, or Roan, I'm just trying to understand things." I wonder if now's the time to ask about the children cargo. Probably not, there's enough on the table already.

"Us, too," Wilde says. "Skye?"

"I'm sorry, too," she says, although I'm not sure she would've said it if Wilde hadn't pushed her to.

"Maybe I can help," I say. "Let me tell you what I know."

~ ~ ~

So I tell them mostly everything, from the beginning. My gambling mistakes, the job, how we learned about the Cure, how Goff is hiding it from the Icers almost exactly like Roan was keeping it secret from the Heaters, about the job suddenly ending and Buff and I going looking for answers and finding

161

Skye and Feve. I only leave out the part about Jolie getting taken and the children being traded for the Cure. I don't even know why I skip it, but Buff doesn't say anything.

"So Goff is keeping the Cure all for himself, too," Wilde says. "Interesting. We thought part of the trade agreement was keeping the Heaters out of ice country so as to not spread the Fire."

"Not spread the Fire?" I say. "The Cold—that's what we call it—kills many of us every year. Something about the snow and ice and cold air slows it down, so we live a little longer, but it still gets us all eventually, like it did my father a while back."

"I'm sorry," Wilde says. "About your father."

"Me, too," I say.

"Goff sounds like our father," Siena says. "Eviler'n a pack of Killers scorch bent on biting their fangs into anything that moves."

"Yah, well, we're learning very quickly that he's not such a good guy," Buff says.

"Where's he get it?" Siena throws out there. "The Cure."

It's another good question none of us know the answer to. "I've taken a fair look at the dried herbs," I say. "But it's nothing I've seen growing on the mountain. But it's possible he grows it right in the palace somewhere."

No one has anything to say to that. A question they'll be able to answer pops into my head. "Why'd you come here anyway?" The question I don't ask is: why'd you sneak in the way you did?

"The Cure," Siena says. "Mostly. We want to get more of it for our people, to stop the death. Whatever's in the air is killin' us all, one by one. We can't barely live past thirty. We were gonna offer a new trade 'greement, a good'un, in exchange for

162

more of the Cure, but he wouldn't e'en listen to us. All he cared 'bout was what happened to my father."

"When we told him Roan was dead, he threw us all back down here," Circ explains. "He didn't look like he'd be letting us out anytime soon."

And there it is. Unless Wes can come through for us, we're all freezed. I'll keep that to myself too.

~ ~ ~

Everyone goes silent for a while after that, each lost in their own thoughts. Mine are like dead leaves in the wind, drifting and swirling and scattering every which way, as haphazard and random as falling snow. Too many questions and not enough answers.

But mostly I just think about Jolie. Whether she's wandering the palace somewhere, carrying a bucket, or planting seeds in the palace gardens that will sprout the stems that'll eventually grow into the Cure plants. Whether she's thinking about me, about ways to escape so she can come home. Whether she's tried to escape and gotten caught, been punished. Whether Wes's seen her around, and is biding his time to get us all out together. Wes has always been so icin' good at protecting us, at taking care of us. Can he do it now?

Then I hear a voice through the hole in the wall, raspy but whispered. "Hey, Icy," Skye says. "You there?"

"It's Dazz," I say, peering through the hole. "And where else would I be?"

She laughs and I see her lips turned up into a smile. She's not looking through the hole—just talking through it, laughing through it. "Good'un. I meant if you were sleepin', but considerin' yer speakin' to me, I s'pose you ain't."

"I ain't," I agree.

"Watcha doin' down 'ere?" Skye asks. "Watcha in for?"

"Didn't I tell you?" I say, trying to think up a good response.

"No, you stopped yer story when you followed us through the woods and found where we got caught."

"We picked a fight with a coupla of castle guards," I say, bending the truth just a little for effect. We didn't actually fight them, although I definitely wanted to.

"You did what? Are you wooloo?" The word rolls around in the hole, clattering against the sides like a pebble. I can easily guess what *wooloo* means.

"Uh, yah, I guess we are," I say, wondering if being crazy is a really bad thing where she comes from.

She laughs and I admire her lips. I could reach through and touch them so easily. Shame I can't fit my head through. I've never made out in a dungeon before. "We're all a little wooloo too," she says. "Hafta be to survive fire country."

I steer the topic away before she asks any more questions. "You know, the only reason you knocked me out in the woods was because I was surprised you were a girl," I say.

"Ha!" Her laugh echoes loudly through the dungeons. "Surprised, eh? Seems to me you were the one chasin' me."

"Yah. But when you turned and you were so—so..."

"So what?" she says, a smile in her question. I wish I could see her face again. All I've got is a memory, a set of eyes, and a pair of lips to go offa.

I laugh. "So...*not* a guy," I say. "Except for the hair."

"Short hair don't hafta be a guy," she snaps.

"Nay, I didn't mean—I'm not saying—" I've never been this rattled talking to a woman before. When I was courting the witch I was as smooth as butter, at least up until the point where she cheated on me and threw me out on my arse.

"What're you sayin'?" she asks, once more laying the pressure on hard.

My face is hotter than fire country. "I'm saying I like it. Your hair. I like your hair. I like everything." Buff chuckles. I realize my voice has risen like the temperature on the way down the mountain. Our private conversation is no longer private.

A hard voice says, "I think you've said enough."

Feve has spoken.

Buff chuckles again. "More than enough," he adds.

# Nineteen

Not much happens for a day.

The dungeon's not so bad, mostly because my cell's right next to Skye's, and she's been pretty set on sitting near our shared hole, so I get glimpses of her all the time. A strong shoulder. A slender neck. Did I mention her lips?

A few times I think I'm doing something wrong by paying her so much attention, because I should be focused on finding Jolie—which I am—but it's kind of hard to find your sister when you're locked in a tiny cell. So I figure anything to pass the time is fair game—at least until Wes breaks us out.

Which he will.

Of that I'm certain.

Well, mostly certain.

When I think it's near the end of the day, Big brings us each a thin metal dish of something gruel-like, but even under the torchlight it's hard to identify what it is. It tastes like a mixture of dirt and bark, so maybe that's what it is, seasoned with yellow snow and fried up in a big old pot, made special for prisoners. Wanting to stay strong, I eat it anyway.

Skye messes with Big on the way out. "Hey, Big," she says.

"Eat your food!" he says.

"I will. It's just, there's this nasty searin' fungus goin' 'round and I been wonderin' if you know anythin' 'bout it."

*What's she up to?*

Big stops sharply. "I'm the one who told ya about it, Woman. When I tossed you in 'ere."

"Was it you?" Skye says, false question in her voice.

"Yah!"

"Oh, I guess I forgot." Skye's voice echoes off the walls.

"What about the fungus?" Big asks, a hint of something that I think is fear in his tone.

"Is that a spot of it on your chest?" Skye says, pointing.

Even under the dim light, I can see Big's face go white. "Where?" he says, frantically searching with his fingers.

"Above that big ol' crater you call a bellybutton," she says.

Big's fingers find the spot, run across his sweaty skin. "Just a mole," he says, relief evident in the way he breathes out as he says it.

"Good," Skye says. "I was worried."

"Now eat your food!" Big repeats, stomping through the doors.

"What was that all about?" I ask Skye.

"Nothin'," she says. "Just havin' a bit of fun. When we were brought in, the big fella was goin' on and on 'bout this flesh eatin' fungus that's been goin' 'round. Seems the only thing he's scared of. Just wanted to put that fear to the test."

~~~

There's not much else to do other than talking, sometimes as a group, sometimes broken up into separate conversations. A coupla of times I move to the front of my cell, stick my head out the bars, look up and down the row, hoping to get another look at one of the others—okay, okay, Skye mostly—but none of them are ever doing the same. Well, except for Buff, who seems to be doing the same thing, except his eyes are always on the cell I suspect belongs to the song-voiced one they call Wilde.

When I make a rude gesture he slinks back into his cell.

So I just sit there, arms draped over the bars, waiting. For Wes. For anybody.

I picture how it'll be when we're reunited with Jolie, how her smile will fill up my heart, how she'll wrap her arms around me and I'll swing her in a circle.

There's movement to my left, from the cell next to mine. The girl sticks her head out. Skye's sister, Siena. She glances my way, smiles a rather pretty smile, and then leans as far to the edge in the other direction as possible, as if I might have the Cold and share it with her. I frown, perplexed as to her strange anti-me behavior, but then a pair of strong arms reaches out from the cell beyond hers. She's barely able to reach them, to grasp them, to hold them. There's something so tender, so longing, so *loving* in the simple touch I witness, between Siena and Circ, that I feel a yearning in my own heart. Not for anyone in particular, certainly not for any of my exes, not even for

Skye—although she has captured my interest—but just for a connection to someone like the one I see between Skye's sister and the Heater boy.

As they continue to hold hands, they whisper to each other, laugh, whisper some more, laugh some more. Everything seems so easy for them, like one was made for the other. Like they never had a choice. Almost like destiny. As I pull back into my cell, I'm left wondering if it's always been that way for them.

~~~

"Psst! Skye!" I hiss through the hole in the wall.

Everything's dark. A few hours back, Big stomped through the dungeon extinguishing all the torches. Everyone's sleeping. I should be sleeping. But I can't, not without clearing something up first.

"Psst!" I hiss again.

"Sun goddess sear it, Icy! This'd better be good." I can sense her face at the hole, her lips turned into a frown that could kill.

I smile in the dark.

"I've got something to say," I whisper.

"Well, out with it, Icy."

"Dazz," I say.

"That's what you wanted to say? To tell me yer name agin?"

"Nay, nay, I'm just saying call me Dazz. In ice country, icy means…"

"Spit it out, Icy. I'm tired."

"Attractive," I say.

"And yer not?" she asks. Is she asking me? Is she saying I am…icy? What is she saying? "An icy Icy," she whispers, floating the words off her tongue. It's the gentlest I think I've ever heard her voice sound.

"Uh," I say.

"Yer smoky, *Dazz*," she says, my name sounding strange coming from her. "But that ain't nothin' where I come from. Not that I mind a-lookin' sometimes."

I almost choke on the wad of spit that's congealing in my throat. I've never had a woman be so…honest with me. Not that women aren't honest, a lot of them are, too honest sometimes, but Skye seems to say every last thought that pops into her head. It's exhilarating in a way, although I couldn't imagine doing the same. If I said half the things floating around in my brain right now, she'd probably never speak to me again.

"Now, are we done, or are we done?" she says. "This feather-hard floor is callin' my name."

"Wait," I say. "Nay, there was something else."

"Well then hocker it up like the lump that always seems to be in yer throat."

Heart of the Mountain, is she reading my thoughts now, too? I gotta get control of things again, if I ever had control of them in the first place. "Look, I just wanted you to know that I'm usually a better fighter. I really was surprised when you turned around and found out you were a—"

"A woman. I know. Full of curves and a mix of hard and soft spots and all the things that guys git all wooloo over. But even if I hadn'ta been a woman, or if you weren't surprised and all that, I'da still've beat you redder'n the fire country sky. You can count on that, Icy."

My jaw drops and I try to lift it back up but it's dead weight. I'm thankful it's dark and she can't see me. "Now wait just a minute, you've never even seen me fight. I've been in more scraps in the last week than you've probably seen your entire life."

"I ain't tryin' to compete, Dazzy. I'm just sayin' truths, which can be hard to hear sometimes. Sleep on it and you'll feel much better in the mornin'."

Sleep on it? You bet your cute little arse I'll sleep on it. And I'll prove to her one way or the other that I can hold my own in a fight. Certainly better than Feve, who's probably who she's comparing me to.

"G'night, icy Dazz," she says, completely disarming me. I lay down with my own shoulder and arms as a pillow, not thinking about proving that I can fight, but about whether she meant icy with a capital or lowercase "i", smiling like a butcher's sled dog.

~~~

Boredom sets in pretty hard the next day. People are used to having the right to come and go as they please, so if you take that right away from them, they get bored very quickly. At least I do.

All of us seem energized after sleeping, though, and when morning comes—in the form of a pathway of torches lit by a lumbering Big, still shirtless and so meaty he looks capable of feeding a village of cannibals for a month—everyone's ready to talk some more. Buff, being Buff, suggests a game of sorts.

"I've got some rocks that broke off the floor," Buff says. "I toss one to whoever I please, and I get to ask them a question."

"A question 'bout what?" Skye hollers down the row.

"Anything," Buff says. "Whatever I want. And the person who's got the rock has to answer, and when they do, they get to throw the rock to someone else and ask their own question."

"What're we, a bunch of game-lovin' Midders tryin' to figure out which boy thinks they're smoky?" Skye says.

I laugh, starting to catch onto the fire country lingo.

I make a suggestion. "We'll play Buff's little game, but let's stick to questions about fire or ice country."

"'Specially blaze about Goff, the Cure, and the Glassies," Skye suggests.

"I'm bored already," Feve says.

"You shut it," Siena says, which makes me smile. I'd love to get a glimpse into whatever history there is between those two.

"I'm in," Circ says.

"It might help us figure things out," Wilde adds.

"Right," Buff says. "First rock's for Wilde." Surprise, surprise.

There's scuffling and scraping as everyone moves to the front of their cells. I stick my head out and purposely look left first, so as to not be so obvious about how icin' bad I want to look in Skye's direction. Siena's head pops out but she looks at Circ, who's grinning at her. Feve's on the opposite side, his bare chest sliced by shadows and markings. He's staring at me like if he looks hard enough he might kill me with just his eyes. Further down the row, Wilde's next to Feve, and she's looking my way, but past me, I guess at Skye.

Don't look. Don't look.

Not yet. Too obvious.

Buff's at the end of the hall, sort of looking at everyone, but definitely favoring Wilde's direction.

Don't look—

—how can I not look?—

—don't. Really, don't.

I look.

I mean for it to be a quick, nonchalant glance, just to see that she's there, but she's looking right at me, a smile tugging at the corners of the lips I've gotten to see the most of over the last day. I don't blush this time, not one bit, just look back, meeting her eyes, feeling something akin to excitement rush through my chest.

She's not icy, like we thought. Nay, her beauty goes far beyond a word like that, which suddenly seems so childish, so ordinary. And she is anything but ordinary. With deep, brown eyes that seem to collect every last flicker of torchlight, strong high cheekbones that fit her right-sized nose and full lips so perfectly, she's a brown-skinned angel, delicate and strong, soft and hard—and grinning.

I've been staring a while.

"Mornin', icy Dazz," she says, soft enough so only I can hear.

"Morning, beautiful Skye," I say, shocking myself at my own boldness.

Skye's grin fades and I can tell I've surprised her too, which is some feat, considering she's seemed one step ahead from the very beginning.

When Buff says, "Catch, Wilde!" she looks past me, and the moment is broken. I turn, too, and watch as Buff chucks the stone awkwardly through the bars. To his credit, it goes in the general direction of Wilde, skipping across the stone and resting in front of her cell, where she picks it up. She looks at Buff, her long black hair draped behind her.

"Ahem." Buff clears his throat. "Wilde, my lady, what are the three most important qualities you look for in a guy?"

Chaos follows the question. I'm laughing, unable to help it. Feve's protesting, yelling something about the childishness of Icers. Siena and Circ are holding hands and more or less just shaking their heads. And Skye's screaming the most, saying things like "...burnin' not what we agreed," and "...searin' wooloo Icies."

Wilde, however, raises a hand, instantly silencing everyone, including me, as I suddenly find myself unable to laugh. "Truth, honor, wisdom," she says, answering.

There's silence for a moment, and then I say, "Sorry, Buff, oh for three."

Laughter fills the dungeon, Buff's being the loudest of all as he nods his head. I catch a glance from Feve and it's not filled with animosity. He's not laughing exactly, but he's not glaring or frowning or shooting eye-daggers, so I guess it's a win.

Skye's laughing, too, which makes me smile even bigger. Score one for the funny man.

We all stop, however, when the door barges open and Big sticks his thick head in. "What the freeze is goin' on in here! Shut yer gruel-eaters 'fore I shut 'em for you!" He slams the door and there's a lot of hands over mouths, as people try not to laugh.

"Now, can we stick to the rules?" Wilde says.

Buff nods sheepishly.

Right away, Wilde turns down the row and says, "Dazz," bouncing the rock along the floor. It skitters to my feet and stops against my toe. I look up expectantly. What will the wise Wilde leader ask me?

"What are you not telling us?" she asks.

# Twenny

I bite my lip. I've told them most everything, but not one of the most important things. They might already know all about it—but then again, they might not. And who am I to be the one to tell them? On the other hand, who am I to keep it from them?

I decide on a more neutral approach, seeing if I can draw what they know out of them.

"My sister was taken," I say.

Silence and stares.

"I'm sorry, I left it out because—well, I don't know why. Just because it's personal, I guess. Her name's Jolie, she's twelve years old, and someone took her away, abducted her in the middle of the night. I couldn't stop them, I couldn't—" My voice breaks and I look at the ground, at the rock at my feet.

Failure written all over me. Plain as day for Skye to see. I couldn't even protect my own little sister.

"Who took her?" Wilde asks softly.

A second question. Do I have to answer? Should I answer? Can I answer?

"I don't know for sure," I say, "but I think…"

I grab the rock, skid it across Siena's cell, all the way to Circ's. "How can the Heaters send their children to King Goff?" I ask, with no attempt to keep the venom outta my voice. I feel heat rising everywhere. My fists clench and I feel my old friend, my temper, urging me to hit something, anything. So much for our fun, laughter-filled game. Maybe we should've stuck to Buff's type of questions.

"What?" Circ says.

"What the scorch are you talkin' 'bout, Icy?" Skye says. There's no question it's a capital *I* in Icy this time.

My eyes meet hers, but there's no anger in them. Or truth. She has no clue what I'm talking about. I scan the faces of the other prisoners and find the same thing in all of them. Confusion. They're as clueless as I was not that long ago. They don't know an icin' thing about any of it, which is a huge relief, because if they did…well, let's just say it wouldn't be something I could forgive. Says the man who delivered the children to the king.

I sigh, close my eyes, feeling the heat leave me.

Eyes closed, I tell them everything I left out the last time.

~~~

When I finish, there's complete silence. Dungeon master Big would be proud.

176

When I open my eyes, I expect everyone to be looking at me, just staring. Hating me. For being the messenger. For not doing anything to stop it. For delivering—actually being a part of taking—the children to Goff.

But they're not. They're looking off into nothing. At the walls, at the floor, at the ceiling. None of them speaking or doing much. Just waiting, as if maybe I'll say, "Ha! I got you, didn't I?" But I can't say that, as much as I wish I could.

Finally, Wilde speaks. "Goff took your sister. Jolie." It's not a question.

I nod, tired of speaking.

"I'm sorry," she says.

"What's he doing with the kids?" Feve asks. I shake my head, feeling more and more helpless. "You don't know?"

"No one does," Buff says, coming to the rescue. "Not even those close to the king. It's a big mystery."

I remember that it's Skye and Siena's father who's as much to blame as anyone. I look at Skye first, but she must have something mighty interesting on her thin, leather shoe, because she's studying it with both her eyes. So I look at Siena, who feels me looking, and turns her head. There's a tear in her eyes, just hanging there, as if it's not strong enough to make it over the edge of her eyelid.

"That's what he was doing for the Cure?" she says. It's a question, but I don't think she's expecting an answer, so I don't say anything. She wipes away the weak tear with the back of her hand, then slams it into her other palm, as if smashing it. "I always wondered what'd be enough to trade for some of the Cure. Some tug meat ain't nothing. Guarding the border? It made sense when we thought there was no Fire in ice country, when maybe fear of it spreading would make the king give a lot for a little. But now it makes sense, in a knocky kinda way. If Goff wanted little kids for some reason, then he'd pay anything for them, even the Cure. No wonder my father was so obsessed with reproducing."

"What do you mean?" I ask.

Siena sighs. "He was so focused on girls growing up and having children," she says. "He told us it was for the good of the tribe, to ensure our numbers didn't dwindle. But really…" Her voice fades away in an echo.

"He wanted more available to trade.

"We still don't know why he wants them though," Circ says, reaching over and grabbing Siena's hand.

"Free labor," Buff says. "Servants, young and fresh and moldable."

That's the theory we've been working under, but even as he says it, I know it's a weak one. Why would the most powerful man in ice country need to kidnap servants when he can buy anyone he wants? "I don't think that's it anymore," I say, wishing I didn't have to say it. I can't think about other possibilities—not now. Not when I'm so close to finding my sister.

"Then what?" Siena says.

I don't answer.

No one answers, because we're all thinking the same thing: something sick, something twisted. An addiction of sorts involving little kids. My throat fills with bile.

"Don't think about all that," Skye says suddenly. My eyes flick to hers, relieved to hear her speak, although I'm not sure why. "What I wanna know is where my fath—where Roan got the Heater kids."

"He just took them," I say. I sense something behind her words, something I'm missing. "Kids go missing and life moves on," I add, knowing full well it doesn't.

"Yeah, he took 'em alright," Skye agrees, "but they didn't just go missin'. We had lots of girls go missin', but they were always older, like Siena and me when we ran away, fifteen, sixteen years old. Never heard of any disappearin' kids."

"Skye's righter'n rain," Siena says. "The only time we ever lost kids was in accidents or early Fire, but they always died…" Her words hang in the air like a dirty piece of laundry blown off the clothesline, just before it's swept away by the wind.

"How old did you say the kids looked?" Feve asks.

I shrug. "I dunno. Seven, maybe eight."

Skye curses. What am I missing?

"Oh, sun goddess," Siena says, her voice a whisper so soft I wouldn't know she said it if I didn't see her lips move.

"That sonofablazeshooter," Skye says, and my eyes dance back to her.

"What?" I say.

Skye looks at Siena. Siena looks at Skye. Siena releases Circ's hand and reaches out toward Skye, as if just by stretching she might be able to touch her. "Skye?" Siena says.

"Their younger sister," Circ says. "She died when she was seven. Her name was Jade."

My breath catches in my throat.

# Twenny-One

"Did you see her body?" I ask, saying the wrong thing as usual.

Skye stands up, grabs the bars, tries to shake them, but they don't so much as quiver. "The baggard. The filthy baggard," she mutters while she yanks at the metal.

"She was taken by a brushfire," Siena says slowly. "Father said the flames were so hot that all t'was left was ash."

"He cried for her, the no-good tug-lovin' baggard," Skye spouts, pacing across her cell.

"They were real tears," Siena says.

"No," Skye says. "No, no, no! There was nothin' real 'bout them." She starts pounding her fist into her hand.

"He didn't wanna give her up," Siena says. "He couldn't. He was forced to. They were real tears."

Skye just shakes her head, continues pacing. "You can think what you want, but if he was 'ere I'd kill him agin."

"Your sister might be alive," I say.

Skye stops short, stops pounding her fist, stops spouting "the baggard."

"She's not alive," Skye says.

"She might be," I insist. "How long ago was the fire that supposedly killed her?"

Skye shakes her head. Siena answers. "Six years," she says.

"It's a long time," Feve says. "Don't get their hopes up." But by the look in Siena's eyes, I can tell her hopes are already up. Way up.

"There's always hope," I say, but it's for me as much as them.

"Skye?" Siena says. She needs her sister now. My words are just words, but her sister's, they're feelings. Beliefs that can become real if she will only speak them.

Everyone looks at Skye.

She's sort of grimacing, chewing on something that's not there, like she's trying to digest the possibility of what a few minutes earlier was impossible.

"I dunno," she says. "I just dunno. But what I do know is that we can't change what's happened, but we can stop it from happening agin, save those it's happened to. Your sister. Maybe ours if she's there too. Jade." I grab each of Skye's words, bundle them in my arms, tuck them away somewhere to look at later, when I'm ready to hope again. I can see Siena doing the same, a big smile on her face.

Skye's given us both the gift of hope. I wonder if she saved any for herself.

~ ~ ~

While we're all energized with Skye's words, I tell them all about Wes, and how he's going to get us out, and how when he does, we'll get them out too. The Wildes and Heater and Marked are all surprised, but pleased, and it only adds to the rising level of excitement.

But then, all of a sudden, it's as if another minute of talking is more than any of us can handle, because we're still confined, still prisoners, so we retract into our cells and our own individual thoughts. Except for Buff and Wilde, who I hear whispering to each other long after the rest of us stop listening. I wonder how that's working out for him—flirting with the unflirtable.

But even they stop eventually, and all goes quiet.

It's so quiet that I suspect at least a few of the group have fallen asleep. I peek through the hole and try to see Skye, but all I see is the cracked and chipped gray blocks of the opposite wall, painted shimmering hues of orange and red by the flickering torchlight.

I want to sleep too, to turn off my brain and let the hours slip by until Wes comes to crack Big on the head and give us our freedom back.

But I can't, so I lay there in silence, worrying about Wes and Jolie, and wondering about Skye's sister, Jade. Could she really be alive after all these years? Somewhere in this very palace?

I hear a sound, a whispered conversation. Buff and Wilde chatting again? Nay, too close. Circ and Siena.

I slither forward noiselessly, till my ear is right against the bars but I'm still outta sight. It's a terrible thing to do, I know, spying and eavesdropping and all that, but I just have to.

Everything about the thing Circ and Siena has intrigues me. They seem younger than me, a year or two perhaps, and yet there's such certainty in each other, in their togetherness. It's fascinating and magnetic and I wonder just how rare it is.

I can't hear their words, but their tone tells me everything. Soft, tender, occasionally broken by laughter. I peek through the bars. They're holding hands again, and playing some game with their fingers, trying to trap each other's thumbs. I smile, watching them do that simple thing in this impenetrable dungeon.

I don't know how much time passes as I watch them. They stop with the thumb fight and just talk and talk and talk, like they've talked this way hundreds of times before, and will continue hundreds of times after. So easy.

Finally, though, Circ rubs his eyes and scoots back, outta sight, presumably to take a nap. Siena stays by the bars, however, flicking them lightly with her forefinger, making a soft *tingl*ing sound.

"Psst!" I hiss, my attention-getter of choice.

She turns, sees me, a snake with its head stuck through the bars.

She crawls over.

"Thank you," she says.

"For what?"

"For telling us what you did. It's bigger news'n when good ol' Veevs got all big with child."

"Sounds like a big deal," I joke.

"'Tis for me," she says. "A year back I had no sisters, thought Skye'd been taken by the Wildes, maybe killed. And of course, Jade was long gone. Now I might still have both. I only wish my mother could've known."

"She passed?" I say.

"No, she's dead," Siena says, looking at me strangely. "You've a funny way of talking, you know that?"

"I could say the same about you," I say.

"'Spect so." She goes back to ringing her finger off the metal bars. The conversation fades for a minute as I muster the courage to ask her what I want to. I feel silly just thinking it, especially since I'm older, probably more experienced with relationships, if you could call what I had with any of my exes relationships.

"You gotta thing for my sister?" Siena says, looking me in the eyes suddenly.

I laugh and if I had any liquid in my mouth I woulda surely spewed it out. Like sister, like sister apparently. Blunter than a lumberjack's axe at the end of a long wood-chopping day.

"Is it that obvious?" I say.

"No," she says. "But she's my sister, so I look out for her, and she does the same for me."

"I don't want to cause any problems," I say, "especially not if she and Feve..."

"Feve?" Siena whispers. She looks across the way to make sure he's sleeping. "She's not with Feve. Skye knows I'd kick her butt halfway to ice country if she was with the likes of that baggard." She scratches her head, as if thinking. "Well, I s'pose we're already in ice country, so I'd hafta kick her back to fire country, but you know what I mean, don't you?"

I nod, smiling. Siena, also like her sister, is a total crack up. "You don't like Feve much?" I ask.

Siena cringes. "We have a bit o' history—and not the good kind," she says.

"Like you and he were..."

She cringes double. "Blech. No, nothing like that. I always been with Circ. Always will." That brings me back to my unasked question. My heart hammers, though I don't know why. It's just a question.

"Siena, can I ask you something?"

"Long as it's not 'bout Feve, I 'spect so."

"Nay, not Feve. Circ. What you two have got seems so…" I say, searching for the right word without sounding like some doe-eyed school girl. Beautiful? Buff would slap me for saying something like that. Magical? A harder slap.

"Perfect?" Siena says.

I nod. "Yah. You just seem to fit each other. I've never seen anything like it before." There are plenny of couples in ice country. My parents, who were better together than most, at least before my father died, still seemed like a round crossbeam in a square fitting-hole. And the three girlfriends I've had, well, they were like ice to my fire. Or in the case of the witch, the opposite. One would melt the other, leaving a big old lake of slushy water. And then whoever was the slushy water would rise up and douse the fire, leaving it a big old mound of wet, muddy ash.

Siena laughs and it reminds me of Skye, which sends a bit of energy zinging down my arms. "Nobody's perfect," Siena says. "Everyone knows that, but I guess with me and Circ it was something like fate of the gods I s'pose. Everything tried to stop us from being together—once I even thought, really truly believed, he was dead—but then some power greater'n anything us humans have, pulled us right quick back t'gether. And we ain't letting go. Never again."

185

She pauses, and I don't have any more questions, but I feel like she's got more to say so I just wait, looking off at one of the torches burning from its fixture on the wall.

"I guess you know when you've found your true Call when everything else just melts away and it's you and them and them and you, and you want nothing more'n to stay like that forever and ever. And then time stops even though it can't, can't possibly, 'cause no one can stop time, but it does, it really stops. You look at them and you see yourself, your past, your future, all at once. And it's enough—no, more'n enough. And everyone acts like it was a choice—and you were so brave for making that choice—but it was never a choice, not really."

I stare at her, shocked, not expecting to hear all that. It's a lot to take in. I haven't ever felt like that around anyone, although Skye's definitely changed my perspective on women and relationships.

There's something about being around Skye that's so icin' energizing. She could just as well punch me in the face as kiss me, and I suspect the effect would be shockingly similar. A jarring so deep it shakes my very soul. She's got a toughness in her you can't teach. You're either born with it or not. She's got something special in her, that's for sure.

But with everything that's happened, first with the notorious cheating witch, to losing all my silver, to seeing what I've seen, to losing Jolie, and now to meeting Skye, maybe my heart's ready to heal. I need to get back on the figurative snow angel, so to speak.

For the first time in a while, everything seems okay, even when I know it's not. But at least now I know it can be. I have hope.

Abruptly, the dungeon door is thrown open. We both look in its direction, expecting to find Big carrying our evening meals of unidentifiable slop. Big's there alright, but not with dinner.

He pushes Wes through the door in front of him.

He's got chains on his hands and feet.

# Twenny-Two

From the beginning, it was my plan, and mine alone. An arrogant plan, one that's doomed us all. My best friend. My brother. Jolie. And these fine people from fire country. Well, mostly fine. Feve's been giving me the death stare from the time Big shoved Wes into the cell next to him, across from me.

"No funny business," Big hollers to Wes, before leaving him to stare across at me.

"What happened?" I say, wondering whether it really matters.

"I got caught," Wes says, managing a tight smile. A bad joke, especially under the circumstances.

Everyone's awake from their naps now, poking their heads between their cell bars. "Who's that?" Skye says. I dip my head, hating to have to tell her. Then she says, "Wait just one Coteenibblin' moment. That's yer brother, ain't it? He's the tugblazin' spittin' image of you, 'cept not so rough-lookin'."

"Everyone, this is Wes, my brother. Wes, meet the people of fire country, the ones you tracked to the palace."

"Hi people of fire country," Wes says.

"Hi, Wes," Buff says.

"Hey, Buff."

"How'd you get caught, Icer, brother of bad-plan-maker?" Feve says without a smile.

I stare at the ground, feeling fire-country-hot all of a sudden.

"It was my own stupidity," Wes says. "This isn't Dazz's fault."

I look up. "It's all my fault," I say, not letting my older brother take my blame away. None of us would be here if not for me.

Wes continues as if I hadn't spoken. "No one really paid me any attention, letting me move about the palace pretty much as I chose, so long as I was there to prepare the meals on schedule. I got too confident, started sneaking places I shouldn't have. Most doors were open or unlocked, and I investigated them all, but they were all just rooms for normal palace activities, like dining or meeting or preparing. Nothing unusual. This was all on the first day, mind you.

"Today I got bolder, seeking out the darkest and the least-traveled places in the palace. After the lunch preparations and cleanup were over, I found a staircase that seemed to lead to nowhere. It spiraled round and round and up and up and into one of the towers, only at the top there was no way in. Just a stone wall and pair of gleaming brass mountain lion heads, mounted on the wall, mouths open in a perpetual growl."

"Sounds like a dead end," Circ says from down the row.

189

"That's what I thought, but when I went to inspect the lions, there were faint cracks running from above and below them, like someone had torn away the rocks at one time, and then put them back together piece by piece, so perfectly you could barely tell they'd been pulled away.

"So I pushed on the lions, hard, with all my might, and guess what? They pressed into the wall."

"Into the wall, Icer?" Feve says.

"Yah. Right in, like there was nothing behind them. But that's not the strangest thing. As soon as the brass lions disappeared, there was the sound of chains pulling, clinking through a pulley. The door started to rise."

"Holy blaze!" Skye says. "A secret room."

"More than that," Wes says, jamming his eyes shut as if they're stinging. When they flash open, there's hurt in them. "A prison," he says. "A child prison. Past the door were little bodies, brown-skinned and every one of them shrinking back from me as if I might hit them, or do worse. I just stood there for a minute, shell-shocked, searching the faces, wishing beyond wishes that she'd be there. Jolie, that is. Do they know about Jolie?"

I nod, my eyes never leaving Wes's face, urging him silently to continue, to tell me the part where he finds Jolie, where he tries to escape with her, where he gets caught and they take her away again. The part where at least she's still alive.

"She wasn't there," he says, and my heart sinks into my empty stomach, beating dully, thumping a hole in my gut.

"Maybe you just didn't see her?" Buff says.

"Maybe," he says. "Before I could go in, really look at them all, someone grabbed me from behind, threw a bag over my head, and dragged me down here."

190

His words are still hitting my ears, but I'm not really hearing them, because I'm back at how he didn't see Jolie, how she wasn't there, how for all we know she's been planted in the ground somewhere, having outgrown her usefulness to the king.

"Any of them children you saw older?" Skye asks, and I want to bang my head against the wall for not thinking to ask it myself. She probably thinks I'm all selfishness and no caring. Always focused on my own problems and no one else's. She's lost a sister, too. We've got that in common, which is what I gotta get through my freeze-brained head.

Wes shakes his head. "They all looked to be seven, eight years old. Nine at the most. No older than that. Why?"

Skye just slaps a fist in her palm, so I tell him what Skye and Siena told me about their sister.

"This whole thing is icin' sick," Wes says when I finish.

"We're knocked," Siena says. "There ain't no way out now. Not unless the sun goddess decides to shine down on us."

I grab the bars, slump against them. The sheet of gray clouds covering ice country will prevent the sun goddess or any other goddess from seeing any of what's happening here.

No one says anything after that.

~~~

I don't even bother with the gruel. It's tasteless and unsatisfying anyway. My stomach rumbles, but I ignore it. The others eat theirs and keep up a healthy chatter, all about how else they can escape, whether there's any other way now that our inside man's a little too far on the inside.

I ignore that, too, throwing all my thoughts into beating on myself, what a failure I am. Everything I've done over the last year has been a complete and utter disaster. Nothing's gone right, nothing's felt right, nothing's been right. Every move's been a mistake, picking apart my life piece by ice-sucking piece.

I'm about to see if I'm flexible enough to kick my own arse, when there's a "Psst!" from beside me. I look over. It's Skye, because, of course, who else would it be? There's no one else over there.

I glance around. The others are still talking, even Wes, passing thoughts back and forth with Siena, Feve and Circ, like he's known them his whole life. That's Wes's way. He's a fitter-inner, always has been.

Surprised, I scoot over to Skye, close enough that if I reached out like Siena and Circ always do, and if she did the same, then we could touch through the bars.

"Ready to stop feelin' burnin' sorry for yerself?" she asks.

I don't know what I expected her to say, but not that. "I freezed everything up," I say.

"You tried," Skye says. "That's all you can do in this sun goddess searin' life."

I look at her and she looks at me and I get lost so quick it's like I'm in another place and maybe there are no bars and no walls and nothing at all separating us. Her hand reaches out into the empty space between us. I stare at it, sun-kissed and full of strength. Strength I'm missing, ever since Wes was pushed through the dungeon door. Strength I need.

I reach out and take it.

It's an icin' good feeling, her hand touching mine, made up of something more solid and realer than the few other womanly touches I've felt since I became a man. Holding her hand for just those few short seconds makes those three other girls seem like distant memories.

She lets go, a smile on her face as she pulls away. "I like you," she says. "Even better when you're like this. Alive."

~~~

The others aren't giving up and neither am I. There's too much at stake, for all of us.

We've got a simple plan, but it might just work. It has to. The only thing left to decide is who—

"I once wrestled a bear with my bare hands," Buff says.

"It was a very hairy, drunken man," I say, "and he ended up passed out on top of you."

"What's a bear?" Siena asks.

"He sure felt like a bear," Buff says, scratching his head.

"You're not the best fighter here, Buff," I say, "so just let it go."

"And you are, Icy?" Feve says, forcing me to duck to avoid his eye darts.

"Why does he keep calling you 'Icy'?" Wes hisses from across the way.

I shake my head, both because I don't know if we'll ever decide who's best suited to carry out the plan, and at my brother, because, well, there're some things that just can't be explained, at least not easily. "I'm not saying anything," I say. "But I doubt if you're the one either."

Feve glares at me, and I glare right back.

"Quiet! Everyone!" Wilde snaps. Her command echoes once, twice, and then fades, along with all our arguments. "Good sun goddess," she says. "You'd think we were from different planets rather than different countries. Let's just take a vote and be done with it."

"Are we all eligible for the vote?" Buff asks.

"Yes." No one has anything to say to that, so Wilde says, "We'll go around and everyone can name who they think is the best fighter."

"I'll start," Buff says. "Dazz. I've seen him take down three knife fighters with just his fists and maybe a head butt or two." I silently thank my friend for the vote of confidence.

"Head and butt seem to go together all too well for him," Feve mumbles.

I bite back a retort. No one's voted for him yet so…

Wilde says, "Skye. She trains my young warriors and she's the best I've seen." I look at Skye but there's no pride on her face. Just belief.

Feve says, "Circ."

"Siena," Circ says.

"Circ," Siena says.

"That's two for Circ, one for Skye, one for Siena, and one for Dazz," Wilde says, recapping.

Wes says, "Dazz." I look at him, surprised, and he says, "I know, I know, I've never seen you fight. But I hear people talk, and no matter how many times I've had to clean up the cuts and bruises on your face, they always say the other guy looked ten times worse." I nod, feeling a burst of pride in my chest. I never realized he listened to the talk about me.

"Skye," I say, knotting the count at two apiece for me, Circ, and Skye.

"The decision is yours, Skye," Wilde says.

She doesn't flinch, just smiles, not one shred of doubt in her eyes. "Me," she says.

# Twenny-Three

Morning comes with a quick step and a dive.

There's plenny of energy buzzing through the dungeon. I even choke down my whole plate of cold gruel, so as to ensure I'm ready for whatever's coming.

As quick as the morning came, the evening meal's like a distant mountain, way off on the horizon, days and weeks and months away. We do different things to pass the time: sleep, throw Buff's rock around (Yah. The question game again.), talk about anything and nothing. Buff even sings a little, in his deep baritone, making us all laugh with his comedic rendition of "The Woman Who Made Me Cry." He earns a bellow from Big for that one. Out of sheer boredom, I expect, Skye tries to taunt Big into the dungeon, but he just slams the door in all our faces, with a final warning to shut the freezin' chill up, or something along those lines.

When the door opens again, we've all been silent for a while, wishing away the minutes until we can carry out our plan. I look up expectantly, and I'm sure the others do too, but it's not Big at the door. It's a small, thin man, and I recognize him right away. The servant who King Goff screamed at on the day Buff and I were captured.

He looks like a mouse, his nose twitching as if smelling his way in, looking for food. "The king requests your audience," he says to the dungeon.

"I'll give you somethin' to say to the king," Skye murmurs.

"Um, I didn't mean you, ma'am. I meant them."

His fingers point in two directions, one at me and one at Wes.

"Us?" I say. "Why us?" What could we possibly be to the king that he would request our audience?

"It is not my job—or your job—to ask questions," the rat says.

"Look, you little weasel," I say, "we're not going anywhere until you tell us what this is all about."

His nose twitches. "I beg to differ," he says. Heavy feet stomp in unison on the hard stone floor as half a dozen sword-carrying guards march into the dungeon.

~~~

The king is resting his chin lazily on his fist when we enter his throne room. I try to keep my face forward, but I can't help glancing around me, at the enormity of everything. The shiny, white pillars are even bigger, both in width and height, than I

196

could tell when we passed from the hallway a few days back. The windows are huge too, taking up half the wall space. The other half is filled with gigantic wall hangings, similar to the tapestries we saw in the main hall, depicting similarly bloody scenes of fights between the legendary Stormers and Soakers.

When we reach a spot in front of the king, I'm still looking around, taking it all in. The soldiers leave us and step as one to the side, looking through the windows, like statues, completely disinterested in whatever's about to happen between us and Goff.

"Who are you?" Goff says, and my gaze drifts to him. His chin's raised now, his hands clasped easily in his lap.

We say nothing.

"Your resemblance is striking…and yet you each came to be in my dungeons by very different routes. Odd," he says. "Wouldn't you say?"

We say nothing.

"Why did you force me to arrest you?" Goff asks, directing his question at me.

I shrug. "Seemed like a good idea at the time."

He laughs, but there's no joy in it. He stands, descends the three steps from his throne, takes another four to stand in front of me. He's an even bigger man than I thought—like his pillars, thick, strong, and tall. His graying facial hair buzzes as he speaks. "You'll answer my questions or die," he says.

I don't doubt the truth in his words for one second.

"Then you'll die with him," Wes growls from beside me, tensing against his chains.

I jerk my head toward him. I've never heard him speak like that, so uncontrolled, so temper-driven. It reminds me of myself.

197

The king sidesteps to face my brother. "Don't be ridiculous. You dare to snoop where you don't belong?"

"I was looking for someone," Wes says.

The king angles his head. "Really? And who might that be?"

"My sister. She was taken a few months back, not long after she turned twelve. You took her." There's fire in his words. Fire fueled by the kindling of truth.

"I'm sure I don't know what you mean," Goff says, but he doesn't even try to hide that he's lying.

"I saw them," Wes says.

"Your sister?" the king says, turning his back on Wes, clearly unafraid of my brother's previous threat.

"Nay," Wes says. "The other children. In your Heart-forsaken tower. Prisoners."

"Are you sure you hadn't been drinking?" the king says. "Seeing things maybe? There are children in the palace, but that's because their fathers and mothers work here. They play in the towers while their parents earn silver to feed and clothe them. I'm a charitable man."

"You're a sick man," Wes spits back.

Goff turns, smiling, as if my brother paid him a compliment. Everything about his demeanor says control, as well it should, considering he's got all the cards on our lives.

"Ever since our forefathers hid in the caves in this very mountain, the Heart has protected them, saved them from what the Heaters call the Meteor god. My bloodline was chosen by the Heart to be your leaders. Something for you to think about while you and your *brother* rot away in my dungeons."

"Is that all?" I ask, suddenly feeling anxious to get back to my cell.

"No. Before you ever stepped foot behind the castle walls I knew who both of you were. You think I'm stupid? From the moment you lost that card game, your sister's—and your—lives were mine, part of something much bigger than the pathetic world you think you live in."

My head starts to spin. *The card game?* What does that have to do with anything? A piece falls into place, then another. I stiffen, my knees locking.

"You chose Jolie because of my debt?" I say.

"Hmm," Goff muses. "You're smarter than you look. But that didn't stop you from destroying yourself. I need you both, you see."

"For what?" I growl, anger rising, cloaking the real emotion I'm feeling. My fault—it's all my fault.

"Your sister is an important trade item, and you're my insurance that she lives up to her expectations," the king says cryptically.

"What's that supposed to mean?" Wes says, taking a step forward.

One of the guards kicks him in the back of the legs and he goes down.

"I can have you killed any moment I choose," Goff says to Wes. "You're not part of any of this. The only reason you're still alive is because I want both your brother and sister to watch when I personally slit your throat."

"You'll have to kill me first," I say, knowing even as I say it that it's an empty threat.

"As much as I'd like that, I need you alive. Like I said, you're insurance that your sister will do as she's told for the rest of her life. Don't you think you'd be dead by now otherwise? At every turn you disobeyed Abe, broke the rules, practically begged me to kill you. You were warned time and time again, but even the small, stuttering man's death didn't stop your insolence. I promoted the two men who were able to place his body so expertly in your path. I have to admit, I was as shocked as anyone when you tried to talk your way inside the castle. Again, my guards would have killed you if you were anyone else. Only my orders to keep you alive stayed their hands."

I want to call him a liar, to believe that it was my own skills and strength that kept me alive all this time, but I know that's the real lie. They killed Nebo, planted him in our path as a warning. The moment I met him he was as good as dead. It was never our fault, not really. I'm nothing but a bug under the king's spotless black boots, to be scraped off and mounted on a board as he sees fit.

"Guards—take them," Goff says. The guards start to move to grab us, but the king raises a hand. "Oh, yes, there is one other thing. Does anyone besides your dimwitted friend—I believe they call him Buff—know about your suspicions regarding where your sister was taken?"

"Nay," I lie, watching Yo slide a tinny of 'quiddy to me in my head.

~~~

When Big brings our one meal, I feel like doing laps around my cell—I'm so energized. I can't take another minute in this place, much less a rotting lifetime as Goff suggested.

And whatever he's got planned for Jolie—her obedience cemented by my own life—I can't let it happen.

Skye's feeling the same, apparently, because she wastes no time throwing our plan in motion.

"Hey, Big," she says, after he gives her a plate of gruel, balancing the others along his enormous arms.

"Shut yer—"

"Pie hole, blazeshooter, yeah, yeah, I got it," Skye says. "I'm just tryin' to help you. But if you don't wanna know 'bout the weird fungus growin' on yer back, then that's up to you."

Big stops, looks in at Skye, who's already ferociously diving into her gruel, as if she don't give two shivers about the dungeon master.

"What fungus?" Big asks, taking the bait.

Skye stops shoveling food, finishes chewing her last mouthful, says, "The flesh-eatin' kind you got growin' on yer back. You'd better git it removed 'fore it kills you."

Big tries to look over his shoulder, but when that doesn't work, he slides the plates of food to the ground, and then swats at his bare back. "Where?" he says.

"Right there," Skye points. "In the center. No, no, you tug-brained fool. You'll never reach it that way. 'Ere, let me. I've removed the nasty stuff 'fore."

Big keeps scrabbling helplessly at his back, but then eases arse-first against the bars of Skye's cell.

"Ooh, there it is, big fella," Skye says. "It's even nastier'n I thought, plumin' out every which way. I can't quite get to it through these 'ere bars. Maybe if you come inside I can git you cleared up right quick."

Pretty obvious what's going on here, right?

Yah, Big's not heavy in the area of brains, or he's just too obsessed with the idea of fungus eating him from the outside in, because he clinks a coupla keys and shoots that door open faster than you can say "moron dungeon master."

Even stretching as far as I can through my cell bars, I can't see what's happening now, so I go to the hole. I can't see much, just Skye's backside, but I keep on looking.

My heart skips a beat, then starts thumping harder than before.

"C'mon over, big fella, let me have a look," Skye says. She shifts out of view and I let out an audible sigh. A giant leg comes into view, as big as a tree trunk. What were we thinking letting Skye be the one to take on this monster? She's half his freezin' size!

Then the leg turns and Skye's leg flashes out, quicker than lightning, all the bite with twice the grace, and Big cries out with a boisterous bellow that reminds me of the goats during mating season.

The ogre doesn't go down, just staggers away from where I can see, screaming the whole way. Skye streaks past the hole and there's a thud and another Big-sized bellow.

They're heading for the door.

I clamber to my feet and rush to the bars, just in time to see Big plow through the opening, bashing a shoulder on one side of the metal doorframe, which twists him around so I can see his face contorted in pain, making him even uglier, if that's possible. Skye's work.

He grabs madly at the door and tries to close it but—

—Skye's there already, kicking it back and—

—it swings and crashes off Big's arm and hits the outside of the cell and—

—it's all happening too fast but in slow motion, like they're both walking through heavy drifts of snow, but then—

—time speeds up suddenly, with Skye a blur of fists and feet and elbows and knees, pounding, pounding, hitting Big as hard as she hit me, except again and again and—

—Big's wailing and covering his head and staggering around like some drunk at Yo's pub, occasionally swatting at Skye, but always missing, always a second too late or a foot too high, but finally—

—just when I think Skye's going to win the fight without any opposition at all, he connects.

A direct hit, right on her jaw.

A blind, lucky swing that sounds like a stomp and feels, even from where I'm standing, like a bone-breaking blow that even the toughest scoundrels in ice country would have trouble getting up from.

"Skye!" Siena cries out beside me.

Skye lifts off the ground, floating, flying for an instant that might as well be an hour, and then jerks to the hard, stone floor, crumpling in a way that makes her look more like a cloth doll than a person.

My mouth's agape and I'm staring, just staring, watching a trickle of blood meander from her nose and over her lip.

She won't get up from that hit.

She won't.

She gets up. Slowly at first, but then faster, almost with a spring, and I can't see her face because I'm looking from behind her, but I know—*I know*—there's fury in her brown eyes.

"Get him, Skye!" Siena says and I'm echoing the thought in my head.

Big's got his hands away from his face, and he's bleeding all over the place, just dripping the red liquid, but his teeth are clamped shut and he doesn't look close to being finished either. It's like she's been pounding on a boulder for the last few minutes, hoping it'll break right down the middle, but all she's managed to do is knock off a few crumbly edges.

Big takes another wild swing, but Skye dances around it, kicks him sharply in the knee, the one he appears to be favoring, keeping his weight off it. He cries out, but steps toward her with his good leg, grabs at her, just missing when she ducks to the side, punching him with a series of quick jabs to the ribs. He hollers again, but not with pain, with anger, as if he hardly even felt the blows and Skye's nothing more than an annoying fly he wants to crush between the flats of his palms.

He turns quicker than I expect him to, swings twice more and Skye dodges, but she's being forced into a corner. She's down to two options: move back into her cell or retreat toward the dungeon door, which Big locked behind him on the way in. I know she won't go back in her cell where Big'll just slam the door shut on our escape plan. I haven't known Skye that long, and yet I know she won't surrender, won't give up. Not ever.

She backs up a few steps, toward the closed door, waits for Big to make the next move. "Finish this, Skye," I say. Her eyes meet mine briefly, but then they're back on her opponent, who stomps toward her.

Getting a running start she moves to meet him.

Just when he swings one of his bear-claw-sized fists at her head, she slides, feet first, skittering off the stone floor, shooting right through the mammoth gap between his legs.

He grabs at her, but she scrapes past, crying out as the harsh stone tears at her exposed flesh, but when she's through—and icin' right, she's all the way through—she pushes to her feet and leaps on Big's back, throwing her arms around his thick neck.

He starts screaming like a murderer on the hanging block, reaching over his head, grabbing at her, trying to find an angle to use to pound her into oblivion.

But he can't find one. Can't get a good shot in. Just like he couldn't reach the fungus that Skye had invented.

Frantic, he runs backward, smashing Skye into the wall.

But she hangs on.

He turns and runs backward into the bars of Skye's cell.

Her body's taking a beating, but still she hangs on.

Skye digs her heels into his skin and pulls harder, choking the life out of him.

He starts bucking, throwing his head back, trying to crack her face with his skull, but she keeps her head low and to the side, safely out of harm's way.

Slowly—

Ever so slowly—

Big stops bucking—

Stands there all dazed-like—

Drops to one knee—

Then to the other—

And finally—*finally!*—flat on his face, with Skye on top.

She did it.

She actually did it.

# Twenny-Four

"You done it, Skye," Siena says. "I knew you would."

Others are saying similar things, encouraging words, excited words, because, well, we're getting out of this Heart-forsaken dungeon.

Skye climbs offa Big's back, turns to look at us, all sweat-gleaming and muscle-tightened. She wipes the blood off her chin with the back of her hand. A woman looking like this, it should be kinda gross, more than a little off-putting, but nay, it's the exact opposite. She's never looked more beautiful.

"Get the keys," Feve says.

Skye nods and reaches down at Big's belt, trying to find them.

The dungeon door swings open.

Goff stands there, filling the doorway, wearing the finest clothes that ice country taxes can buy. In the cracks and crevices between him and the door I can just make out the dozens of armed guards behind him.

"You really thought you could just walk out of here? Haven't you learned that I control everything? Ice country is my game board, and you are the pieces."

"Go to scorch," Skye says, even as I'm wondering why the king himself would stoop so low as to visit the dungeons. Something about it doesn't feel right. Doesn't he have people to do this kind of work for him?

"Oh I will," Goff sneers. "But not for a very long time, not with the Cure in my possession. But you, my dear fire country animal, are heading there sooner than you think."

"Stay away from her," I growl.

Goff glances at me, a look of surprise flashing across his royal face for a moment, but then morphing to amusement. He laughs. "Interesting," he muses. "Making friends with the natives I see. What's this girl to you?"

When I don't answer, he takes a step forward. "Guards! Please escort her back into her cell."

Skye stiffens and I think she might take on all of them, Goff included, but then she wisely steps into her cell, says, "I'm goin'," and even closes the door herself.

A guard moves forward and locks it behind her.

"Is he dead?" Goff says, motioning to the pile of flesh at his feet.

The same guard that locked the door bends down, sticks a couple of fingers to Big's throat, says, "Just unconscious, your highness."

207

Goff smiles an ugly smile. "You couldn't even kill him?" he says, looking in at Skye, who's far enough back from the bars that I can't see her.

"I chose not to," she says.

"An important difference to you, I suppose," the king says, "but to me, it shows your weakness just the same. In any event, attacking a palace guard and attempting to escape are sufficient crimes to leave me no choice as to the punishment."

He pauses, looks down the row, calm as a windless day, meeting each prisoner's eyes. I'm pretty sure none of us flinch away.

"Let this be a lesson to you all. Foolhardy escape plans and a bunch of children carrying them out will be the death of each and every one of you. Starting with her." He points a stiff finger at Skye.

Dread fills me, blackening my soul like a fire darkens the inside of a fireplace.

"No," Siena whispers. "No. You can't do that."

Goff laughs, which is beginning to annoy me. "My dear, I'm the king. I can do whatever I want. She'll be hung at dawn."

~~~

"Skye?" Siena says for the fourth time. There's no answer.

I take another look through the wall hole but Skye's tucked in a corner somewhere, outta sight.

"Skye, we'll find a way out of this," I say. I mean it, although I don't have an icin' clue how.

"There's no way out," Skye says, finally breaking her silence.

"There is," Siena says, almost pleadingly. "I lost you once, I won't again."

"Goff's one sick man," Feve says. "He'll make us watch."

"Yeah," Circ says, latching onto the thought. "We'll all be there. We'll fight. We'll do everything we can to break you out."

"So you can be hung right after me?" Skye says. "Sear it all to scorch, don't be foolish. Jade and Jolie are as good as dead if we all die. We're the only ones who know."

"No," Siena says. "No. You can't die. You can't."

"Oh, don't you worry, Sister, I'll fight like a Killer. They won't get me that easy. I'll fight 'em with my every last breath, and then keep fightin' even after I got none left."

I close my eyes as reality sets in. There's no escapin' what's comin'. The king probably knew exactly what would happen with all of us born fighters in the dungeon together. He wanted us to try to escape, so he could have his fun. So he could give us hope and then snatch it away. So he could make us watch him kill one of our own. With a jerk I realize that's who these people from fire country are to me. My own. All of them, even Feve. He may not like me, and I may not much like him, but we're in this together now.

And Skye, well, there's something with her that's worth exploring. I can't let her slip away so fast. I just can't. But there's nothing for it. There's no plan that'll work. There's no spy I can call upon. There's just me, Dazz, who's failed at everything I've tried for the longest time. Except fighting. So like Circ said, that's what we'll do. Every last one of us.

Fight until they stick us in the ground.

~~~

There's no dinner tonight. My stomach's all clenched up, aching and aching, but it's not because I'm hungry. Every last ache is for her.

Every beat of my heart seems to ring out, louder than ever, like a dull bell ringing, counting down the moments on her life. I squeeze my chest tight, try to slow down my heart's frantic pace, but on and on it beats, never ceasing, speeding up if anything.

Big's gone. It took half a dozen guards to carry him out.

Siena and Skye talk across my cell, but I shy away from it, staying against the back wall, because I don't want to intrude. I'm nobody, just an outsider, someone they met by a strange twist of fate that left me with a bloodied nose and a black eye. And Skye with a death sentence.

They talk about all kinds of things, stories from their childhood and all that, and although her voice hides it well, I can sense the tears on Siena's cheeks. Skye, however, is herself, as tough and stalwart as ever, talking as if it's just another night, rather than the night to end all nights for her.

"Siena," she says. "You take good care of Circ, you hear me? Treasure him like you always have. Don't ever take him for granted. Guys like him don't grow on pricklers these days."

"I will," Siena sobs, and I feel a hot tear slip down my cheek, the first in a long time, since the Cold took my father. I wipe it away with an angry hand. Wes stares at me across the hall, brows heavy.

"And you, Circ," Skye says, a little louder, "don't let me hear of you doin' anythin' to hurt my lil sis, or you know I'll find a way to kick yer butt from wherever I am."

"I won't," Circ says.

She's not stopping there. Everyone's getting a turn. "Feve," she says, "you've done some searin' stupid things in yer time, and you've hurt me and my sister more'n anyone, save fer my father, but yer more'n yer past, more'n what you done. Throw it all behind you and be the man yer capable of."

"I'll make you proud," Feve says.

"Wilde, my sister," Skye says. "You might have a different mother, a different father, but you'll always be my sister." Another freezin' tear splashes below me and I scrub at my eyes with my fists.

"I know, Skye. And you mine. Go with honor," Wilde says.

"Buff," Skye says, and I stop rubbing my face. I didn't expect us to be included in her goodbyes. We're just Icers. "You seem like a good fella, and you've got a good friend sittin' 'ere 'side me. He seems like he's got more thunder in him than a storm sometimes. Help him control it 'fore he searin' gits himself killed, will ya?"

I can't hold back the laugh that chokes outta my throat. "I'll try," Buff says, as if he's just been given the biggest challenge of anyone.

"Uh, Dazz's brother," Skye says.

"Wes," he reminds her, watching me when he says it.

"Thank you fer tryin' to help us. When you think of me, I hope you think of someone who tried to pay you back, who tried to fight fer you the same way you fought fer me."

"I will," Wes says, tucking his head in his hands. He barely knows her at all, and yet I can tell he feels her, the truth in her. The realness.

"Now git yer rest everyone," she says and I stop moving, stop fidgeting, just sit there like a stone, waiting. Has she forgotten me? She mentioned me in her speech to Buff, so

211

maybe that was all she had to say. I hang my head, knowing full well I shouldn't expect more than that considering we're only a few days from having met each other.

But still—I'd hoped.

Selfishness. That's what my thoughts are, plain and simple. She's gonna be hung and I'm worried about whether she's thinking of me the night before she dies.

But still—I'd hoped. I won't sleep tonight.

Not one wink.

~~~

I musta fallen asleep because my eyes jerk open suddenly. The wall torches continue to burn, because Big's probably not conscious enough to put them out. Everything's quiet, except I know something woke me up.

A stone clatters around my feet, which are sticking out into the middle of my cell, away from my head, which is resting uncomfortably against the wall. I look at the rock, changing color from orange to red to yellow and back to gray as the flames flicker.

*Clatter, clatter.*

Another stone careens across my cell, skipping all the way to where it rests by my side. I curl my fingers around it, retrace its path to where it musta come from.

The hole in the wall. Skye's hole.

I slide on over to it, blinking away the sleep I didn't expect in the first place.

Skye's looking at me. "Icy Dazz," she says. My toes curl slightly.

"What're you doing awake?" I say.

"Hard to sleep on yer last night," she says. I cringe, wondering how I manage to consistently say stupid things through this hole.

"I'm sorry, I didn't me—"

"I'm just kiddin' ya," Skye says. "Don't git yer—whaddya call the small clothes you wear under yer other clothes?"

"Skivvies?" I say, like a question.

"Sure. Whatever. Don't git yer skivvies all in a knot."

"Skye, I—"

"No," she says. "It's my night to do the talkin'. 'Cause if I'm talkin', I ain't fallin' apart, I ain't losin' the dignity I found when I left my father behind to join the Wildes. I won't lose that, not tonight."

"I'm sorr—"

"What'd I say?" she says, showing me the finger she's got to her lips.

I don't say anything. Just wait.

"Better," she says, sending her eyes through again. "I know we ain't hardly more'n strangers, but I've got feelin's for you, Dazz, I'll go right on out and say it, 'cause, after all, what do I have to lose, right?" I nod, feeling a burst of something good in my chest. I don't say anything because she told me not to.

"I don't go chasin' after guys. I don't got a Circ, like Siena. I've never..." Her voice falters for the first time. "Dazz, I've never kissed a guy," she says.

Not what I expected her to say. How could a girl like her not have kissed anyone? She should have fire country guys leaping over each other to get to her. I don't say anything, because, well, you know why.

"Well, ain't ya gonna say somethin'?" she says.

213

I almost chuckle, but I hold it in. "I thought I wasn't allowed."

Now she does laugh. "You take my words pretty seriously, don't you?"

"I do," I say.

"Why?" she says. "I ain't smart, the sun goddess knows that as well as anyone. I got things to say, but they're probably not always the right things."

I gawk at her brown eyes through the hole. The right things? She's worried about saying the right things when every time we speak I'm the one bumbling along. "You're wooloo," I say, turning her fire country word back on her.

She laughs again. "Ain't that the truth," she says. "Did you see how I rode that big fella like a searin' tugbull?"

"I did," I laugh. "I was most impressed."

"Ain't you wonderin' why I've never kissed nobody?" she asks, changing the subject quicker than a rabbit hopping to his hole when he hears the hoot of an owl.

"I wasn't going to say anything," I say. "But yah, I figured you'd have kissed dozens of guys by now."

"You callin' me a shilt?" she says, her tone darkening.

"What? Nay! I mean, I don't know what that even is. All I meant was that as beautiful as you are I'd think guys would be lining up across fire country for a chance to win you over."

"Flattery won't git you far with me," she says.

"How about honesty?" I say, finally feeling the words flowing the way they're meant to.

"I wanna kiss you," she says matter-of-factly, like she's saying she wants another plate of gruel, or the sky is red, or ice country is cold, or any of a dozen other normal things to say.

"You—you do?"

"Scorch yes, I do, Dazz. Yer smoky, you make me laugh, I 'spect without even tryin', and you got a good heart." Be asleep, Buff. Be asleep.

"We should try," I say, feeling my blood rushing all over the place, waking up my whole body.

"This is a searin' thick wall," she says. "And this hole ain't big enough to git more'n a hand through." As if to demonstrate, she sticks her fingers through. My confidence is roaring like a just-woken beast, and I feel like the old Dazz, the one who could catch girls' attention, even if he couldn't keep them. I grab her hand, kiss it, stars flashing behind my eyelids. Ice this wall! I've got the urge to pound my way through it, fist by fist, without regard for my bones breaking.

I give her hand back, look through at her. There's a wildness in her eyes and I know everything I'm feeling is mutual, and she's considering pounding away too, meeting me in the middle, in a big old pile of dungeon rubble. "Bars," I say, but she's already moving in that direction, gone from sight.

I rush along the wall to the bars, jam my head and arms through, feeling the metal poles cinch around me, stopping me. Her head's through too, and she's reaching for me, and our hands are touching, and now our arms—I've got one hand in her hair, running through it wildly, and the other on her jaw, cupping it, touching the dark bruise where Big hit her.

I strain against the tightening bars, feeling the dull pressure of the metal as it bruises my ribcage, but keep pushing, getting another inch, Skye doing the same, trying, trying, icin' trying to—

—meet in the middle where—

—her lips can meet mine, where—

—she can get her first kiss, and me, my first *real* kiss, her lips closing in, so close I can see the pink tinge on them but then—

—we can't go any further, and we're just dangling there, hugging each other awkwardly, wishing we had another inch. Just one more inch.

The dungeon door creaks open.

# Twenny-Five

We stop moving. Stop struggling against the bars.

"What do you think yer doin'?" a familiar voice says.

Can't be.

Can't.

I'm dreaming up the whole thing. Skye's words—*I wanna kiss you*—weren't real, at least no realer than my imagination made them.

I pull back, and Skye does too, strain on her face as she wedges back between the bars. I do the same, grunting as the metal tightens, tightens, tightens, and finally releases me. The whole time I'm trying to look past Skye, but I can't see anything except the top bits of an open door, dark and empty, and then—

Still dark. Still empty. The darkness is trying to creep into the dungeon while the blazing torches fight it away. And then—

A big old head fills the space, towering close to the top of the door. The head grunts and I know it's true.

Skye slips back into her cell and all is revealed.

Abe stands there grinning, or at least I think that's what it is, all crooked and honest-like. Behind him is Hightower, rising a head higher, the head I saw filling the dark, empty space, grunting a greeting, like he always does. And the biggest shocker: Brock's there too, scowling, looking like he'd rather be anywhere else.

"What the…?" I say. And then in one breath, "Whatthechillareyoudoinghere?"

"You know them?" Skye says, looking back at me sharply.

"Of course he knows us," Abe says. "I was his master not that long ago."

"His master? Dazz—these're the men you worked at the border with?"

I nod. Skye's face clenches with anger. "I'll kill 'em," she says.

"Do that and Daisy here'll spend the rest of his days rottin' in this cell," Abe says.

"What are you doing here, Abe?" I ask again. "There are guards all over this place. If they catch you…"

Abe raises a hand, silencing me. "Don't worry 'bout the guards. We're 'ere to git you out."

"Out?" I say. "What are you talking about? Why would you—"

"Don't question it, kid, we ain't got much time." As Abe stomps over to my cell, he jangles a set of keys in his hand.

218

"How did you—what did you…?" I can't get the words out, because I'm so confused it's like I'm standing on the ceiling, and everything's up instead of down, right instead of left, backwards and twisted. Abe's helping me? I mean, he already did, but now he's really helping me, like if-he-gets-caught-his-head-will-roll kind of helping.

"Later," Abe says, turning a key in the lock. The cell door swings open.

I hear, "Abe?" from down the row. Buff stands up, rubbing his eyes, probably thinking he's dreaming too.

"Yah, Fluff, it's me and the whole gang." He leaves me to gawk at Tower and Brock, who're waiting by the door, Tower looking the other way. There's a click and a moment later Buff's by my side, as free as I am.

Everyone's waking up now, making tired and curious noises. Wes crawls over to the bars, eyes as wide as if he's been awake for hours. Abe says nothing, just opens his door too.

"We gotta go, kid," Abe says to me. "We ain't got a spare second 'fore more guards'll come."

I look at Skye, who's looking back at me, horror all over her face. "What about them?" I say. *What about her?* I add in my head.

Abe shoots me a look, rolls his head around. "C'mon, kid, really? You expect me to break out a bunch of Heaters?"

"I'm the only Heater," Circ says. "You can leave me if you like. Get the others out."

"No," Siena says. "If he stays, I stay."

"You're all stayin' as far's I'm concerned," Brock growls. "Abe, we gotta go. Now!"

"You comin' or what?" Abe says, staring at me and my two brothers, one by blood, one by everything else.

I look at Buff, then Wes, and last at Skye. *Go,* she mouths.

"Not without them," I say. "All of them."

~~~

It doesn't take more than a minute for Abe to unlock all the cell doors. He doesn't seem happy about it, but I think the thought of leaving empty handed is worse to him than leaving with his hands way fuller than he expected.

"Why're you doing this?" I ask him as he snaps open the last lock, Skye's. She's watching us both curiously.

"Later," Abe says.

"Thank you," I say, clapping him on the shoulder.

"Don't get all snowy on me or I'll throw you back inside and eat the key," Abe says.

"Thank you, too, Tower," I say. Hightower, well, he does his usual. "And Brock," I add, half-joking.

"Shut the chill up 'fore I smash yer face in," Brock says. I shut up.

Abe moves for the door and so does everyone else, but I let them go past. Brock hands each of them a weapon as they pass by, a sword or an axe or a knife. The weapons gleam bright and new and look suspiciously like the ones the guards are always carrying.

The only one who doesn't move is Skye, still in her cell. "This is our only chance," I say.

"Them fellas, they delivered the Heater children to the king?" she asks.

"Yah. And so did I," I remind her.

"But you only did it once. And you told us why. They probably did it again and again and again, countless times. They mighta been the ones who gave him my sister."

"Maybe," I say, "but I don't think they wanted to. There's something I've been missing. And they're helping us now—that's more than anyone else has done. We can describe your sister to them, maybe they'll remember her." I'm pleading now, trying to get her outta that cell, so we can escape together, so maybe one day we'll be able to finish what we started before Abe showed up.

She swallows hard, steps out, so close to me, closer than we've been since I chased her in the forest. Dangerously close. My heart drums harder. The feelings from before return. There's no time for this but I have to touch her, have to do something, before it's too late. She brushes past me and Brock hands her a short dagger.

"Aren't you the icy one," Brock says.

"Shut yer tughole," Skye says.

Smiling, I say, "Don't mess with her," and slap him on the back, ignoring both the look he gives me and the axe he tries to.

~ ~ ~

There's blood and bodies on both sides of the passage, littering the path beneath our feet. I look back at Brock with a question, and he says, "Don't get Hightower worked up. It ain't pretty."

Walking behind Skye, I step around and over the bodies, staying close, feeling her closeness like a promise. A promise of what could be if we ever get outta the palace.

221

We climb the steps leading out to the main hall, but I have to stop halfway up when Skye stops in front of me. Everyone stops, and I see Hightower bending his neck to look around the corner. Then, without even the smallest grunt, he motions for us to follow.

With soft footfalls, we sneak into the hall, leaving the piles of bodies behind us in the dungeons. Skye and I walk stride for stride, while Brock jogs past us, cradling the axe I refused, moving toward the front of the column, as if he's just itching for us to run into more guards.

"Follow my lead," Skye says as we approach the high, white archways that lead to the palace courtyard. *I plan on it*, I think to myself.

The archways fly away overhead and fresh, cold air fills my lungs, sharpening my senses.

A cry goes up from one of the watchful tower guards. A dozen other wall guards turn and let out a chorus of shouts, alerting the groundsmen, who are lounging in the yard, probably not expecting any action from behind the safety of the high, stone wall.

Our group breaks into a run, scattering across the yard, making us each an individual target. An arrow zips past my head, so close its tail feathers leave behind a buzzing in my ear. The wall guards are shooting at us.

I dart left, following after Skye, who's moving faster than the wind now that we're outside, opening up her long strides, just a blur of brown and grace. A guard stands waiting, clutching a two-headed battle axe, his face harder than the metal of the weapon he's carrying.

Skye closes in.

He swings—

—but she's already ducking, ramming into him shoulders and head first, knocking him flat on his arse, the axe spinning away over his head. She raises her knife over her head, slams it down without hesitation.

I gawk at her as she climbs off the dead guard, making the act of killing look so easy that I wonder how many times she's done it before. More times than my zero, that's for sure.

While I'm acting my usual idiot-part and standing around watching Skye in action, I see a shadow closing in from my left. I turn sharply, catching the glint of metal before I see the face of the guard wielding the long sword.

I jump back, narrowly avoiding getting slashed to ribbons as the guard brings the sword chest-high across the empty space I was just standing in. Anger floods my face with warmth as I rock back on my heel and then spring forward, using my arm and hand like a club, bashing him over the head. I finally see his eyes, but only when they widen and roll back into his head. He slumps to the ground.

I pick up his sword.

I throw it back down, having never really used one before.

Another guard rushes me, wielding a battle axe. Maybe even a fool with a sword woulda been better than what I am now: a weaponless fool.

I dodge his first slash and, getting inside his weapon's arc, crush my elbow into his jaw. But he recovers nicely, jabbing my nose with the butt end of the axe. It hurts like chill and I see stars for a second, feeling the discomfort and metallic taste of blood running from the inside of my nose down my throat.

When I grab the handle of his axe, he pulls back on it sharply, trying to wrench me loose, and we grapple with it for a few seconds, him pulling, me pulling, the axe slicing around at a blank spot of air.

When I'm sure he's pulling with every last bit of his strength, I let go. He goes flying, taking two stumbling off-balance steps before rolling onto his back, still clutching at the axe handle, as if he thinks it will protect him against—

—cracking his head off a pillar. He shoots me a final helpless look and then his eyes close, his shoulders weaken, and his fingers uncurl, letting the axe slide away. Two down.

There are grunts and cries all around me. I whirl around, trying to take it all in, but it's too much. Everything's a blur of movement and fighting and killing. This is no pub fight. This is real. People are dying. And then—

like the strange distortion of a nightmare becoming real,

everything twists

and turns

and comes together

in one moment of clarity, as the curves straighten and the blurs sharpen. And what I see is this:

Skye standing over a growing pile of bodies, wiping her dripping knife on her hip;

Siena dodging a punch from a guy twice her size, diving, rolling, snagging a satchel of arrows and a bow from a fallen guard, stringing one, shooting the guard through the neck;

Circ sword fighting another guard, taking a blow to his off-shoulder, but swinging his own sword across his opponent's chest, striking him down;

Feve, moving as fast as Skye, running from enemy to enemy, eliminating them with seemingly no more than his bare hands and a short knife;

Wilde, using a long dagger to hold her own against two medium-sized guards with swords, but getting pushed back, back, back toward the palace, until—

—Buff charges from the side tackling the guards, laying down a barrage of punches on one of their faces while the other lies motionless, his own sword sticking from his chest;

Abe getting hit in the leg by a wall guard's arrow, going down, Brock standing over him and screaming obscenities at the foursome of guards that surround them, holding them off until—

—he gets stabbed through the gut and his eyes go white, and he falls, falls onto Abe, who's injured but not dead, a dead man covering a living one, but then—

—Hightower is there, swinging a huge club in one hand and a battle axe in the other, chopping down guards like small trees, throwing his axe down, rolling Brock off his brother, picking Abe up and slinging him over his shoulder, arrows filling the air like sleet, hitting him once, twice, thrice, shoulder, chest, thigh, but he's running, running like a raging bear, using his club to knock away the guards in his path, another arrow, this one in the arm with the club, which he's forced to drop, reaching the gate crank, kicking the guard who's manning it, and finally, finally, using one arm to spin the crank faster than anyone's probably ever cranked it.

The gate starts to open.

It slides higher and higher, rising up into the hollowed out wall. We all hear it—and so do the guards, who begin running toward it to make their last stand. The wall guards abandon their posts and throw ropes over the wall, slide down them. There are only a half-dozen left.

225

Skye yells, "To me!" and there's no doubt that she's the leader of the fighting portion of our escape.

I start to run to her, but then I realize that in my moment of clarity, there was one person missing. The person I should've been looking for first, who, was I thinking clearly, I would've sought out. My brother. Wes.

I stop and spin around, searching, searching—frantically freezin' searching—and not finding. The others rush past me toward Skye, stampeding over any guards in their path. Buff grabs my arm, tries to pull me. "We gotta go!" he says.

"Wes," I say. "Have you seen him?"

"What? Nay. He's probably with the others…" We both look to where the others are standing, Skye shouting quick orders. He's not there.

"C'mon!" Skye yells in our general direction.

I push Buff toward them. I run the other way.

# Twenny-Six

I hear a cry behind me but I don't look. The others are storming the gate, fighting their way through. I should be with them, helping, not running away, but I can't leave him. I can't.

I run through the courtyard, tossing aside bodies of guards piled on bodies of guards, desperately trying to find the man who clothed and fed Jolie and I when my father was dead and my mother stricken with something worse than death. But he's not here. He's not here.

Then, suddenly, Buff's beside me, pulling at bodies, searching alongside me. "Go!" I yell at him, right in his face. "Go, you can't be here!"

"I'm not freezin' leaving," he says, and I know he won't.

The sound of death burns near the gate, but it seems miles away, the cold windless night becoming eerily calm around us, like we're in a normal place, doing normal things. But my erratic heartbeat and ragged breaths tell me everything I need to know about the desperateness of our situation.

We're out of time. More than out. If we're going to escape, it has to be now.

"We have to go," Buff says.

"I can't leave him," I say.

"We'll come back for him."

"When?!" I shout. "He's already got my sister. I can't let him take Wes too."

And Buff nods grimly because he knows. He knows I can't. He was just saying what he had to as my friend.

We keep looking while someone dies at the gates.

But we've looked everywhere—there's nowhere else to look. Every body's been turned, examined. Nothing. No Wes. It's like he disappeared.

We look around us helplessly, trying to find somewhere we've forgotten to look.

That's when we hear it. A groan. Amidst the cacophony of battle noises, it's faint, and I think I mighta imagined it until I see Buff's head tilt to one side. He hears it too.

"Hurry," I say.

We fan out, listening intently, moving toward where we think it might be. We close in on the opposite sides of a pillar near the palace entrance, which is full of shadows.

"Uhhhh," the voice says.

I run toward the sound, circle the pillar, find him, find Wes, back against the stone, clutching his blood-soaked side, streams of red running between his fingers and down his leg, more blood than I've ever seen.

"Nay," I say.

"I'm dying," Wes says.

"Nay," I say.

"Leave me."

"Nay."

Buff grabs his feet and I pick him up under his arms and he screams louder than I've ever heard him scream, even louder than when we were kids and I pegged him with an iceball and he fell offa a wall and broke his leg. And he screamed plenny loud then.

But we have no choice. No choice. We leave him, he dies. We take him, there's a chance. Slim, yah, but a chance nonetheless.

We run sort of sideways, sort of front ways, Buff on one side, me on the other, my brother airborne between us. In front of us is carnage.

Bodies are strewn every which way, but by the looks of it, we've won the night. Several weaponless guards are staggering and stumbling away from the gates, holding bloody arms or putting pressure on blood-spouting stomach wounds. Skye's waving to us to hurry the chill up, or the scorch up, or however they say it in fire country.

We run, hobble, stumble across the flat area outside the castle walls, reaching the White District a minute later. We duck behind a tall, snow-covered wall to catch our breaths and assess our injuries.

Although I'm sure everyone contributed to the fight, it's clear that Hightower, despite being stuck with more arrows than a shooting range target, did more than his fair share. He's down on one knee, panting heavily and loudly, soaked in blood that's surely equal parts his own and his enemies'. Abe's standing over him, a broken arrow sticking from his leg. "Can you walk, Tower? Can you?"

He grunts and pushes to his feet. I think every single one of us just stares. He's a sight to behold, what with half a dozen arrows sticking from him and more slash and cut wounds than the rest of us combined, he looks like the magnificent warrior that he is. The hero that he is.

"Is yer brother alright?" Skye says, looking right at me.

"He's not good," I say. "We need to get help fast. Hightower'll need it too."

"Circ too," she says, motioning to where Siena and Feve are holding Circ up, his arms draped over their shoulders, hobbling on one leg.

"My people say the cold helps heal," Feve says.

"And what do you know about it?" I say sharply.

"I know of healing," is all Feve replies. He leaves Circ to Siena and bends to grab a handful of snow. "Pack this in your brother's wound," he says. "It might help with the bleeding."

I don't know if I can trust him, but I'll try anything that might help Wes, so I only watch as Buff grabs the snow and pats it on Wes's stomach.

"We gotta get to the Red District," I say. "There are healers there who know how to be discrete."

"We can't," Skye says. "This ain't our country. We hafta git back to the desert."

"Trust me," I say. "Healers first. Desert after. We'll go together."

Wilde steps forward, a wicked gash running from her ear to her chin. "He's right, Skye. We all need help."

Skye's fierce brown eyes are uncertain for a moment, but then she nods, says, "Move out!"

Before we charge through the White District, I look back, wondering if, at any moment, a horde of guards will pour from the gate, descending upon us like a swarm of demons.

Instead, I see only one man, high atop the wall. He holds a child in his arms.

With a slow, drawn out motion, he slides his thumb across his throat.

And it's hard to see, because it's dark and snowflakes are falling, but I know…

*I know.*

It's King Goff and he's—he's got—

He's got Jolie.

And I don't know if his death decree is meant for me or for her.

~ ~ ~

We run, walk, limp, hobble, and carry each other to the Red District.

It took every last bit of my self-control not to run back to the palace, to demand that Goff hand over my sister, to fight him and the rest of his guards, all of whom will be awake and called into action.

But if he hasn't hurt Jolie yet, it's unlikely he'll hurt her now. He told me himself that he needs her, that she's some special trade item, whatever that means. And Wes is in trouble *now*, so he has to be my top priority. But even as Buff and I struggle along, carrying him, watching him fight in and out of consciousness, babbling like our drug-plugged mother, Jolie's all over my thoughts. She's calling to me, asking me why—

*WHY?*—why did you leave me behind when you were so close to finding me? I thought you loved me?

It's all I can do to whisper, "I'm sorry," and push onwards.

Although it's the middle of the night when we reach the Red District, there're lights on everywhere, music playing, men laughing. A man crashes through a swinging door, landing face first in a pile of snow. "And stay out, you drunk!" a gruff voice calls after him.

A door to our left creaks open and there's Lola, looking as provocative as ever, something thin and silky tied up top and around her waist. "By the Mountain Heart," she murmurs when she's sees us leaving bloody footprints in the snow. She slinks back inside, slamming the door behind her.

Skye glances at me and I shrug. Just another normal night in this place.

"Turn here," I say as we approach a cross road.

Around the bend we stop at the second building on the right. There's no sign, no placard, not even something spray-painted on the wall to describe what's here. You either know it, or you don't. Thankfully, after Wes demanded that I never come home again looking like I'd been through a war, I found this place. They've stitched and bandaged me (and Buff too) up more times than I can count even with both shoes off and my toes warming in front of the fire.

"Here," I say.

"Here?" Skye says.

I nod. She shrugs and pushes the metal door open, holding it for me and Buff.

We carry Wes inside.

It smells like 'quiddy and burnt ice powder inside, but it's not an underground drug and booze house. The alcohol's for sterilizing wounds and the burnt ice powder is a natural anesthetic, although I wouldn't recommend using it for that purpose very often. As my mother has shown time and time again, it's more addictive than a woman's smile.

Maddy, the rough-edged woman who runs the joint, is sitting at the desk when we barge in. "Good Heart!" she exclaims. "Dazz?"

"Mads," I say with a nod. "Wes needs urgent medical care. So do some of the others." I wave a hand back at the ragtag group behind me. Her eyes widen. "All of us need treatment for one injury or another."

"We're all full up," she says, frowning, her eyes jumping between Skye and Feve, who are standing next to me.

"Mads," I say, not even attempting to keep the desperation out of my voice. "Please."

"I don't even know where these—these strange people come from," she says, her eyes narrowing on Feve's markings, which curl out from beneath his skins and around his neck.

"Fire country," I say. "They come from fire country, and they need your help. I need your help."

Every line in her face crinkles. "You got silver?" she asks.

"Nay," I say, and I see her frown deepen. "I mean, not on us. But you know I'm good for it."

"Ain't got no silver, ain't get no service," she says crossing her arms.

My arms are burning from carrying Wes and all I want to do is collapse right here on her floor, refuse to move, force her to help us, but then Abe hobbles up next to me and says, "I got plenny of silver and yer icin' gonna help us or so help me Mountain Heart, I will make the rest of yer days a livin' chill, Woman!"

233

Well, Mads pretty much jumps into gear after that, yelling for all her healers to come to the front immediately and stop helping the drunks with bruised knees and even more bruised egos. At least ten women come out, all wearing less-than-clean aprons—which I expect at one time were as white as snow, but which are now a yellowish-reddish-brown—about one per each one of us, although those of us with minor injuries refuse treatment until Wes and Hightower and Circ and Abe are taken care of.

They usher us beyond the desk, through a door, and into a large room, full of beds. As it turns out, the place isn't even close to "full up", as Maddy said, and nearly every bed is empty. There are only two fellas being treated, each with similar looking head wounds that look suspiciously like what you might expect a gash from a shattered bottle over the head to look like. The way they're glaring at each other, I suspect they hit each other at about exactly the same time. Well, Maddy tells them to get the chill out, and they do, pushing and shoving each other the whole way.

The rest of us get a bed. Hightower gets three, two side by side to accommodate his width, and one sideways along the bottom for his length. His feet still stick off the end. He wiggles his toes and grunts. The three healers that surround him are scratching their heads and wondering aloud at how they're going to treat his many wounds. I also hear them say something about whether Tower might be descended from the Yags.

Abe's in a bed of his own, yelling orders and curses at the two healers that look scared to be treating him.

Siena opts out of her bed, standing by Circ's side, holding his hand, saying something that makes him laugh and then wince when one of the healers does something to his injured leg.

Feve skips the bed, too, standing by the door, his eyes dark, as if the king himself might come through. Mountain Heart help Goff if he does.

Buff, now naked from the waist up, sits next to Wilde, chattering away as a healer looks at a dark and mottled bruise that covers half his abdomen. She looks amused, but her eyes keep flicking around at the others, like she's concerned for them too, while another healer bandages her head.

Skye and I stand across the foot of the last bed, where Wes lies twitching in a fitful sleep. Every few minutes he moans.

"How'd this happen?" Maddy asks, breaking her own number one rule: don't ask questions. But this is a night for rule-breaking.

"I don't know," I say. "One minute he was there, fighting alongside us, and the next he was missing. And when we found him he was like this. Did you see anything, Skye?"

Skye shakes her head and Maddy stares at her for a good, long while, so long that Skye flashes her a warning frown. "I'm sorry," Maddy says. "I've just never seen anyone from…"

"From fire country," Skye finishes. "Well, truth be told, until a few days past, most of us ain't never seen any of yer kind either."

"Please, Mads. Can you just focus on my brother?" I plead.

The other two healers are using small knives to cut away Wes's shirt. At least their instruments look clean and rust-free, I think.

When they peel away the fabric, I feel a shockwave of fear lock my bones up tight. There's so much blood that we can't even see the wound. Despite the snow, which is red and melting, the blood's pouring outta him like a bubbling spring, soaking his pants and the bed and the healers' hands, which are dabbing at his stomach with thick cloths that fill up with blood in an instant.

"Pressure!" Maddy says and one of the healers starts pushing on his gut with both hands, while Maddy and the other healer finish cleaning up the blood. "We need more hands!" she says, and one of the healers who was helping Buff rushes over. "Get anesthetic, pain killers, a sewing kit, and more freezin' cloths," she orders. "The good stuff. Only the good stuff," she adds.

The healer runs to a cabinet and flings the door open, scattering vials of liquids, which shatter like crystal on the floor, spilling their contents. She ignores the broken glass, rummages through the box, gathers the desired items and brings them back over, setting them on a table next to the bed.

When Maddy says "More hands!" again, Feve wanders over.

"I can help," he says.

"You know about healing?" Maddy asks.

"Yes. I have herbs," he says. "They'll help with infection and pain."

"Whatever you've got, we'll take it," she says.

Feve reaches inside his thick coat and extracts a small sachet.

At the same time, the assistant healer grabs the cloths and helps to wipe away the blood, while Maddy uncorks a vial of a clear liquid, tilts my brother's head, and forces it down his throat. He chokes, gasps, but she holds his head back, pinches his nose, and the liquid goes down. Then she opens another glass bottle, selects a needle and thread from a small box, and wedges herself between two of the other three healers.

"Herbs," Maddy says.

Feve pours out the contents of a small skin, sprinkling black and green flecks onto my brother's torn skin. Are they magic from fire country?

"Would you shut up!" Maddy says sharply in my direction. "He can't hear you anyway."

It's only then that I realize that I'm rubbing Wes's leg, saying, "It's gonna be okay, it's gonna be okay," over and over again, even while I'm watching them try to save him. I stop, noticing that Skye's not across the table anymore, but next to me, a hand on my back, looking up at me.

"Yer right," she says. "It's gonna be okay."

# Twenny-Seven

But neither Skye nor I was right. We never were. Nothing is okay. Nothing will ever be okay.

Wes died that night from an axe wound to the stomach. They worked on him for three, four hours, dabbing away the blood and stitching him up, both stuff on the inside and the skin on the outside. By the end of it my legs were shaking and I could barely feel Skye's hand on my back, her other hand gripping mine.

The blood was gone. He was whole again. And then he took his last breath.

I collapsed, fighting all the way to the floor even with Skye trying to hold me up. She lay down with me, curled up, her arm around me, holding me, as I sobbed and shook.

Sobbed and shook.

Now I'm all cried out, torn and broken on the bed that Buff and Feve carried me to. Skye's never left my side, not once, but even her caring can't bring my brother back. I didn't even get to say goodbye.

And it was my plan—my stupid freezin' dimwitted plan that caused it.

So my head's down, my face pressed flat against the bed, as tight and low as I can make it. I tried to get lower twice, attempting to throw myself off the bed and onto the floor, but Skye wouldn't let me. She held me up, her strength like a rock, bearing all the weight of my body and my grief in her arms. Then she rolled me back on, where I am now.

A few of the others, those able to walk—Buff, Siena, Circ with Siena's help, Wilde—have come over to offer me words of sorrow, how they wish it hadn't happened, how they're sorry. But none of that'll make things right, or bring Wes back.

I wish for more tears, a whole lake of them, enough to make the sum of my sorrow worthy of my brother, of the man that he was. But try as I might, I can't squeeze one more out, my eyes burning with salt and fatigue and despair.

When Skye pushes onto the bed and right up next to me, I finally sleep.

# Twenny-Eight

I need to take a break from my brain, but every time I try to push my thoughts away, they come roaring back all the harder, pushing against my skull like they're trying to burst out, flying away on wings of sadness and winds of ache.

I've been awake for at least an hour, but I haven't moved, haven't opened my eyes. I don't want anyone to know I'm awake, because I can't take their *sorrys* and *regrets* any more than I can take the awful memories that my brain is spinning around.

Jolie needs you.

Wes is dead.

Jolie's not.

Wes is.

Jolie.

Oh Jolie, Jolie—are you there? Are you really in the palace or did I dream up Goff holding you high on the wall?

With questions lingering still in my mind, I open my eyes to the sound of voices. Abe's, harsh and definitive, rises above the others.

"You can do what you want, but I fer one ain't goin' back to that place," he says. "Hightower neither. King Goff'll roast us alive."

Skye, Siena, Circ, Wilde, and Feve stand in a semicircle, watching the argument.

"They've got Dazz's sister," Buff says. "He's just lost his brother, if we can…if we can only get her…"

"Good luck with that," Abe says.

"I'll go on my own if I have to," Buff says and I see him cross his arms across his chest. "Is anyone else with me?"

Silence. There are quick glances between the people of the Tri-Tribes.

Wilde says, "We've talked it over…"

Skye scrapes a foot on the floor, looking down the whole time. I notice she's shaking her head slightly, as if she doesn't necessarily agree with the decision that's been made.

"…and we think it best to return to fire country, to gather as many able-bodied men and women as we can, and to come back in force."

"Nay," I croak. I intend it as a shout, a cry of defiance, but it comes out all garbled and raspy. When everyone turns to look at me, I say it again, even softer. "Nay."

Buff strides over. "I'm going with you," he says. "We're going to get Jolie. We'll break down the gates and kill every one of Goff's men, and then the king himself."

I smile, my lips dry and chapped. "Yah. We will," I say, clasping his outstretched palm. "Raising chill and kicking arse. Like always."

"Like always," he says.

"No," says a voice from behind him. Buff moves aside to reveal Skye, who's moved within a few steps of my bed. In my mind flashes memories: we strain through the bars, touching each other's arms, desperately trying to lock lips; she brushes past me in the dungeons, so close I could touch her, if I'd only reached out; her warmth against me, her arm around me, providing an alternative to my grief. "You need to come with us," she says, and the memories come crashing down like a fallen star.

"We're going after my sister," I say, my voice strengthening. I sit up, swing my feet over the side, plant them firmly on the floor. "With or without you."

Our eyes lock and we're both fighting it. The need we felt in the dungeon. Amidst everything—all the turmoil, the strife, the *death*—still there, pulling, pulling, banging, crashing through everything we say, everything we do, everything we want, like an avalanche, an unstoppable force of nature. But I fight it and I can see in her fathomless brown eyes, she's doing the same. Me with thoughts of saving my sister and avenging my brother's death, and her with doing right by her people, both of her sisters, one who's alive and one who might be.

"Don't," she says.

I want to give her the option to come with us, but I can't. I can't ask that of her when it's suicide, when it's crazy. When it's what I have to do.

"I can't," I say.

She turns and walks back to her people.

~~~

Buff and I know as well as anyone that we need to let things cool down a little before we go back to the palace.

So that leaves us to escort the others to the border, where we'll bid them farewell. Each of them—save for Feve—has already promised me multiple times that they'll return with many warriors. Wilde even offered her own promise, and I almost believe it coming from her. I thank them and smile, when in my heart I know that by then it'll probably be too late.

Abe and Hightower have the worst injuries and will stay at Maddy's for a while longer. Before we leave, I stand between their beds. "Thank you," I say to both of them, my head bouncing back and forth. "For doing what you did."

Abe sighs, opens his mouth, says something I'd never expect him to say in a million years. "I hate that bastard, King Goff."

"But you're his—"

"Slave?" Not what I was going to say. "Look, kid," Abe says, "I know you think we're the king's evil little helpers and all that, but that's not really us. We do what we're told because the king's had leverage over us from the start. He had my wife, Dazz."

I can't help raising my eyebrows, both because Abe called me by my real name and because he's not who I thought he was. Not even close. Then I realize: He *had* my wife.

"What happened to her?" I ask, dread creeping into my cracking voice.

He just shakes his head. "Kid, you must think I'm a monster. Taking all those kids, giving them to the king." I did think him monster-like, but not anymore. "Was my wife's life more important than theirs? I could only hope the king wasn't hurting them, was treating them okay, was using them as servants. He said he'd kill my wife if I didn't help him." There's sadness in his voice, laced with shreds of remorse. But he still didn't answer my question. I don't ask again.

Abe continues anyway. "I always said I'd make up for the many wrongs I'd caused, but I never really believed I would. It's just what I told myself so I could sleep at night. But then…" His eyes cloud and his voice turns whisper soft. "Then, last night, when I showed up for my weekly visitation, part of my agreement with the king, she was gone, my Liza, her chains left in a pile in her cell, which was in one of the towers. The guard passed along the king's regrets, how they'd tried to save her, but that her self-inflicted wounds were too serious to reverse. I grabbed Tower and Brock and marched straight to the dungeons."

I tilt my head to the side, bite my lip. Abe could've fallen into a dark pit of sorrow, left us to rot in the dungeons. But he didn't. He didn't. He came for us.

I grasp his hand. "I'm so sorry," I say. "You have more than made up for the sins of your past."

He squeezes back. "Kill that bastard king," he says. "If it's the last thing you do."

"I will," I say. "I'll do it for Liza, for Wes, for the kids. For my sister."

He nods and lets go.

Hightower grunts and holds out a big hand, which I take, squeezing it firmly.

"To Brock," I say, raising a fist. They each raise a fist of their own and I knock mine against them, each in turn.

"To Brock," Abe mumbles, "the no-good scoundrel."

~~~

I stop in front of Maddy on the way out. She's pretending to busy herself in the cabinet, rearranging the supplies.

"Thank you," I say.

She doesn't turn around. "Abe paid me good silver—"

"Thank you for trying," I say.

She returns to fiddling with the supplies and I walk on, but when I look back she's watching me go, her face streaked and glistening with tears.

Outside, I push Wes outta my mind so I don't breakdown or break someone's face. I focus on Jolie. *I'm coming for you, girl,* I think.

We take backstreets—nay, streets that are behind the backstreets, streets that no respecting king or his guardsmen would ever find themselves walking down. Beggars and those in a drug coma rest against the walls, enjoying a bit of summer sun that breaks through the dense cloud cover. There's still snow on the ground, but it's not cold snow.

The Red District disappears and we enter the forest. A snowbird speaks to us in whistles and light tones. If it wasn't for my icin' memories, I could almost be happy on a day like this.

A forced silence sets in on all of us, as if we believe the songbirds and the trees are the king's ears, and if we speak they'll fly or march to the palace to tell him what we said. It gives me plenny of time to watch the people I'm with, the people I wish were coming with us.

Feve's well ahead of the group, steady and calm. Everything about him seems so self-assured, so confident. I can't read him though, and every time I look at him I feel like he's struggling to read me too.

Siena's walking along next to Circ, who's limping a little but seems to have recovered well. His leg is heavily wrapped but it must be a flesh wound, not a bone or muscle injury. We all got pretty lucky, considering. All of us except for…

I shake my head around, tell my brain to *freezin' leave me the freeze alone or I'll freezin' slam you against the next freezin' tree I see!* That shuts him up for a few minutes and then he says, *Wes.* I bite my lip, hard enough to draw blood, and go back to watching.

Siena's shivering pretty badly, although her skins are thick. Funny though, I never really noticed any of them being cold until now. I take off my coat and give it to her. She doesn't say anything because her teeth are chattering so much, just takes it and wraps it around herself like a blanket.

Buff's walking next to Wilde, because that's what he does, and she's already wearing his bearskins. What are the chances? A guy like him with a woman like her. *Zero,* I think, and hold in a laugh. I hope he gets the chance to prove me wrong.

Skye's been avoiding my gaze since we started walking, and frankly I'm glad, because I'm not sure I can bear it right now. I feel so raw, like my skin's been scraped away, partly by the fighting and the violence, but mostly by losing Wes, seeing Jolie in the king's grasp, leaving everything underneath poking out, emotions and nerves and blood vessels sticking every which way. It's like the littlest thing might set one of them off, make me go crazy, crying or laughing or burning hot with rage, or a mixture of all three, laughing and crying while punching King Goff in the face.

Skye strides ahead of us and I watch her go.

She doesn't look cold at all, as if she's radiating her own heat from within. Or she just bears it well, like she seems to bear everything so well. I want to chase after her, to talk to her, even if we only look ahead and avoid eye contact while we're doing it, but I don't.

She catches up to Feve.

*He tried to help save Wes.*

I shake away the thought because it shouldn't matter one way or the other, not when Wes is…

I watch as Skye and Feve talk, wishing it was me instead.

~ ~ ~

When Siena starts talking to Buff and Wilde, Circ comes over to me. He's limping and I can see a grimace every couple of steps, which he's unsuccessfully trying to hide.

"You alright?" I ask.

"I'll live," he says with a forced grin. "I've had worse during Hunts."

"For the tug?" I ask, wondering what a tug even looks like. Like a bear maybe? By the time the meat gets to ice country it's already butchered and wrapped in skins.

He nods and I try to imagine how different their world is to ours. "What's it like?" I say.

He raises an eyebrow.

"You know, living in fire country," I say.

He nods, almost to himself. There's a solidarity in his eyes and expression that makes me feel like he's someone you can depend on, someone who'll cover your back no matter what. It reminds me of the way Buff is, only with fewer jokes.

"It's hot," he says with a straight face.

I stare at him for a second and then laugh, realizing he's joking, but not. Maybe he's even more like Buff than I thought.

"It's beautiful, in its own way," he says. "On a warm spring day when the wind is blowing, the prickler are growing, turning green, the burrow mice are scavenging in the sand, and the desert floor is rolling in every direction, it's home. Especially if you've got someone special beside you, leaning into you."

"Siena," I say, picturing the two of them so close even when separated by bars and stone, holding hands, playing their thumb game. I try to take that memory and stick it in the desert.

"We go back a ways," he says, almost wistfully.

"And Skye?" I ask, trying not to look at her ahead of me, whispering to Feve.

"I've known her just as long," he says. "They've both changed over the years, but Skye more than Siena."

"How do you mean?"

He laughs, a hearty chuckle that's full of fond memories. "Well, Siena's always been the way she is. You know, the way she has with words, always making me laugh, always wishing every day was full of more hours I could spend with her. She's got a real unique way of looking at the world. The only thing she's ever lacked is confidence in herself, which is the biggest change in her. Ever since she joined the Wilde's, she's got that spark, like she knows she's more than just a stream of words, that she's actions too."

I take it all in, nodding to myself as I remember how quickly Siena made me laugh, and also how quickly she strung her bow to protect the lot of us against the guards. Yah, I've seen firsthand everything that Circ just told me. "And Skye?" I say.

"She's always had the confidence, always had a lot of friends, was never afraid to speak her mind to anyone and everyone that'd listen."

"You don't say," I reply, laughing.

"So you've had a taste? Well, that's pretty normal. She'll tell you what she's thinking in a heartbeat, not caring whether you like it or not. And if you cross her or her family..."

"Watch out," I say.

She sounds perfect, I think to myself.

"Dazz," Circ says, and I hear the sadness coming in his words, the compassion.

"Don't," I say, unable to hear another *I'm sorry* from anyone.

~~~

We're almost to the border.

We stop to rest in a blank spot in the woods. People are finally talking again. Buff to Wilde. Siena to Circ. Skye and Feve. I'm the odd one out for the moment. I stalk off into the woods, find a clearing of my own, big enough to fit me and my temper, which is rising for no reason at all.

I grab a stick off the ground, snap it over my knee. Too thin—too easy. I pick up a thicker branch, do the same with it, relishing the *snaaaap!* as it shatters into two pieces. I imagine it's the king's leg or arm or *head*.

"Argh!" I yell, and I'm sure the others will hear it, but I don't give a shiver anymore. I'm done crying, I'm done mourning. My anger will sustain me now.

I hear sticks cracking in the forest and I look away from the sound. It'll be Buff, my best and most loyal friend in all of ice country, hearing my temper-induced cry, who'll come running to make sure I'm okay.

I can't look at him, not by any fault of his. I can't look at anyone right now.

The twigs stop snapping and feet scrape into the clearing.

"I'm fine," I say to the forest. "Leave me alone."

"I tried to git 'em to go back to the palace," Skye says.

A tremor runs through me. Anger? Excitement? Both? Neither? Something else entirely? My emotions, while surface-deep, are like a labyrinth, a maze of false walls and trapdoors.

I stare deep into the cracks of a tree trunk, not seeing anything.

I don't say anything.

"That was yer sister on the wall, wasn't it?" Skye says. "With the king."

I stare straight ahead, like a statue. She looked back too. Saw what I saw. I didn't imagine it.

I don't say anything.

"It's a seven day journey," she says. "Across the desert. A day to prepare and gather provisions and warriors." She pauses and I can't help but like the way *warriors* sounds in the rasp of her voice. "Then seven days back. It sounds long but it's only half a full moon. We'll come back stronger. We'll crush that baggard." I like the way she says *crush*, too, but I can't enjoy it, because all I can see in the lines of the tree trunk is Wes dying while I watch helplessly.

"Why are you leaving?" I ask.

"I trust Wilde," she says. "The others do too."

I can see that, but still…I can't wait two weeks for them to return. I can't. "More like you're scared of Goff," I say, my words an obvious lie.

She frowns again, takes a step forward. "Yer not thinkin' straight. What happened to yer brother, it's—"

"Don't speak of my brother." Fire's burning in my chest, hot and cold and fast.

"—cloudin' yer judgment," she continues as if I hadn't spoken.

"The only thing that's clouding my judgment is you," I say, taking my own step forward. Three steps away. I could almost touch her if we both reached out.

"We're all tryin' to help you 'ere." Stop there, I think. Just stop there.

My eyes are burning but I don't blink either. "Yah, I've heard that one before," I growl. "But people don't always come through for you, do they?"

"Are you sayin' I'm lyin'?" Skye says, getting that look in her eyes, the one I saw just before she leapt on Big's back in the dungeons.

I ignore it, goad it even. "Just confused. Wooloo," I say in a mocking tone.

She pushes me away with both hands. "Go to scorch," she says.

I scowl at her, take a step forward.

She charges, grabbing at my arms, trying to get ahold of them, to pin them, but I twist away and grab back, clamping my fingers on her shoulder for a quick second before she slips away. Arms outstretched, she manages a firm grip on my arms, and I grab her back. We grapple, frantic-like, as it turns into a wrestling match, and she's strong, so strong, stronger than most guys I've fought before.

I push and pull and try to get an edge, but she's pushing and pulling and doing the same and then dropping suddenly,

251

throwing off my center of balance and I'm falling, falling, slamming into the dirt, scrabbling at her as she holds me down, throwing her offa me, rolling, getting on top of her and then I realize I'm not angry, I'm not angry, I'm fighting her but I'm not angry—least not at her. My guard falls away and she takes advantage and throws me to the side, gains the upper hand. But I'm not seeing her, at least not the *her* that's here, who's fighting me, I'm seeing the Skye who's arms were reaching out through the bars, grabbing mine, want in her eyes and on her lips, and I don't want to fight anymore, not one second longer, and so—

—I'm holding her and I think she's holding me back and—

—my hands draw up her slender neck, run along her jawline, cup her chin, and then—

—I'm kissing her and she's kissing me and the world blinks away as I close my eyes and—

—it's just Skye, all around me, but she's brown skin and short, dark hair and not gray and cloud-covered like the other sky and I think she's the *real* Sky and—

—it's like for this moment, for this one moment, Wes isn't dead anymore and everything's okay and we might be able to rescue Jolie and I'm happy and—

"Feve has a family, you searin' Icy fool!" she snaps abruptly, pulling back.

I look at her but her words aren't angry and she's almost laughing. "What?" I say, breathing heavy, unable to decipher the meaning of anything but her lips, which I desperately want to kiss again.

"Feve," she says. "He's a married man. He wants to help you, but if we go back to the castle like this he'll die, and his family will be left without him. If it was just us to worry 'bout, we'd be with you in a heartbeat. All we wanna do is get more warriors so we'll have a chance."

"Oh," I say, feeling my face go warm.

"Is everything all right?" Buff's voice says. I turn my head and he's pushed aside a leafy branch and is watching us, amusement splashed all over his face.

"Fine," I say. "Skye was just teaching me a thing or two about fighting."

Skye rolls her eyes, but I can tell she finds it funny.

"Sure," Buff says. "If you say so. We're heading out now, so unless you want to keep...*practicing*...up here all by yourselves, with no one within miles and miles, you'd better get moving."

I look at Skye and she looks at me, and then she rolls offa me and we head toward Buff. He turns to fight his way back through the woods and Skye turns to me. "That was one scorch-of-a good first kiss, Icy Dazz," she whispers through those lips of hers.

Although I'm still catching up on fire country lingo, I'm pretty sure it's a compliment.

# Twenny-Nine

Kissing Skye doesn't make my emotions any less frayed. If anything, it forces them even closer to the surface.

I want things to be normal, for Goff to be a distant memory, to get Jolie back, to get to know Skye. To *really* get to know Skye.

But that's not where I'm at. That's a dreamland, so far away that I'll have to grab a passing cloud to get there.

We keep on traipsing through the forest, down, always down, until we reach the borderlands. With the air warming, Siena returned my coat a mile or so back, but it's too hot to wear it now so I've got it draped over my shoulder.

Skye and I haven't said a word since her comment about the kiss, but I'm glad for it. Words can only screw things up right now.

Fire country stretches out like an endless blanket of sand, while ice country rises up behind us like a ghost. And the two are stitched together by us, as if we're the only link between two worlds.

"We'll be back as soon as we can," Wilde says.

Buff looks like he wants to do something, maybe hug her, but he just rocks back and forth awkwardly.

"We'll be waiting," I say, a promise I have little control over. Skye's eyes are all over mine and I can tell we're sharing memories, clinging to them like the branches of a tree that's about to be chopped down.

"Fight like the Killer hounds of scorch are at your heels," Siena says and I smile at her way with words.

"That's just what we'll do," I say.

Circ thrusts a hand out and I shake it. Feve offers a firm nod, but it's clear he's ready to move on, to get back to his family.

As Skye moves in close, the others look away, already moving off into fire country, while Buff pretends to be looking at a bird at the very top of one of the border trees.

She whispers in my ear. "Find yer sister," she says. "Find her and we'll find you."

"And then we'll find your sister," I say. Her cheek slides back against my skin and then she brushes her lips against mine, lingering for a second, causing my blood to flow and my emotions to swirl.

I grab the back of her head and pull her in, kissing her exactly the same way I kissed her before. We both come up gasping and open-mouthed.

That's when a swarm of black swamps the edge of our vision.

"Skye," I say, but the others have seen it too, are already running back toward us.

For a moment Skye and I just stare as the horizon fills with black, an avalanche of darkness, a single roiling mass, close to the ground, sending up clouds of dust all around them.

Dark like the tapestries on the palace walls; the dark men on dark horses, burning, burning everything, slaughtering Icers and the strange water riders as easily as if they were pulling leaves off a tree.

My first thought is: are they coming for us? But I shake that one away as quickly as it comes, because the black mass shifts to the right, turning, dust billowing behind them, as if marking their trail. They're heading for…They're heading for…

They're heading for ice country.

"Oh, Heart," I say.

"Who are they?" Skye asks, looking at me—looking right at me—like she expects me to know. Like I *should* know.

But I don't. I don't have a Heart-icin' clue.

The others surround us, watching—nay, *gawking*—as the black horses gallop across the border, into the forest, their dark riders urging them on by sticking their heels into the horses' sides. It's not a friendly advance, like the Glassies coming to pay a visit, wandering silently up the mountainside. As the last of the dark men plunge into the woods, the sun catches the steel in their hands, glinting like silver coins in the distance.

Swords. The men are all carrying swords.

Ice country is under attack.

~~~

There's no discussion, barely a word other than *Go!* and *Run!* as we charge back the way we came, back under the cover of the trees, back up the slope that seems to want to do anything to slow us down, seeming steeper and thicker with undergrowth than when we came down it in the first place.

Just by coming with us, the people of the Tri-Tribes have proven their mettle. They're willing to help the Icers even at the risk of their own lives.

Even though we've got another couple hours before we reach the village, everyone who's got a weapon has it out, ready, as if the dark men and their horses might be lying in wait to ambush us.

Buff, breathing heavy beside me, says, "What do they want?"

I don't know, but if the tapestry was any indication of reality, there's only one thing: "Blood," I say.

Buff doesn't ask any more questions after that. In fact, no one says much, just keep running, getting slower as we tire. I've got half a dozen cramps, from a dull ache in my calves and shoulders, to a sharper pang in my side. I fear by the time we reach the top we'll be too exhausted to do much to help anyone.

I bite away the pain and try to focus on the situation at hand. If these men are here to attack ice country—and what else could they possibly be here to do?—then they'll go for the palace first. It's the only real threat to stopping them, what with the well-armed and trained guards, the thick, stone walls, and the head of the dragon, King Goff, hiding behind it all. Which means that—

That—

I can't say her name, can't even think it, but I know it's the truth.

She's in grave danger. More than she is with Goff.

"We'll save her. We'll save Jolie," Skye says, on my other side.

I say nothing, just keep running.

The day is dark as the clouds seem to thicken for war. At some point snow starts falling, but I barely notice it. Then it starts falling harder, thicker, and I look up at the sky, feeling cold and wet all over my face.

Autumn has arrived.

I put my head down and keep running.

~~~

Before we reach the town we can smell it. Burning. Fire. Destruction. Violence.

It hangs in the air like a haze, coating everything; every breath, every movement, blackening our skin and our hearts. Smoke rushes in living columns above the trees, far thicker and heavier than the exhaust created by fireplaces, a stark contrast to the whiteness of the falling snow. Smoke caused by fire that's eating bigger things than a few logs of firewood.

I throw the weariness and fatigue off me the same way I discard my coat, which has become too hot and heavy, as stifling as the dense forest.

Quickly and completely.

I half-notice Siena picking it up and pulling it tightly around her shoulders.

Exhaustion is nothing. Pain is nothing.

My sister is everything.

Jolie is everything.

Saying her name in my head stings me like the nettles on a pine branch, and I wince, but I don't stop. Will never stop until she's back in my arms.

Finally—freezin' finally—we break through the trees and see the village standing before us, spotted with snow. The Brown and Red Districts sit heavy and low at the base of the slope, with their rows of small, densely clustered houses, while the houses of the Blue and White Districts rise above, with their tall columns and pointed roofs, generous gaps between each residence. All burning, swept with orange and red and the darkness of the black riders, ripping holes and tears in the blanket of snow covering everything.

And above them all…

Above them all, the palace, an impenetrable barrier protecting the king and his men.

Smoke pours from beyond the gates.

"Hurry," Skye says, grabbing my arm with one hand, a blade gripped tightly in the other.

I lead the way into the Brown District, where most houses are burning, spitting mountains of black clouds. A dark rider and his horse run off a ways, and we watch as he closes in on a group of Brown District Icers, who have organized themselves and are brandishing planks and clubs. The rider sweeps past them, slashing with his sword, cutting them down one by one. They don't get one good shot in before they fall. I scream something indecipherable and I think Buff does too.

The enemy rides on, seeking out his next target. A cluster of children run from a burning house, shepherded by a slightly older, but still young, girl. Her mannerisms are so familiar, surprisingly mother-like despite her young age. A wad forms in my throat when I realize I know her.

"Darce!" Buff shouts, warning his sister of the rider that's now only a few gallops away.

But she doesn't hear, not amongst the children's cries and the crackle of flames and the pound of horse's hoofs—and the screams of the men not five houses down.

Buff takes off and the rest of us do too, because we're not separate people now, not anymore, we're like a single living, breathing creature, with lots of arms and legs and more hearts than anyone could ever break.

But we're also too slow and too far away and too late. Far too late.

The rider closes in, his sword out, level with Darce's neck. Buff screams and screams and screams—

And I think I'm screaming too, my throat hoarse and dry—

And the rider raises his sword—

And my body's all tensed up, preparing itself for the *slash, slash, slash* and more *slashes* that'll destroy Buff's life far worse than mine's been destroyed, that'll change him forever—

But it never comes.

It never comes.

The rider gallops on, a shadow passing down the road, cutting up the slope toward the upper lofts of the Brown District.

Toward where I live. Where my mother, even now, is likely in a drug-induced stupor and oblivious to the world falling down around her.

# Thirty

We leave Buff to take care of his family, his brothers and sisters. His father, who was in the group of men defending themselves, is lying in the snow bleeding, being worked on by a group of healers.

There's nothing more we can do to help them.

But we can still help my mother.

Can still save my sister.

(Can't we?)

Buff thinks so and he pounds my back before we leave. I think he's trying to boost his own morale, because of his father bleeding in the snow. I say, "I can stay, Buff," even though I know I can't.

"Nay," he says. "Fight."

I try to smile, but it comes out all crooked. "Even now, I fight with you," I say.

And he says, "Cut the cosmic shiver. Just get it done."

Up the hill we go, stepping in the snowy horse prints, seeing spots of red where blood's dripped off the rider's sword. Buff's father's blood, so fresh the rapidly falling snow hasn't had time to cover it.

I'll kill that rider. I swear to the Mountain Heart I will.

We reach Clint and Looza's place, which isn't burning, which, if you look just at their house, appears to be separate from the battle that ravages everything else. Untouched. Pristine. Just another house in a snow-covered village.

I burst through the door, nearly snapping it off its hinges.

Clint and Looza, who are sitting in the dark, look up sharply, their eyes wide and white. "Dazz?" Clint says. His eyes flick to the posse of brown-skinned people behind me.

"My mother," is all I say, my eyes darting everywhere and seeing no one else.

"She's here," Looza says, pointing to a pile of blankets on the floor. "She passed out and we couldn't bear to wake her."

"There are riders," I say.

"They came here," Clint says.

"What?" I say. And then again, "What?"

"One of them barged in just like you did. We just sat here looking at him, not moving, not doing nothing at all, and he left, like he couldn't see us. He left."

"Oh, he saw us all right," Looza says. "He looked me right in the eyes and I could see him deciding, like he was working out whether we were any kind of a threat, which of course we aren't. I guess he decided the same, because he left us alone."

"Thank the Heart," I say. I bend down, pull the blanket away from my mother, touch her cheek with my knuckles, kiss her once on the forehead. "Wes is dead," I say, and both of their mouths open, as if they might say something, but then they don't. They just nod. "Don't tell her. I have to tell her."

They nod again and I leave, out into the autumn snowstorm. There's only one place left to go: the palace.

~~~

We don't see any more riders as we run through the Blue District. They've come and gone, leaving burning buildings and bloody bodies in the snow, who are being tended to by healers, of which ice country seems to have plenny; they're crawling like insects out of the woodwork.

Every rider seems to have moved on, focusing everything on the final goal of taking the palace.

Where Jolie is. Trapped with Goff, who's surely the riders' ultimate target.

The gate's been cranked wide open, but the guards didn't just open it up and let the riders in. There are signs of a major fight littered all over the ground. Hundreds of arrows lie in bunches, some on their sides, some stuck in the snow, some poking from the dozens of black-skinned bodies of riders and their horses, which lie at a dozen different angles, forcing us to weave our way through the carnage.

There's red and white and black everywhere.

Long ropes are slung over the walls, which explain the gate being open. The riders dismounted, fought their way up and over, and then cranked open the gate for the rest of the riders to pass through. Several lengths of rope are coiled at the base of the wall, riders tangled in them, stuck with arrows. The rope would've been cut by the archers, sending them to the earth before shooting them.

We move for the gate, an Icer, a Heater, a Marked, and three Wildes. A strange and deadly combination.

Before we pass through the opening, we see the battle in the courtyard. Compared to this, our own fight to escape was child's play. Men play the parts of murderers in a game of death.

Skye pulls up short, raising a hand, and we all stop with her. This is her game.

I want to look at her, but my eyes are glued to the fight. With a hack of his sword, a rider slices off a guard's hand, which falls like a rock to the ground, still clutching an axe. Weaponless, the man runs, bleeding from his wrist, which is now just a stump, but he only gets three steps before the rider plows into him, trampling him beneath his horse's feet.

"Dazz," Skye says.

But the rider doesn't get far, because as soon as he kills the guard, an arrow pierces his chest. He clutches at it with his hands, his mouth agape as if surprised, his eyes and teeth looking as white as the snow against his dark skin. He slumps back, back, back, hanging from his horse, which keeps running with a dead man bouncing on its back.

"Dazz," Skye says again, and I manage to pull my gaze away from the dead rider, the trampled guard. Skye's eyes are fixed on mine.

The others are watching me too, waiting patiently. Perhaps only a moment has passed, perhaps several.

Skye says, "We'll stay in front of you, protect you."

"Nay," I say, shaking my head. "We'll move through together."

"Yeah, we will," Skye says. "But you need to stay alive so you can git to yer sister. Leave that to us."

I close my eyes.

They were on their way home. A week-long trek across the desert, a day to rest, and a week back. Fifteen days they wouldn't have been here, having to fight an enemy they don't even know—fifteen days to be alive. And now they're going to die today? For me? At risk of what Buff will say later, I want to throw my arms around all of them, hug them, thank them. For me, for Jolie. For Wes.

"We're doin' this," Skye says, as if she thinks I'll try to stop her. That's what I should be doing. Stopping them. But I can't.

I won't.

Not when the king's in there with my sister. Not when the riders are fighting their way to the king.

"Thank you," I say.

~~~

Amidst the swirling snow, we enter the courtyard in a line, with me behind them, like I'm someone important, someone worth protecting. I should be at the front, fighting alongside them, but—

Jolie.

I swallow my pride and try to keep up because they're moving fast. They've all got weapons from before, but a few of them traded up for the weapons of those dead outside the palace walls. Circ and Feve found shiny new swords and Siena grabbed a bow and a satchel of arrows from beside an Icer archer who was so bent and broken he must have fallen off the wall.

Guards are everywhere, swinging double-bladed battle axes, shooting arrows, jabbing swords at the dark, mounted warriors, who are deflecting them with their own swords, which are long and heavy. For the first time I notice the black riders are not only men, but women too, fierce and carnal and full of brutal violence that even Skye would be proud of.

The fight slams into us from all sides.

Circ gets thrown back into me by a heavily armored guardsman who's using a metal shield like a battering ram. Skye deflects a blow from a passing rider with her blade. Siena starts shooting arrows at anything that moves.

We're fighting two armies. Having sun-kissed skin here means everyone wants you dead. And I'm with them, so I'm a target too.

An arrow whistles past my ear and I duck instinctively even though it's already behind me.

Distracted by the arrow, I'm falling behind already, the others pushing forward. Everyone's got their hands full.

Circ manages to discard the guard with the big shield, slipping past its edge and stabbing hard and deep, practically splitting him in two. I look away.

On my other side, Feve and a dismounted rider circle each other, their eyes wary. Their swords ring out as they parry but the sound is immediately swallowed by the clang and grunt and screams of the battle around them. Feve blocks an attempted kill stroke and then aims one of his own, which the rider swats away too easily. Another jab by Feve, another block. Then a flurry of strokes by the rider has Feve on his heels, retreating, blocking, retreating some more.

"Dazz!" Skye yells. "This-a-way!" She's found a seam, her and Wilde and Siena, a weak spot in the battle, a place where I might be able to slip through to the palace. They're holding it open for me, keeping the path clear, swinging blades and shooting arrows and kicking and punching.

My eyes flick back to Feve, to the black-garbed rider. Feve's losing, getting knocked back by a heavy onslaught of sword strokes, barely keeping his footing as he steps backwards over a dead body. But then he slips, is forced to use his hand to keep his balance, giving the rider an opening, which he gladly takes, swinging with enough force to crush stones, slamming his sword into Feve's with a fierce

*CLANG!*

and Feve goes down, rolling onto his back amidst blood and bodies, trying to scramble to his feet, but being forced to scrabble backward while blocking another swipe from the rider's blade.

Feve's dead—

If I don't do something—

Dead.

"Dazz!"

Do something!

I run toward the rider, weaponless, except for my fists.

The rider doesn't see me coming. He's a mountain lion with a mouse trapped under his paw and nothing can disturb him from his meal.

He swings again, harder than any of the other blows, so hard that Feve—even Feve—can only throw his sword up in a last-ditch effort to protect himself.

*CLANG!*

267

Feve manages to block the strike, but he can't hold onto the handle any longer, and it skitters out of his hand, creating a sword-shaped hole in the snow, disappearing.

I keep running.

The rider raises his sword over his head—

I keep running, still too far away.

—thrusts it down—

I keep running, and I'm screaming now.

—and Feve rolls away, narrowly avoiding the kill attempt.

Hearing my scream, the rider turns just as I barge into him, leading with my shoulder, smashing into his chest, which is as hard as iron, perhaps from muscle or from some hidden form of body armor. He lands on Feve with me at the top of the pile. Feve grabs at his face from behind, poking his fingers into the rider's eyes, doing anything he can to help from his precarious position.

The rider rains down a barrage of punches on the back of my head, his sword not in his hand, disappearing just like Feve's. But I don't feel his hits. This is my territory now and shots to the head are a way of life.

I lay into him, punching him first in the gut, and then in the face.

Gut and face. Gut and face.

I get a rhythm going while he continues to pound from the back and squeeze his eyes shut against Feve's raking fingers.

Buff always said I had a head harder than an ice sculpture, on account of how many bar fights I won with my signature finishing maneuver. I crank it up now, still pounding away with my fists, leaning my head back slightly, waiting for the perfect moment...

Feve's hands slip away from the rider's face as he's crushed underneath him. I snap my head forward, butting the rider's skull like a goat defending my young. I hit him so hard—too hard probably—seeing stars myself and feeling an instant throb in my temples, but my pain's nothing compared to what the rider's feeling. He screams, clutching at his forehead, wailing something fierce. Then he stops screaming and lies unconscious.

I pull and Feve pushes and we get the rider offa him. We look at each other and it's one of those moments when you think you should say something, but it's impossible because another rider's swooping in and you're both dead if you don't get your arses in gear.

Feve cracks a strange grin, dives for the snow, somehow finds his sword, slashes at the rider, and knocks him off his horse, which keeps on running without him. When I just stand there, Feve yells, "Go!" and I take off, sprinting in the direction I last saw Skye.

But she's not there anymore and any path is all closed up. There are so many bodies, alive and standing and fighting, dead and crumpled and broken, that I don't see how I'll get through them all. Then I spot them, Skye and Siena and Wilde, and now Circ too, moving off to the side, looking back for me and Feve. Skye spots me.

She waves me over and I run, run, run, ignoring a fallen guard with a sword in his gut who cries out for help from the ground, leap over the lean flanks of an injured horse, which blows steam out of its nose, whinnying in pain, give a wide berth to an axe-wielding guard who's facing off against a sword-swinging rider.

While Siena continues to let arrows fly at anything that gets close, Skye, Circ and Wilde hack their way to the wall. And then Feve is with us again, still grinning, his sword slick with red.

We move along the palace wall, only having to fight foes on one side now, which makes all the difference. None of the guards or riders get anywhere near me, because the others are so good at keeping them away. We inch our way forward, skirting the battle, which continues to rage hot and fierce, neither side seeming to gain an advantage. Small wooden supply structures burn along the edge—the source of all the smoke we saw earlier—but we run past them, barely feeling the heat.

I'm coming. I'm coming, Jolie.

We reach the pillars that hold up the roof just before the palace entrance. A wall of guards blocks the way, fifteen, twenny of them. Too many to fight our way through.

But it's not just us. The riders want to get through just as badly.

A half a dozen riders charge the line.

We charge the line.

# Thirty-One

An axe arcs over my ducking head.

I raise a heavy boot and kick the guard in the midsection, launching him back into a mess of other guards who are attempting to hold off a pair of riders.

Something slices at me from the other side and I turn too late, only seeing the rider's sword in time to watch it cut me into Dazz-steaks.

But then he slumps over before he can finish his swing, dropping his sword at my feet. His horse keeps running and I see the arrow sticking from the rider's back as he passes. Siena stands back a ways, wearing my coat, bow strung with a new arrow, as if saving my life was just a small act, and she's already pushed it from her mind. Her arrow flies and pierces the shoulder of a guard who's fighting Circ. The guard staggers back and Circ slashes him down, flashing a smile in Siena's direction.

I search frantically for an opening in the mess of bodies, but it's all just violence and falling snow and armor and swords and—

There.

A rider cuts down three guards in quick succession, splitting the wall of men in half. He charges through, riding right into the palace. He's going for the king!

*Jolie!* I scream in my head as I charge through the gap, ignoring the killing that continues on either side. I'm two steps from the door, two steps from getting inside, but then I see him.

A rider, hot exhalation steaming from both his and his horse's mouths, galloping toward me, sword raised. It's the same rider who cut down Buff's father, who let my mother and Buff's brothers and sisters live. The merciful murderer.

Heat flares up in my chest as I charge him.

~~~

When we're so close that I can see the individual spots of blood on his sword, I dive to the side, narrowly avoiding getting trampled by his horse, which pulls up sharply, lifting its hoofs in the air, bucking at something that's spooked it.

With a cry, the rider falls back, tumbling off and landing awkwardly. The horse returns to all fours and gallops away, leaving a clear view beyond. Skye stands stalwart, her blade raised, her brown skin steaming in the cold as her sweat vaporizes the moment it leaves her skin.

I stride toward the fallen rider, but Skye says, "Go. Save your sister."

I glance at the rider, who's struggling to his feet, looking dazed, then back at Skye. She walks toward him.

I run through the doorway.

Tapestries flash past me as I run, full of blood and dark men and violence—all of it having come to life just outside the doors. One of them, the one depicting the battle between the people living on the water and the riders, is shredded in half, each side hanging limply from its frame. Sliced by the rider who already came through.

Fear rises up, dwarfed only by the red hot anger that continues to pulse through my veins. As I pass the throne room I can't hold back the images. Wes in chains, being led into the dungeons; Wes holding his bloody gut; Goff on the wall holding my sister. Goff. Icin' freezin' Goff.

The fear disappears and I'm all anger and it's okay—it's okay this time. Necessary. Right, even.

The steps to the dungeon go by on my left and I keep running. A ceramic vase lies broken in jagged shards on the floor. Knocked over by a horse that's not used to running inside?

I turn a corner to find a staircase and a horse. The horse chews on something, ignoring me, as if I'm just another person and today's just another day. The stairs wind up and up. A tower staircase. The central palace tower, the one that splits the clouds and allows the king to see the sun even in the worst storms, like the one today.

Rushing by the horse, I take the steps two at a time, tripping once, banging my knee, but scrambling with my hands to stay on my feet. Two steps, two steps, curving, climbing, around and around and around. Higher and higher, my lungs burning, my mouth dry, my hands fisted, higher and higher.

There are windows every twenny or so steps, but I can't see anything except gray and white.

Higher and higher, around and around.

My legs are aching, not in one place, but in *every* place—but that's nothing. Nothing.

I realize I'm speaking out loud between ragged, heaving breaths. "Jolie. I'm coming. I'm coming, Jolie. Don't hurt her. Don't. I'm coming."

I don't stop running or mumbling. Both things are all I have and they give me hope.

I reach a landing and there's a door, a vacant room beyond. I keep going.

My legs aren't working the way they should and I have to switch to one step at a time. With each stride they protest, but I tell them *Only one more step*, and then I take it. Repeating my empty promise, I take another. And another. And another.

Just when I think the tower goes even higher than they say, stretching all the way to the stars, I step onto a landing. My head's down, between my knees, but I manage to tilt my chin enough to look up. And there aren't any more stairs. Just a stone ceiling.

The top of the tower.

A door stands open. I walk toward it just as the screams fly out.

~~~

I'm in no shape to fight, too exhausted from my harried flight up the stairs, which is exactly why the king is probably hiding out here.

But I enter anyway, taking it all in with a single glance.

The horseless rider is surrounded by guards, slashing and blocking and hacking at their spears and axes and swords, killing one with a slice to the throat, stabbing another through the gut, fighting like someone who can't be defeated.

Small windows are cut at intervals along the walls, barely letting in any light at all, and certainly no sun—nay, not one speck of sunlight; at the other end of a room that seems too big to be held up this high, Goff stands in front of a huge, stone throne on a raised platform like a god, eyes blazing, his arms around...his arms holding...

I choke when I try to speak, gasping for air and words, because he's got her, he's got...

"Jolie," I say.

It's not loud enough to reach anyone's ears beyond my own, not against the battle cries in front of me.

Another guard dies with a scream, the rider vanquishing his enemies one by one.

"Jolie," I say again, this time louder.

Both Goff and Jolie look across the room at me. "Dazz!" Jolie screams.

And King Goff smiles. He actually smiles. His whole world is crashing down around him and he doesn't seem to care one bit, as if he's entertained by it. Jolie strains against his arms, but he's got her tight, so tight, and I start to run toward her, but then Goff reaches back and when his hand returns it's gleaming and it's holding a knife, jabbing it under Jolie's throat, and he's still smiling and his eyes are too, warning me to *Stay away, stay away, back off, or, or…*

*…she dies.*

There's nothing I can do but stop. Rage is throbbing in my head and in my blood and in my heart, but I have to stop, because he's got her and he'll kill her—that much I can see in his eyes.

But Jolie's pleading, pleading with her own eyes, giving me that hopeful look that she always has, like having a knife at her neck isn't anything if I'm there. Her protector.

A body crashes to the floor behind me and I jerk my head to the side and down. Another guard, not yet dead, but on his way, blood gurgling from his lips as he tries to breathe through thick, red liquid.

I raise my head to see the rider standing alone amidst a circle of bodies. He's killed them all—every last guard. A warrior, his strength far beyond my pathetic and useless bar-fighting talent that I once held such pride for.

He steps forward, his dark skin dripping with sweat, his black robe dragging at his feet, his sword held with both hands in front of him, the tip almost touching his chin.

I won't let him get Jolie without going through me first.

"You're here for the girl?" he asks, his voice a deep rumble. I step back, as if his words are far worse than his sword. He says it like it's a normal question, the start of a normal conversation, as if he hasn't just killed ten men on his own.

"She's my sister," I say. "He took her from me."

He nods. "He's a bad man," he says. "I can't let him live." But what about Jolie?

"I'll kill her if you come any closer," the king says, and in his tone is a promise. I see him drawing his thumb across his neck, high atop the wall.

The rider steps toward him.

"I swear to the Mountain Heart, I'll do it!" Goff screams, pushing his blade into Jolie's flesh, drawing a trickle of blood.

"Ow! You're hurting me!" Jolie cries.

"Don't!" I shout, both to the rider and to the king.

The rider looks back, but there's no uncertainty on his face. I see him slip a knife from his belt, using the width of his body to hide the motion from Goff.

I signal *No!* with my eyes, but he ignores it, turns, throws the knife toward the king and my sister.

The sound of the knife embedding in flesh and bone is sickening.

Blood flies.

The king slumps over, still clutching his knife.

Footsteps thump onto the landing outside the door.

With a whirl of his cape, the rider leaps past me, his sword raised. I spin around as he deflects an axe, a metal club, and a sword, each of which come flying through the entrance in short succession.

Past him, hordes of guards clamber up the stairs, pushing forward. The rider swings wildly, forcing them back, throwing them back, looking over his shoulder, looking right into my eyes. "Save her," he says.

With a sharp yank, he ducks through the door, pulling it shut behind him.

I rush to it, slide the thick, metal latch across, locking us inside.

Before I can spin back to Jolie, I hear the most awful sound.

It's a laugh. The king's not dead.

~ ~ ~

I turn to face Goff, my heart skipping a beat when I see the truth.

Goff *is* dead—at least the man I believed to be the king, the tall, strong, throne-sitting man—lying in a red pool, a knife embedded in his heart.

But another man has replaced him, shorter, older, more grizzled, with a wispy beard and unkempt hair that stinks of crazy, jutting out from his golden crown at odd angles. He looks anything but kingly, and if not for his red, satin robe and glinting crown he might be no more than a castle soothsayer. He must've been hiding behind the heavy stone seat, the throne.

"You can't save her," the real king says.

"Dazz?" Jolie says, like she wants to know if what the king says is true.

"Everything's okay, Joles," I say.

The king laughs. "Okay for whom?" he asks.

To the king I say, "Who was that man?" The dead man.

Goff laughs, his eyes blue and filled with a wild glee. "Captain of the guard," he says. "You really think I'd stoop so low as to cavort with commoners? While my men obey, the king can play."

So stupid. I've been so stupid. I knew it wasn't right that the king would speak to Wes and I, that he would venture into the dungeons to stop our original escape attempt. But I didn't listen to the warnings in my head. But now I know. A second chance to make things right.

I know I can't go right at him. He won't hesitate to kill her and then take his chances with me. There's only one thing to do: try to distract him until I can make a move.

"Where are the other children?" I ask, taking a step forward.

"That's far enough," Goff says. The trickle of blood reaches Jolie's neckline. I stop, take a deep breath, fighting my urge to rush at him.

"You want to know about the *other* children?" he says. "That surprises me, Dazz. Why do you care so much about them when your sister's right in front of you?"

I grit my teeth and try to stay focused. "I don't care about them," I lie. "I just need to know why. Why do you take them? What do you do to them?" I can't keep the rage out of my voice, bubbling up like a spring. I swallow it down.

"Oh-ho! You're worried about whether I've done anything to your pretty little sister here. Why she's still here even after all the other children are gone. Is that it?"

The other children are gone? Does he mean—I swallow again—dead?

Goff laughs again. "Kid, you look like you've swallowed a frog. If you're thinking I killed the rest of them, you're mistaken. I might be a monster, but even a monster has a heart. I sold them, like I have for years. What do I need a bunch of snot-nosed Heater kids running around here for? My servants wait on me hand and foot. My guards protect me...well, *try* to protect me, although they're not doing the best job of it lately, are they?"

I'm dumbfounded, speechless. *He sold the Heater children? To who? And for what?*

"Mountain lion got your tongue?" Goff says.

"I'm just surprised," I say, trying to keep the conversation going.

There's a heavy thud on the door behind me, which doesn't bode well for the rider. He lasted a while, but never had a chance against so many foes—not really. I don't look back.

Goff smiles, looks past me to the door. "Seems we're finally winning," he muses. "Should we let them in and end this quickly?"

"Nay," I say. "Not until I understand." *And freezin' kill you*, I add in my mind.

There's a heavy thud on the door and the metal bar rattles in its fixture.

Goff smiles, but I'm not sure if it's at the door or at what I've said. "As you wish," he says. "It's simple, really. The Stormers want children."

"The Stormers? But they're…"

"Attacking us?" the king says, smiling. "I guess I'm not delivering enough of them, or the children aren't strong enough, who knows? Although this one"—he squeezes Jolie harder—"is a real firecracker, always trying to escape, fighting the guards—I wonder where she gets it from?" He kisses the top of her head.

"Let go of her!" I scream, my rage rising up quicker than I can bite it down.

"Oh-ho, are you forgetting who has the knife to whose neck? Another outburst like that will get her killed," Goff says, his green eyes gleaming maliciously, as if he's hoping he gets just such a chance.

*Thud, thud!* The hammering on the door is getting louder, more persistent. If Goff's guards get in, it's over.

"You wouldn't," I say.

He laughs and that answers my question. He would. He has. Killed children. Enjoyed it. "Don't be so naïve, Dazz," he says.

I grit my teeth. I shake my head, trying to take it all in. "Why children?" I ask, pushing the conversation forward. The second it ends Jolie dies.

"How should I know? I don't even give them our children, just natives from fire country, but I'm sure you already know that."

*THUD, THUD!*

I ignore the pounding, keep things moving. "And you give the Heaters the Cure."

"*Gave* the Heaters the Cure," Goff corrects. "Since Roan was killed, the situation has changed, become more complex. But I never gave him much, just enough to get the children. I keep the rest for me and my men."

"What do the Stormers give you for the children?" Food, goods, what? Nothing seems to fit.

"Are you slow, Dazz?" the king says. "The same thing I gave Roan, except in much larger quantities."

The air goes out of my lungs. The reason the bags of dried plants looked so unfamiliar, unlike any plant I'd ever seen growing in ice country, was because they weren't from ice country.

"The Cure comes from…" I don't finish the statement.

"Of course. It comes from storm country. Those plants only grow on the shores of the sea."

The pieces click, snap, lock, and then *weave* together, into a sickening and screwed up tapestry that somehow, somewhere came to include my little sister, Jolie, ending with a knife to her throat.

*THUD!* The slam on the door is the loudest and heaviest yet, but I barely notice it, barely notice the metal bar bending under the pressure.

"Why *her*?" I say, spitting out the words, feeling a fresh wave of anger boil to the surface. "You said you only traded Heater children, but then you—you—" Memories of the night I went to visit Jolie at Clint and Looza's hits me like a punch to the gut. Finding them tied up, silence and darkness surrounding the house like a suffocating blanket. Seeing them drag Jolie out the back. Running, running, a knock to the back of my head, falling, falling, *failing* the only one I ever wanted to protect...

I can't speak another word or I'll lose it.

"I took your sister," Goff says. "Well, not me personally, but some vile men I dredged up from the Red District. They'll do anything for silver there."

"Why?" I growl, pushing him to get to the point.

*THUD!* I'm vaguely aware of voices shouting behind me, where a crack's opened up in the door.

"Let's just say she caught my eye," he says, licking his lips.

"Liar!" I roar. "That's not what your captain of the guard told me."

"What exactly did he tell you?"

"That she's a special trade item. That I'm the insurance to keep her in line," I say.

The king raises an eyebrow. "I didn't authorize him to say that. I'd have needed to punish him if he weren't already dead," he muses. "No matter. What you know now is of no consequence to me. In a short while you'll be dragged across the border with your sister. And she *will* obey her new masters, because if she doesn't it'll be *you* that pays for it with pain."

"I won't let anyone hurt you, Dazz," Jolie says.

"I know, Joles," I say. "So you can't hurt her, Goff. If she's so special, surely you can't just kill her here and now."

"Tsk tsk, Dazz," the king clucks. "I thought I warned you about being foolish. If she dies, I'll find another little girl to replace her in an instant. And another brother or sister or friend to force her obedience."

Something doesn't make sense. The Heater children were both boys and girls. "Why a *girl?*" I ask

The king smirks. "Now you're asking the right things. Because she'll be betrothed to a young man, of course," he says.

"Betrothed?" I say, the word sounding foreign because it was so unexpected. "The Stormers want my sister to marry one of their boys?"

"Yes." One word. The king may have lied about a lot of things, but this one word rings true. "But not just any boy. I suspect it's a boy of some importance to them. A son of a king or the equivalent."

"Why? Why an Icer?"

"Like I said, they want to ensure her cooperation and subservience to her master, her husband. Perhaps the young women of their lands are not as…easy to control. And the brown-skinned Heater children are their servants, so it wouldn't be appropriate to use one of them." I remember the unchained wildness of the dark riders, many of whom were women.

There's a series of sharp cracks against the door. Goff glances at the door, then back at me, smiling wider than ever. "Don't make me out to be such a bad guy," Goff says. "She's only one girl, no one will even notice she's gone."

"You stupid, stupid man!" I shout, taking a step forward even as there's a massive *THUD!* behind me.

"Not another step or I'll—"

But I'm not listening, not to the pathetic icin' King who's got my sister, nor to the incessant pounding at my back. Not anymore. "She's a *child*," I say. "Someone's daughter, someone's *sister*. My sister. You didn't think anyone would notice? You're insane."

I step forward, spurred on by another massive *THUD!*

"Not one more step, kid," Goff warns.

I hesitate, not because I'm scared of the king, but because it's still my sister he's got, still Jolie, biting at her lip and trying not to cry.

"Dazz?" she says, her question full of a thousand other questions, none of which I can answer without lying.

Men's voices pummel the door, even as a series of vicious pounds erupt behind me.

*THUD, THUD, THUD, THUD!*

I glance back at the door. The bar is fully bent now, the crack in the door widening with each hammer of the battering ram. "It's okay, Joles, everything's okay," I say, wondering how it will be, how I can speak something I don't believe myself.

Now is the moment. My moment. My one chance to make up for everything, for all the mistakes, for all the pain and hurt and anguish of the last few days, weeks, months, *years.*

I step forward and Goff lifts the knife from Jolie's throat, pulling it back in a slashing motion, as if he wants to shove it all the way through her neck, not content to simply slit her throat.

I have no choice but to act.

# Thirty-Two

This is it. This is it. My final failure, the ultimate mistake that will leave my family broken into a million pieces, so many that my drugged-out mother and me will never be able to pick them all up, fit them back together again.

I charge forward, shouting something at the top of my lungs, something familiar, something powerful—a name—

*Jolieeeeee!*

—feeling time and distance and life slowing down, stopping, freezing more solidly than the ice-coated peaks of the mountain—

*Jolieeeee!*

—urging my muscles to go, go, go, faster, faster—

*Jolieeeee!*

—watching with dread as the knife starts its downward arc, gleaming brighter than the eyes of the wicked, wicked man wielding it—

*THUD!!!!*

—hearing the loudest pound on the door yet, but knowing it doesn't matter, not now, not ever, prepared to face death if I don't save her.

No time, no time, no freezin' time, the knife right there, right there, and she'll be, she'll be…

Two small hands flash up, grab at the king's arm, hold it off, barely, barely, but it's still moving as Goff's look of surprise changes back to determination, but I'm still running, getting closer, even as the knife gets closer, but he's winning the battle—the king is winning the battle—pushing the knife to within inches of my sister's fragile skin, and then, and then—

—Jolie bites him, sinks her little teeth into the flesh of his arm and he cries out, *yowls* so loudly it momentarily drowns out the pounding on the door.

But he doesn't.

He doesn't drop the knife.

I'm close now, close enough to

(stop him.)

Close enough to

(save her.)

The thoughts are there but I can't think them with the full extent of my mind, just let them slip around the edges, not letting myself believe that we could, that we could

(win.)

I swing hard, putting everything I have left into the punch, aimed well over Jolie's head, at his face, at the malicious eyes of the demon who holds her, even now still trying to stab her, and—

My fist connects, crushing Goff's temple, just on the edge of his eye, snapping his head to the side and back.

He releases Jolie, falls away, his arm stabbing wildly at the air behind her as he crumples to the stone floor.

Jolie's left standing there, tears in her eyes, a stream of blood running down her neck.

"Dazz?" she says.

There's something in her eyes—

"Dazz?" she says again.

Something's not right—

"Dazz?" she says, once more, and I step toward her, ready to take her in my arms, to tell her everything really is okay, that I'm here, that the king won't hurt her anymore, that—

She falls to her knees, her head slumping forward, right into my arms as I dive down to catch her, to stop her from hitting the floor.

That's when I see it.

That's when I see it.

*Jolie? Nay, Jolie. Nay.*

The blood down her back. The knife embedded in her skin, gleaming, always gleaming, laughing at me with the voice of the broken king beyond it.

"Jolie!" I scream, grabbing her, clutching her to me.

"Dazz, I'm cold," she says into my chest, which should be a funny statement, because we're in ice country so we're always cold, but people don't say stuff like that here, because it's a given, like trees have leaves or winter has avalanches.

Jolie doesn't speak like that.

"Dazz?" Her voice again, so innocent and sweet, sounding weaker than before, less vibrant, my sister's voice but not, changed somehow.

I kiss her cheeks, wetting them with the tears that are streaming down my own face, over my lips, salty and fresh.

She's *not* dying. She's not. Not on my watch.

A surge of strength and determination and *anger*, red hot and fiery, courses through me, but I ignore the anger. Revenge will come later. Now I have to stop the bleeding.

I lay Jolie down gently, resting her head in my lap. There's so much blood—so much I can't think, can't speak—but I know I have to stop it, have to stop the life from draining out of her.

I've got nothing to use but myself. I clamp my hands around the handle of the knife—the king's knife—and put pressure around it, try to keep the red liquid from spilling out past the wound, being careful not to push the blade in farther. Jolie cries out but I have to ignore it, although I'm sobbing and shaking and wanting nothing more than to hold her and kiss her.

"Help!" I scream, but I know no one will answer. The pounding on the door has stopped, but the men outside are still yelling, still shouting meaningless words, full of rage and murder. But the murder's already happened and Heart of the Mountain save them if they make it through that door.

"Help, please," I sob, my tears falling on the backs of my hands, which are white with effort and strain. The blood's not coming out as fast anymore, but Jolie's stopped speaking, her back barely rising and falling with each exhalation. No matter how much pressure I put on her wound, without help she's

(dead.)

"Help…" The word dies on my lips, but I won't give up, won't stop sealing the wound with my own flesh.

The king groans nearby.

Rolls over.

Starts to get up.

"You shouldn't have done that, kid," he says, rising up, bigger and taller this close, when I'm slumped to the floor like an animal. There's a nasty gash on his forehead where I hit him, spilling blood down his cheek, some of it getting onto his lips, into his mouth, coating his teeth with a red sheen. His eye is puffy and turning purple. His other eye is full of crazy.

I don't stop the pressure on Jolie's back, try to ignore Goff, pretend he's not there. If I take my hands away from her back, she dies.

Goff raises a boot in the air, hovers it over Jolie as if he might step on her, but then levels it out so it's even with my head. I close my eyes and brace myself for a kick to the face, determined not to let go of Jolie.

No matter what.

The blow never comes.

I open my eyes.

Goff's boot is lowered and he's fumbling at his belt, searching for something, for…

Another knife.

He holds it up, lets its sharp edges catch the light, shows it to me.

"I'll kill you," I say.

"If you let go of her, you'll kill her," he says.

"And then I'll kill you."

He shrugs. "Maybe so, but I'm the one holding the knife."

An impossible decision. If I let go of Jolie, she might die, but if I don't, Goff will kill us both anyway. I have to fight.

It has to be a quick one, or I might be too late to save her.

"I love you," I whisper to Jolie, but I don't know if she hears me.

Then, weaponless, I stand.

~~~

King Goff slashes at my throat, leaping over Jolie's small body.

I jump back, surprised at the suddenness and intensity of his attack.

But I'm not on my heels for long, not with the rage that's been roiling beneath the surface of my skin since this day began, since Wes died. Finally—finally!—I can let it out, all of it, the fear for Jolie's life, the anger over Wes's death, the burning need to take revenge on the wicked man who threatens my whole world, who's done unspeakable things.

He feints left, feints right, and then comes up the center, flicking his blade across my abdomen. I'm fast and full of energy, but he's faster, a man possessed, and he slices my skin, sending a fierce burn into my gut.

The blood pours out but it's nothing, a flesh wound, nothing compared to the knife embedded in my sister's back. The knife that's killing her while I continue to waste time with the king.

I leap back, hardening my jaw at the smile on Goff's face. He moves in, still smiling, gaining confidence.

But when he slashes again, I'm ready, letting the knife slide past me even as I grab his arm, twist it, wrench it in an unnatural way that leaves the king screaming out as his bones snap.

Following through, I crush a forearm into his skull, aiming for the same spot I hit him before, feeling him rock back under the force of the blow. I land on top of him, punching with all my might, swinging and swinging, blood misting in my face as his nose explodes, his lips crack open, still swinging, fists hitting the face of pure evil, not ready to stop, not wanting to stop, but remembering, remembering…

Jolie.

It can't wait any longer. I have to get back to her, but first Goff has to die.

His knife lies discarded on the floor. I reach for it, grab it.

I've never killed before, but this is a good place to start.

I raise the knife just as there's a final, stone-crushing *THUD!* and the door crashes open.

~~~

I whirl around, knife still raised, ready, so ready, to fight them all. A hundred men couldn't stop me when I'm this close to saving her.

My arm drops when I see her.

Skye.

Blood-spattered and fierce-eyed and *here*. The bodies of dozens of guards are scattered and broken on the floor behind her. She came. She came for me—for us. For Jolie and me.

She looks at me, at the king, at Jolie's body, taking it all in.

The king groans and I turn back. One of his eyes is slitted open and he's staring at me. His hand lifts, slides toward me as if beckoning for help. Instead I raise the knife once more.

"No," Skye says, suddenly by my side, taking my hand, taking the knife. My fingers don't protest as she uncurls them. I am powerless against her. "Go to your sister."

My whole body numb, I manage to stand, unsteady on my feet, shaking, stumbling my way over to Jolie, seeing moving bodies around me, barely able to recognize them as the others. Siena, Circ, Wilde, Feve. They're all here, all fought through the hordes of guards to get to me.

But they're too late. We're all too late.

Right where I left her, Jolie sleeps.

That's how I want to see her—asleep—just resting, a child in her bed, dreaming a child's dream.

My eyes play the trick, and play it well, but when Feve rushes to her side, coated in a thin layer of sweat, his markings glistening in the light, the truth returns.

Jolie, broken. Jolie, lying in a pool of her own blood. Jolie, covered in red and black, a knife sticking from her...from her beautiful...from her beautiful little body, and I can't speak, can't think, can't remember another word about her, because it hurts too much, and I'm by her side, like I floated there, because I can't remember walking, and I'm cradling her head in my arms and I'm crying into her hair, and there's nothing left in this world.

Nothing.

And then Feve opens a leather pouch at his side, removes little glass jars and skins of herbs.

And then he reaches for the knife, the knife in my sister's back...

"Don't!" I shout, my voice husky and heavy, grabbing his hand, stopping him, meeting his eyes. "Don't touch her," I say.

"Trust me," Feve says. He puts a hand on my shoulder. "It's her only chance."

Siena kneels beside me, says, "Feve's saved me 'fore. Let him save her." Coming from her, it means everything. She's the one who doesn't even like him.

A dead girl doesn't have a chance, but my shoulders slump and I release Feve's arm. He couldn't save Wes, but perhaps my brother's life was too far gone. Maybe the Marked have magic. Maybe they have miracles. But I won't hope for it; my heart can't be broken twice.

Feve's hand goes back to the knife handle.

I hold her limp head, brush her sweat-damp hair away from her face.

"Cloth, Circ!" Feve orders, and then takes a deep breath, adding a second hand to his grip on the handle. I hear cloth tearing behind us and it sounds like the rending of my own heart.

"Oh, Joles," I murmur under my breath, touching my forehead to hers. "You can't go. Please stay." But she's not breathing, not moving, not sleeping like I want to believe.

Circ slides next to us with a panel of cloth. He uses a blade to cut it into long strips. Feve looks at him. "You ready?" Circ nods. "When I pull it out, hold some cloth firmly on the wound. You've got to be quick, she can't lose any more blood." Circ nods again.

"One…"

I kiss Jolie's head.

"Two…"

I close my eyes.

"Three!"

Jolie's body shudders and my eyes flash open to Circ covering a deep stab wound with cloth, holding it in place with the heel of his hand. Jolie gasps suddenly, coughing in my face, her eyes shooting open, wider than the base of the mountain.

"Jolie? Jolie?" I say, holding her, but her eyes drift closed slowly, her head heavy once more. Lifeless.

But wait.

Wait.

Please, wait.

Her breath's on my face. It's weak, so frighteningly weak, but still there.

Feve pushes in next to Circ, lifts the bandages, which are already tinged with blood, pours clear liquid across the wound, refolds the cloths, and presses them back down, closing Circ's hands on them once more. He looks at me. "To help close the wound," he explains.

I want to know more, how he knows to do what he's doing, how he's going to save Jolie's life, but not now. Now, all I want to do is feel her breath on my hand, on my face, as I watch her sleep.

Really sleep.

# Thirty-Three

She hasn't woken up and I haven't left her side, sitting in an uncomfortable wooden chair that hurts my back and my arse in equal measure.

Three days have passed with her little chest rising and falling, rising and falling, but other than that, she hasn't moved more than a whisper, not even stirring for the dark dreams that surely plague her sleep.

Mother's oblivious to everything.

I've held Jolie's hand for hours and hours, just in case she can feel it and draw strength from me. And in case she can hear me, I speak to her, tell her memories of growing up together, when Father and Wes weren't dead, when Mother wasn't a ghost of a human. Good stories. Stories I can't tell without feeling melting snow in my eyes.

Feve comes every day, gives her herbs in a drink that we dribble on her tongue, both for strength and for healing. I help him replace her bandages and watch as he sprinkles his strange medicines on her wound. Every day I hope it'll look better, but it never does.

And every day I get plenny of visitors. Buff, Siena, Circ, Wilde—even good ol' Yo from the pub comes by. My friends from fire country are staying at Clint and Looza's with my mother. I never ask them how *that's* going and they don't offer the information.

Skye comes by more than anyone, at least six times a day. It's weird, seeing her on a daily basis outside of the prison, outside of the woods, outside of battle. She can be so different when she wants to be. So much less strong, more tender. Sometimes she holds my hand while I hold Jolie's, and I can almost feel her strength running through me and into my sister.

She might never wake up.

I think it all the time, but I won't say it out loud, even when Feve cautions me that it's a possibility. "There's no way to predict how a body will react to something like that. And she's so small," he says.

"She's strong," I reply back, but still the thought is in the back of my head.

(She might never wake up.)

I'm so tired, so freezin' exhausted, both mentally and physically, that all I want to do is curl up in a ball next to Jolie and sleep forever with her. But the bed's too small and I'm too big and I'm afraid of crushing her in my sleep.

For the third night in a row and with tears in my eyes, I drift away into an uncomfortable sleep filled with dark riders, burning houses, and the king stabbing my sister.

I'm still sitting in my chair.

But I'm still holding Jolie's hand, too.

~~~

I awake with tearstains on my cheeks and Buff punching me in the shoulder.

"I brought you breakfast," he says, and he doesn't even call me a sissy-eyed snowflake-lover for the tracks of white salt on my face. That's how I know everything's changed.

"How's your gut-slash?" he asks, and I know what he means. It took him asking me that three times before I realized he was asking about Jolie, not me. After all, Jolie's the gut-slash that hurts me the most, deep under the surface, in the pit of my stomach, worming and gnawing away.

"No worse, no better," I say, my standard response that I hope will change one day soon.

He nods and we're both silent for a moment, just watching Jolie sleep. "So, uh, you said something about breakfast?" I ask. I'm not hungry but I need something to distract me.

"Rolls again," he says. "Harder than rocks. Less tasty too," he adds with a grin. He hands me a hunk of bread from his satchel. It really is like rock.

For a few minutes we scrape at our rolls with our teeth, trying to get some kind of sustenance from them. Watching Buff gnaw away, I almost laugh, but my lips don't turn up so quickly these days. "You make these?" I ask, raising my eyebrows.

"Shove it up your snow-blowin' arse!" Buff says. I glance at Jolie, who's as silent and motionless as ever. If she can hear us, she's getting a topnotch education on the intricacies of cursing. Buff's as good a teacher as anyone.

"Sorry," Buff says, covering his mouth with a rock-roll. "It's easy to forget your…gut-slash is there sometimes."

"Stop calling her that," I say, feeling a flash of heat for the first time in three days. "Her name's Jolie."

"I know, it's just hard—"

"And quit forgetting she's there," I interrupt. "She's still a person. She's still my little sister."

Buff nods a heavy nod and right away I know I've been too hard on him. It's not like he doesn't have problems of his own. It's not like he doesn't care about Jolie. The fire in me dies quickly, like it was no more than a spark anyway, and I find myself backtracking. "Look, man, I'm sorry, it's just…seeing her here like this, day in and day out, it's getting to me."

"Don't apologize to me, Dazz. Everyone's on edge. It's natural. And she'll…*Jolie* will come out of it. I know it."

"Thanks," I say, nearly breaking a tooth as I try to bite into the roll again.

Buff grins. "Alright, alright, I made them. But only because Darce was busy cleaning my father's injuries."

"How is he?" I say, wishing I'd asked right away. It's so easy to get stuck in the snowdrift of our problems sometimes, so deep and cold that you can't see anything else at all, even the important stuff.

"The slash he took from the rider should've killed him," Buff says. "Even the healers can't explain how the rider, in that position, didn't manage to do more damage. It's like he only did enough to keep my father from hurting him, so he could get past and on to the castle. The men he was with had similar injuries, none of them fatal. They're healing up nicely."

"That's good," I say, managing a weak smile. "And his leg?"

Buff frowns. "Not so good. When the horse stepped on him, his leg shattered into a whole lot of pieces. He won't be able to work for a long time. But even that…" Buff trails off, staring at Jolie.

"What?" I say.

Buff tilts his head thoughtfully. "It feels like even that was an accident, like the rider didn't want to hurt him badly."

Now I frown. "Buff, that rider was lighting houses on fire, stampeding through the village with a sword, chopping down good men like your father. That's no accident. It was the Stormers who took the children, too. I told you what the king said, they wanted my sister to marry one of their boys. They were going to force her to obey him. They're evil."

"The king was evil," Buff says, "he might've lied to you."

I close my eyes because I know Buff's right. "Some of it was the truth," I say. "He had no reason to lie." *Like the part about my sister being betrothed.*

Buff sighs. "I know, I'm just saying it's weird. My father said the horse was bearing down on him, about to stomp all over him, and then the rider pulled up sharply, like he didn't want to step on him. The horse turned as best it could, but wasn't able to avoid my father's leg."

"He still trampled him," I say. "He still slashed him."

"But didn't you say one of the riders saved your life? That he left you with Jolie and gave his life to hold back the guards? That he told you to save her? Why would he do that if they wanted your sister? It doesn't make sense."

Vivid memories flash through my mind: the rider, dark-robed and menacing, stepping toward the king and my sister; his words, "You're here for the girl?"; then, watching him leap past me and into the flow of guards, fighting them back while I barricaded the door. He did save my life. Maybe Jolie's too. But why?

"He thought it was over," I say. "He thought he'd killed the king, which apparently was what the Stormers were after in the first place. And he didn't take Jolie because he knew he couldn't possibly escape *and* abduct her."

"Maybe," Buff says. "But no one else in the village died. Other than the castle guards, casualties were zero. The Stormers massacred or injured almost every guardsman and then galloped off with their own injured on their backs. They could've taken over the entire village if they'd wanted—but they didn't."

"But the burning," I say.

"Only houses with no one in them."

"But why?"

Buff cringes, closes his eyes—opens them. Says, "I don't know."

"Aren't the people angry?" I ask.

"At King Goff mostly," he says. "Now that the truth is out, people are saying he brought a curse on our country."

"I meant, aren't they angry at the Stormers?"

Buff chews his lip. "Yes and no, but mostly no," he says. "Sure they're angry that they have to rebuild, but mostly at Goff for bringing the curse on our people. Already the Stormers are falling back into myth and legend. There are rumors that they rose out of the ground, formed from clay, and returned to it, like inhuman shadows."

"I saw them. They're as real as you or I. They're evil," I repeat. "Child stealers. Don't you get it?"

Buff nods. "I do, but the rest of the villagers won't be so easily convinced. At least they didn't get your sister."

"Thank the Mountain Heart," I say.

"Do you want to know what's been going on at the castle?" Buff asks, changing the subject.

I raise my eyebrows. I've been so set on watching Jolie and praying for her to wake up, I've almost forgotten there's a whole world out there, one that's broken into a thousand pieces. "The king?" I say.

Buff nods. "You gave him quite a beating, but he survived it. The truth is out though, and already the people are calling for his head on a platter. A consortium's been created with an equal number of representatives from each of the Districts, which the White District folks aren't too happy about, but given the situation they haven't fought it too hard."

"Who's included from the Brown District?"

There's a twinkle in Buff's eye. "Yo, for one," he says, and I smile. I couldn't think of a better choice. He's always had more wisdom and kindness than most.

"Good," I say. "What'll this consortium do?"

"Decide on what's to become of the king, and then what's to become of the Icers. Yo says they'll be announcing the king's execution any day now."

I feel like I should smile, but I can't, not with Jolie the way she is.

"And then what?"

He shrugs. "Not even Yo can predict, but he expects things'll get better."

"They could hardly get worse," I say.

Buff leaves after that.

~~~

Skye comes shortly after Buff leaves. She's wearing thick snow pants and a heavy coat, borrowed from Looza, so they hang from her like extra skin, way too much material for her lean frame. But at least she's warm. And she still looks beautiful, breathtakingly so.

"She'll heal soon," she announces when she sees the frustration on my face. "Feve's a searin' good healer." She flips Buff's chair around, straddles it backwards, her leg close to mine.

Her words give me hope, which surprises me.

With her leg tapping on the floor, always moving, I feel the warm sensation I get inside me whenever she's around. "Skye?" I say.

"Yeah?" She tilts her head to look at me.

"Why're you doing all this?" It's a question I've been holding for a while, but with everything happening, I haven't had the chance to ask it.

She shrugs, keeps on tapping her foot. "Why not," she says. "We were 'ere. The village needed help." *You needed help.* The rest hangs unspoken on her pink tongue.

"I'll do whatever I can to help you get your sister back from the Stormers. Jade."

"You'll stay 'ere with yer sister," she says. "We'll take care of it."

"I need to know the truth. Who wanted my sister. And why."

"You want revenge," Skye says, right on point as usual.

"Wouldn't you?" I ask.

"Yes," she admits. "But we can give you that. You need to stay with her." She motions to Jolie.

"When are you leaving?" We haven't talked about what comes next, but I know it's got to be coming soon. Skye's not the type to wait around for heroes to rescue her. She is the hero.

One side of her lip turns up. "I know what yer thinkin' in that pretty little Icy Dazz head of yers," she says. "You'll follow us, you'll find a way to stay with us till we realize you ain't takin' no fer an answer. Am I right?" Before I can answer, she adds, "Yer not comin'." She's got that locked-jaw look that says it's the end of the conversation. Only for me it isn't. She was exactly right. I'm going with her if I have to follow like a shadow from a distance.

"If you say so," I say, laughing. I cut off short, however, when I realize it. I can't laugh, not when Jolie might be dying beside me.

Can I really leave her like this?

"I do say so," she says, getting that look in her eyes, the one where she narrows them and you know there's no way you can change her mind, so it isn't even worth trying.

So I try anyway. "You helped save my sister, so I'll help save yours. This has nothing to do with us."

She punches me lightly on the shoulder and gets that *other* look in her eyes, the one where her eyebrows raise, pulling her big brown eyes open a little wider than usual, and you know, just know, she's about to say something that'll surprise you, because it'll be so honest, so straight to the heart that you wonder where she came from, how she can wear her emotions on the outside like that, when most people are hiding them deep inside, locking them in a box, throwing away the key.

"Dazz," she says, and I wait for it breathlessly.

"Yer a real icin' fool sometimes," she says, and I burst out laughing, both because she's right and because she used one of our words, the one that I think means the same thing as *searin'* in her language.

~~~

After Skye leaves I feel that hole in my soul that always seems to appear when she's not around. I don't know what's wrong with me, but maybe Skye is right, that I'm a real icin' fool for thinking I should leave the side of my unconscious sister to go on some wild hunt for a Heater girl I don't even know, who's probably not alive anyway.

Call it foolishness, call it the need to pay the Heaters back for what they did for me, call it a hot desire for *revenge*, call it bear crap for all I care, but that's what I know I need to do.

The Stormers can't get away with stealing children, not from ice country, not from fire country, not from anywhere. We'll make them stop.

I'm staring at the floor thinking about it all when there's a heavy knock at the door, so heavy I think the guards are back with their battering ram, trying to smash straight through our hut. "Ice it all to chill!" I hiss under my breath, striding to the door with snow water in my veins.

I throw the door open, ready to knock whoever's disturbing my thoughts and my sister's peaceful slumber all the way into fire country.

I suck in a quick breath when I find myself staring into the chest of a giant.

He grunts and I look up. Hightower stands over me, a foot taller and twice as wide.

Abe steps around him, leaning on a stick and smiling the nastiest smile I've ever seen, all bite and no warmth. A smile that makes me smile back. "Hey, kid, mind if we come in?"

I chuckle. These are the last two people I expected to show up on my doorstep. "It's not like I can stop you when you got him leading the charge," I say, motioning to his Yag-sized brother.

"Icin' right," he says, pushing past me. I step aside and let Hightower grunt his way inside, having to duck and turn sorta sideways to get through the narrow entrance.

"To what do I owe this pleasure?" I say when I close the door.

Abe smiles wickedly. "Tell 'im, Tower."

I frown and look at Tower, who I've never heard speak even a single word. The monstrous man reaches a big ol' hand into a deep pocket in his bearskin coat. There's a jingle when he pulls out a fistful of bright, gleaming silver.

I gawk at the sickles, more wealth than I've ever seen in my entire life.

"But where...how...what..." I say, unable to pull my eyes off the shiny coins.

"Exactly," Abe says. "All of that. This 'ere, kid, is yer share."

I keep on staring, wondering when I'm gonna wake up. "Share of what?" I finally say.

"The silver!" Abe says. "Ain't you been payin' attention?"

I manage to tear my eyes from Tower's hand, look at Abe. "Nay, I mean, what's it for? I didn't realize we were in business together."

Abe laughs and then stops suddenly, seeing Jolie's resting form in the bed against the wall. "Poor kid," he says. "I heard what happened. She'll be all right?"

"I don't know," I admit.

Tower grunts something. "My brother offers his well wishes," Abe says. Before I can even wonder how Abe can understand anything his brother says, he continues. "When the riders tore through the castle, not to mention you and yer strange friends running about, it was like a free fer all fer all the lowlifes in ice country…"

"What does that have to do with you?" I say.

"Well, thank you for sayin' that, kid, but I'm proud to be a part of such a rowdy and mischievous bunch. Anyway, we snuck our way in like rodents, keepin' behind the melee. It took ten men and Hightower 'ere to break into the palace vault, but we did it. Now I'm richer than the richest snow-blowers in the White District. Tis only fair that you get a share for everythin' you been through. Consider it payment for killing my biggest enemy, may the king rot in a shallow grave."

"Did you know the king was hiding behind a puppet figurehead?" I ask

Abe chews his lip. "Well, I had my suspicions, but never enough to prove anything. But now one's dead and the other ain't far behind, so enjoy the spoils."

Feeling the weight of the coins in my hands, I lift a hand to my forehead, feeling the room spinning. "I don't know what to—"

"Don't say a freezin' thing, kid. Just take it," Abe says, smirking. "I'm not usually this generous, so be quick 'fore I change my mind."

I don't have to be told twice. I cup both hands together, knowing I'll need two hands for one of Hightower's. Abe's brother tilts his palm and lets the silver fall like shimmering rain into my hands, piling up and filling them to overflowing, and yet still they fall, clattering to the floor, scattering.

"Thank you," I say, misty-eyed, but I'm talking to Abe's back, because he's already at the door.

"Hope the kid gets better," he says, opening the door and stepping outside.

"I'm sorry about your wife," I say, but I don't know if he hears me.

Hightower lingers for a moment, staring off at Jolie. Then he starts to lumber over to her. "Whoa there, Tower," I say, springing in front of him. Luckily he stops, because if he didn't I'd be human paste under his feet. "The door's that way," I say, motioning to where Abe's waiting outside.

Tower grunts, points to Jolie. I look up, way up, into his eyes, which are crystal-blue, and ogre-sized, like everything else on him. I never realized his eyes were blue, and for some reason it surprises me. "You want to see her?" I say, replacing *see* with *eat* in my head.

He nods. I hope he means *see* and not the word I was thinking.

I chew on my mouth for a second. Hightower, despite his somewhat scary and threatening appearance, has been nothing but good to me, other than when he held Buff back so Abe could beat the living shivballs out of me. But I probably deserved it then, and he did save my life on at least two occasions. If nothing else, he's earned my trust.

I step aside to let him pass, watching his every move like a hawk.

He approaches Jolie, kneels down—which means he's still almost as tall as me—reaches toward her. My spine stiffens, but I don't stop him. His movements are slow, almost gentle, if gentleness is possible from such a large person.

He touches a single finger to Jolie's forehead, runs it along her skin, pushes a few strands of loose hair away from her eyes. And if all that's not surprising enough, his next move is so shocking I swear a lightning bolt hits me in the head. He kisses the same finger, and then places it on her forehead, as if kissing her with his lips would be inappropriate coming from such a gargantuan.

He stands, grunts something, I think a farewell, and then ducks through the door and is gone.

# Thirty-Four

Three days later Jolie still hasn't moved.

With only two days before Skye and her gang leave to find the Stormers, Feve's been teaching the healers what they'll need to do for Jolie after he's gone.

Skye insists I'm not coming with her, but I am. At least that's what I'm telling Buff.

"I'm going," I say.

"You sure you want to leave Jolie?" he asks for the third time.

I shake my head. "I don't *want* to, Buff, ice it! By the Heart of the Mountain you know that's true. But I have to. You know I do. I owe Skye, Siena, all the others. I owe it to Jolie to find out the truth."

"But isn't Skye telling you not to come?"

"Yah, but I'm freezin' going anyway, okay?"

"Okay, okay. I'll watch out for her while you're gone."

"Nay. Clint and Looza already said they'll do it. You've got to come with us."

Buff's face falls. "Dazz, you know I want to, more than anything, but I can't. Father, he's not getting back on his feet anytime soon and I have to get a job—a *real* job—or Darce and the others are gonna starve."

I smile. Not at the thought of Buff's bed-ridden father or of his brothers and sisters starving, but because I have a solution. Compliments of Abe and Hightower. Buff takes my smile the completely wrong way. "Something funny?" he says, his fists coiled at his side.

Things must be really bad at home if his temper's gotten as bad as mine. I speak quickly. "What if I pay you in advance to help us find Skye's sister?" I say.

His eyebrows shoot up and he stares at me like I've been punched in the head one too many times, which I probably have. "Pay me? I don't want to come as part of a job. I want to come because you're my friend."

I feel a bit of foolish warmth in my heart so I smack a fist in my hand to compensate. "Not like a job," I say. "Like a donation. To your family. So you can come."

"You've barely got more silver than me, and you'll need to give it all to Clint to take care of Jolie and your mother while you're gone."

I keep smiling as I tell him about Abe's little visit. He doesn't believe me until I show him the pouch of silver coins. "Holy mother of all shivballs!" he exclaims. "You're rich, Dazz!"

I nod because I am, and because sickles solve problems. "So you'll do it?"

"Chill yah, I'll do it," he says, all smiles and taut muscles.

~~~

"Sear it, I'm gonna miss you when we leave," Skye says, running a finger along my hand.

I laugh. "You know, I really love your honesty, Skye, but I'm coming with you."

"You ain't."

"Think what you want to," I say.

"My fists say you ain't," she says, and I laugh again.

"You can't fight me," I say. "Remember what happened last time? We might as well skip the fighting part and go straight to the other part."

"You want to?" Skye says, her eyes bold and sharp as they cut into mine.

This time I really hope Jolie can't hear us.

Skye leans into me and I scoop a hand around the back of her neck, slip it under her coat, feel the warmth of her smooth skin, pull her even closer. Her forehead touches mine and we look at each other, all the way in, closer than close, her brown chestnut eyes bearing her soul to me, and I can see—nay, *feel*—how much she wants me, how when she looks at me she feels the same way I do when I look at her.

I touch her jaw with my other hand, just below her ear, running my thumb along her brown skin. And then we kiss, more tenderly and slowly than the last time, when it was all adrenaline and urgency and—

I pull back, glancing sharply at Jolie, who I thought I saw move.

"What?" she says, following my gaze.

Jolie continues sleeping as still as a stone, just like she's been the whole time.

Feeling foolish, I say, "Sorry, Skye, I thought—I just thought I saw…"

"It's okay," Skye says with that raspy voice of hers that makes me shake with desire. She touches a gentle hand to my face, brushing the scruff of my beard. "Time'll heal everythin'," she says.

~~~

One day till Skye leaves. (And me with her?)

I know, I know, I've been saying all along how I'm going, how Buff's going with me, how I owe them and have to help Skye and Siena find her sister…but…but…

*Jolie.*

How can I leave my sleeping angel sister alone in her bed, maybe to wake up one day without me there by her side? After all she's been through, how could I ever do that? The warmth of the fire is making me sweat.

I'm brooding over my thoughts, changing my mind again and again, when there's a knock on the door. Usually Skye and Buff and the others just come right in, so it surprises me. Abe again maybe?

I wipe my sleeve on the frosted glass so I can take a peek. My breath hitches. What am I seeing?

I rush to the door, thrust it open, slamming it off the wall, but not caring, not caring, because—

—standing before me is my mother, practically withered away to nothing, all skin and bones and as pale as the Glassies, but that doesn't matter, because she's standing on her own two feet.

"Dazz," she says, her voice as whispery as it always is, like when she's murmuring nonsense at the fire. But there's no nonsense in it, because it's her—it's really her. Not drugged-out Mother, but the real one, the one who was always there, always around when father was working in the mines, who only left us when he did.

My brain's telling me to turn her away, to tell her to come back when she's been clean for more than a day, a month at least, but every instinct in my body is saying different. And after everything—Wes and Jolie and Skye and the king—I can't, I can't be the firm hand on her now, because I need her, maybe every bit as much as she needs me.

I step forward and curl my arms around her, feeling my heart beating firmly against her head, which rests on my chest. I hold her and hold her and hold her, and I feel her body shaking as she sobs into me, but then I realize I'm shaking too, just letting go, letting everything out of me, because she's my mother again, and she can make all the bad stuff go away.

I don't know how long we stand there, just hugging, just being mother and son again, but by the time we pull apart there's snow on our eyebrows and in our hair from the big, fluffy flakes that have begun to fall, coating everything, including us, in white.

"Want to come inside?" I ask.

She bites her lip and nods, frozen tears on her pale cheeks.

Her tears melt from the warmth of the fire while we sit next to each other, watching Jolie sleep. We don't say anything, except when, from time to time, Mother strokes Jolie's hair and murmurs, "My baby, oh, my sweet baby."

I just watch her, wonder how things could've been different had my father not died, or if mother was able to cope with it better. Would we be different, Jolie and I? How much was lost by my mother's actions, by her weakness? Although I don't want it to, my red, red temper starts to rise.

I clench my fists in my lap to try to squeeze it back down.

Mother's eyes flick to my hands. "I know, Dazz," she says. "You're angry. You have every right to be." She won't look at me, keeps her eyes on Jolie, and I don't blame her. I'd be scared of me too if I were in her position.

"You as good as abandoned us," I say through my teeth.

"I know."

"Father didn't have a choice—it was the disease that took him—but you—"

"I know."

"You could've been stronger, could've taken care of us, helped us through the loss that hurt us every bit as much as it hurt you."

"I know, Dazz."

"Jolie was just a little girl...*is* just a little girl. And Wes...Wes had to become a man, take care of all of us, well before any kid should have to. And now he's..." And I can't say it, can't say it, not one more time.

"I know, Dazz."

"You know nothing!" I rage, burning a hole in the side of her head with my eyes. Still she won't look at me, because she's too weak, like she's always been. "Look at me!" I demand, and she flinches a little, her cheek raised, turning red, like she's been slapped.

314

Slowly, so slowly, she turns to face me, her eyes filled with moisture and failure. "I'm sorry, I—"

She reaches for me, but I'm not ready to touch her, still hot and quivering with anger.

"—I hate myself for it," she says, the tears dripping out of her eyes and falling all the way to my feet, splashing on my boots.

The hurt, the anger, the accusations, all of it, falls away from me, leaving me as bare as if I was naked, stripped to my very soul. Before me sits a broken woman, my mother, who's punishing herself for what she's done far more than I ever could. And she won't...nay, *can't* get through this without me supporting her, especially with Father and Wes gone. All we've got is each other and Jolie, and that has to be enough, will be enough. I'm sure of it.

I push into her arms for the second time, clutch her tighter than before.

When I pull back, I say, "Let me make you a cup of tea," and her teary smile warms me more than the fire, or a cup of tea, ever could.

~~~

"Thank you," I say, having spoken those words many times before, but never meaning them as much as now. Mother told me how Wilde helped her over the past few days, how without her she'd never have defeated the drugs.

"I'm just glad I could help," Wilde says, and I can tell she means her words too.

It's just us, walking through the woods on the edge of the village, while my mother, Skye, and Buff look after my sister.

It's the first time I've left the house in days, and the cool chill of the air makes me feel alive again. And going with Wilde…that was my request.

"Wes and I," I say, my voice cracking slightly, as it always does when I say my brother's name, "we tried so many times…"

"It's okay," Wilde says, taking my hand, squeezing it, making me feel better with only those two words and her simple touch.

I can't help but think about how different someone's touch can feel from another's. When Skye holds my hand, it's like my whole body's on fire, reaching for hers, pushing for her, needing to be closer to every part of her. And when I held my mother's hand earlier today, it felt warm and safe. But now, holding Wilde's hand, it's different still. A whole world of different, like nothing I've ever felt before. So full of caring and mystery and *strength*, like she's giving me her strength through my glove, through my skin, charging it into me. And although she only feels sisterly to me, I can see why Buff is so taken by her.

"How did you do it?" I ask. I have to know, in case my mother ever falls again—so I can save her myself.

Wilde releases my hand, extends her palm, and catches a snowflake on it. We both stop walking as she studies it, as if committing every last detail to her memory. I watch her, somewhat awkwardly, unsure of what to do or say.

When the snowflake finally melts from the body heat coming through her glove, she looks at me and says, "Everything beautiful must die eventually. And to her, your father was the most beautiful thing in the world. All she needed was to understand that."

And, of course, that explains everything and nothing, but I'm thankful for it either way.

~~~

I still feel sort of awkward being alone with him, but I couldn't put it off any longer, so I pulled him aside.

Feve stares at me with dark eyes, waiting expectantly. "Are we just going to look at each other all day, Icy?" he asks.

I take a deep breath. "Look, I know things have been...*rocky* for us from the start, but I want to thank you. I don't know if my sister will wake up, but she'd be dead without you; and you never backed down from a fight that wasn't really yours in the first place. So thank you."

Feve raises his chin, cocks his head to the side, looks at me thoughtfully. "I still don't like you much," he says, "but I accept your thanks. And you did save my life once. Who knows, maybe we'll become friends one day."

*Not today*, I think. "Maybe," I say, nodding.

# Thirty-Five

They're leaving later today, Siena and Circ and Wilde and Feve and *Skye*.

Going to find the Stormers. To find Jade, if she's still alive. It may be the last time I see any of them again. Buff's going too, even though I'm not. He said he'll get my revenge for me, as long as I take care of his family.

I'm scared of losing all of them, but I won't abandon my family, not when we're so broken to pieces, and yet feeling like we have the potential to be whole again.

Skye said she'll come around later to say goodbye, but I think she's delaying it as much as I am.

Mother's out. I know, it sounds weird even to me. She hasn't been out in a long time, doing normal things. The bakery, which was burned to the ground during the Stormer attack, has been temporarily relocated and is back up and running, so she took some of Abe's silver and went with Wilde to buy some fresh bread. I'm thankful we don't have to eat Buff's hard rolls anymore.

I'm holding Jolie's hand, just holding it, telling her a story. A story about her brother's bravery, about how Wes was her hero, trying to break down walls to get to her, to save her. How he gave his life to save hers. My tears are flowing before I'm even halfway finished.

That's when I feel it.

A twitch. Her finger moves beneath my grasp.

I swear it does.

I stop speaking, stop moving, wait.

Nothing.

Nothing.

My imagination or a random muscle spasm. Nothing more. I can't hope for more.

So I go back to telling my story, hoping for the day when a twitch is real and turns into more—

She twitches again and I know this one *is* real because right after it her mouth opens and she yawns—really yawns!—lifts an arm above her head and stretches—

And I'm staring, just staring, tingling all over, my mouth gaping open, but sort of turning into a smile, but sort of not, because I could wake up anytime and it could all be a dream, but then she's opening her eyes, pushing the sleep—the long, long sleep—out of them with a little fist, the way she always has and—

—looking at me, really looking at me, with adoring eyes that I've missed so much, missed more than I even realized until I see them right now, at just this perfect, perfect moment.

"Dazz?" she says, and it's the same voice that spoke to me when the king had her, when he was stabbing her, trying to take my whole life away from me for no reason other than he could. But she's not in his grasp anymore, won't ever be in his grasp again, and I drop to my knees and I hug her, feeling an explosion of warmth and love running along and through every part of me, concentrating in my chest, right where my heart is beating furiously for my sister. My sister who's alive.

Alive for good.

~~~

I've been arguing with Jolie for near on an icin' hour now.

After all the tears and the hugs and the mourning for Wes and the big family reunion with my mother, Jolie demanded I tell her everything. So I told her the whole story, and I told her the parts about Skye—leaving out certain details, of course—three times over, because she wanted to hear them again and again, and I'd do pretty much anything for her right now.

That's when the arguments began.

"You have to go with them," Jolie insists again, trying to sit up.

And, of course, that's the one thing I won't do for her right now.

I gently guide her head back onto her pillow. "I'm not leaving you," I say, refusing to back down. "Either of you," I add, looking at my mother, who's standing—actually standing—her hands on her hips.

"I'm fine now, Dazz, I swear it," my mother says.

I roll my eyes. "I've heard that before," I say, "but without Wilde here to work her magic, will you really be fine?"

She nods but even she doesn't have much belief behind it. Whatever influence Wilde has on her ability to stay clean, it's stronger than I think either of us fully understands.

There's a knock on the door and I know it's time. Time for Skye to say goodbye. Time for everyone to say goodbye.

But it's not. Not quite yet. Only Wilde stands at the door when I open it.

Her timing is so uncanny I'm beginning to think she really does have magic inside her.

"I've made a decision," she says.

"I have too," I say, inviting her in with a sweep of my arm.

My mother greets her with a fierce hug. "How are you feeling?" Wilde asks.

"Better than ever," Mother says. "I've got my daughter back." She motions to the bed, where Jolie's sitting up, even though I've told her time and time again that she needs to rest a bit longer.

"Are you...are you from fire country?" Jolie asks, eyes wider and whiter than snow-covered boulders.

"I am," Wilde says, approaching my sister with graceful steps. She takes Jolie's hands in hers. "It's a true pleasure to finally meet you."

Jolie stares at her, as if mesmerized, taking in every part of her, from her long black hair to her brown skin. "You look strange," Jolie says and I suck in a sharp breath.

"Jolie!" I say, feeling embarrassment flush my skin.

"Sorry, I didn't mean anything by it," Jolie says, not sounding that sorry. "I mean you're beautiful, but not like my mother is beautiful. Different."

"It's okay," Wilde says. "You're beautiful, too, in a way that's different too. A very good way."

At that, Jolie smiles, and I'm happy she's getting on with one of my new friends, but it doesn't change what has to happen today. "You said you came to a decision?" I say.

Still holding my sister's hands, Wilde says, "Yes. I've decided to stay."

"What?" I blurt out. "Stay where?"

"Here. With your family. With your mother, for a little while."

Her words float across the room, but they're strange and I get the sense that they'll drift all the way into the fire and burn to ash if I don't grab ahold of them. "But the others, they need you," I say.

"No," she says. "They need *you*."

Jolie claps her little hands. "See, I told you, Dazz."

"Nay, I can't," I say. "I can't."

"Yes, you can," Wilde persists. "You needn't worry about a thing while you're gone. We'll stay here for a while, until your sister recovers, and then they'll travel with me to fire country. My people need me now more than ever, and I fear I've been gone too long already."

"To fire country?" I say.

Wilde nods. "If they're willing."

"Oh, Mother, can we?" Jolie says, practically squirming with excitement.

"Mother," I say sharply.

She looks at me, at Jolie, at Wilde, and then says, "We can and we will."

~~~

322

It's almost time to go and I still can't believe I'm going. I still don't know if I should. But iced if I can argue with Jolie, she's got a stubborn streak a mountain high and wider than fire country.

Jolie's met everyone, and although she still seems somewhat in awe of my friends from fire country, she seems perfectly at ease with them too.

First she thanked Feve about a million times for saving her life, which was sort of funny to watch because he didn't seem that comfortable with all the praise. Eventually he left to wait for us outside.

Then, when she saw Siena and Circ holding hands, she thought it best to investigate their relationship, asking every question she could think of about how it started, how long they've known each other, and everything in between. Her curiosity made me laugh because it wasn't that different than my own, when we were in the dungeons.

When she got tired of that, she latched onto Skye and now appears intent on talking her ear off.

"What's it like to live on sand? I don't really know what sand is, but it sounds nice. Saaand. It's even fun to say the word. How hot is it where you come from? Hotter than summer here? Is my brother a good kisser? I bet he is. Will I like fire country?" Jolie continues to let loose a random assortment of questions, answering half of them herself, as Skye scratches her head. Even she's baffled by what to make of my sister.

"Uhh…" she says, probably wondering which question to answer first.

"I think that's enough for one day, Joles. I'm sure Wilde'll be happy to answer your many questions over time, while we're gone," I say, sitting on her bed next to Skye.

"You'll be back soon, right Dazz?" Her nose crinkles up earnestly.

"I'll do my best," I say. "But you'll be safe with Wilde and with Mother." I can't believe I'm saying it and actually meaning it, but it's true. Mother's better than she's been in a long time and I have a feeling this time it might stick.

Jolie's nose uncrinkles and her eyebrows lift, her eyes widen. "Dazz, you find her, you find that girl, and all the rest too," she says, hugging me tight.

I hold her close, feel her warm little body, so real, so alive, her heart pumping. The world is right again. So right. "I will," I whisper into her hair. "We all will."

I stand up, trying to hide the tears in my eyes. Mother awaits.

"You don't worry about anything at all while you're gone," she says. "I'm better, and with Wilde here, I'll stay better."

"I'll hold you to that," I say, embracing her, feeling her frail body fold into mine. "Goodbye, Mother."

"Goodbye, Son."

Somewhat solemnly, we leave, Siena then Circ then Skye then Buff.

I start to follow but then turn in the doorway. "Thank you, Wilde," I say. "Thank you for everything."

She just nods and smiles. "Go," she says.

Out in the autumn-cold, I pull in a deep breath of cool, crisp air, hold it for a second, and then push it out in a cloud of steam. Watching me, Skye says, "I still can't get over how we all breathe smoke up 'ere."

I just smile and drape an arm over her shoulder, which earns me a punch in the gut that I think is meant to be soft and friendly, but which hurts like chill and leaves me gasping. I try to hide how much it really hurts while Skye laughs.

We make our way through and out of the Brown District, ignoring the stares we get from all the Icers who still haven't gotten used to seeing brown-skinned folk walking around town. You'd think after having the dark riders charging around they wouldn't bat an eye, but sometimes change don't sit so well with folks. After a couple of glances though, they go back to whatever it is that they're doing—repairing burnt houses, shoveling snow, or chasing their kids around.

Cutting across the space that connects the four Districts, we head for the White District. Entering the upscale area, it's strange to see so many of the beautiful houses devastated by the fires set by the Stormers. A roof missing here, a once-beautiful mahogany door charred black there. But the really interesting thing: there are Brown District men repairing everything. Even after all that's happened, the rich folk can't bring themselves to do an honest day's work, relying on the sweat and muscle of the lower classes. Things are changing alright, but sometimes change is slower than you want, while other times it's faster than a dark rider's gallop.

As we pass a familiar house with a red door that evidently escaped the Stormers' fires, I see a familiar scene. The door is thrown open and a guy pops out, chased by a vase, which hits him in the back of the head, sending him tumbling out into the snow. "And stay out!" a shrill, witch-like voice hollers after him before the door slams, jarring clumps of snow off the roof.

I laugh when I recognize the guy. Soft-hands LaRoy, previously known as girlfriend-stealer. Little did he know he was doing me a favor. It seems things didn't work out for him and the witch so well after all.

I approach him, chuckling to myself.

When he sees me he shrinks back into the snowdrift, hands above his head. I fake a punch and he shrinks further still. Smiling, I extend a hand, which he stares at with the most disturbed look on his face. "Take it," I say.

After a moment's hesitation he does, and I pull him to his feet, using a hand to brush the snow off his back. "Trust me," I say, "you're better off without her."

He shrugs and then flinches when I fake another punch. Despite all that's happened, it'd feel good to hit him just once, but I won't today. There's always another fight to be fought, and although I'm looking forward to the next one, I now know I can control myself.

I return to Skye's side. "What the scorch?" she says, raising her eyebrows.

"Long story," I say. "Maybe I'll tell you on the way to storm country."

She punches me in the ribs again and I'm beginning to think that means she likes me, which is good enough for me.

We leave the village, and with the setting sun trying to push red light through the thick, gray cloud cover, we march into the forest, two Icers and four fire country natives, off to save the world, or at least a few kids. They're someone's daughters, sons, brothers, sisters—special to someone. Special to Skye and Siena.

And I'll do everything I can to save every last one of them. Just like my sister.

Just like Jolie.

~*~

Keep reading for a sneak peak at the action-packed sequel, book three of the Country Saga (a Dwellers sister series), *Water & Storm Country*, coming June 7, 2013!

# Acknowledgements

As always, I have to thank all the readers, new and old, who have stuck with me through this series. Between the three books in the Dwellers Saga and the two so far in the Country Saga, I know it takes a huge level of commitment to be a part of it, and for that I thank you. But we're not done yet! I'm especially excited about the third book in the Country Saga, *Water & Storm Country*, which will answer a lot of your questions about the Cure and who's behind, in Siena's words, *the 'spiracy*. And then, of course, *The Earth Dwellers* will smash the two series together in a final seventh book (may the sun goddess and Heart of the Mountain be with me as I attempt to not screw this up!), in what I hope will be an epic end to a long adventure. Thanks for sticking with me!

My wife, Adele, gets the biggest hug ever, for being the ultimate supporter and challenger, keeping me from making stupid (and cheesy) decisions in my stories. You are more than just a friend and wife, you're my soul mate and partner for life and beyond!

Thanks to Rhomy at Black Lion Book Tours, who put together the perfect blog tour to get the word out!

To my remarkably talented cover artist, Regina Wamba, you've created the perfect book cover to contrast the cover for Fire Country, and I'm sure your two covers will grace many a bookshelf. Thanks for your dedication to my vision and to the series.

Next, a rapid-fire thank you thank you thank you to my beta readers. You really rocked on this book, taking it to levels even I didn't realize it could hit. So thanks to Laurie Love,

Alexandria Theodosopoulos, Kayleigh-Marie Gore, Kerri Hughes, Terri Thomas, Lolita Verroen, Rachel Schade, and Ventura Dennis for being awesome. And a special thanks to Mr. Anthony Briggs Jr. for pushing me to develop my story in ways I never imagined. Many of the jaw-dropping moments in the book are a result of your gentle but honest feedback.

To my super-secret street team (shhh, don't tell anyone who you are), thanks for being even more vocal (if that's possible) in promoting my books than ever before. I get tears in my eyes when I see what you do for me on a daily basis. Your friendship is for a lifetime.

Discover other books by David Estes available through the author's official website: http://davidestesbooks.blogspot.com or through select online retailers including Amazon.

<u>Young-Adult Books by David Estes</u>

<u>The Dwellers Saga:</u>
Book One—The Moon Dwellers
Book Two—The Star Dwellers
Book Three—The Sun Dwellers
Book Four—The Earth Dwellers (coming September 2013!)

<u>The Country Saga (A Dwellers sister series):</u>
Book One—Fire Country
Book Two—Ice Country
Book Three—Water & Storm Country (coming June 7, 2013!)

<u>The Evolution Trilogy:</u>
Book One—Angel Evolution
Book Two—Demon Evolution
Book Three—Archangel Evolution

<u>Children's Books by David Estes</u>

The Nikki Powergloves Adventures:
Nikki Powergloves—A Hero Is Born
Nikki Powergloves and the Power Council
Nikki Powergloves and the Power Trappers
Nikki Powergloves and the Great Adventure
Nikki Powergloves vs. the Power Outlaws (Coming in 2013!)

# Connect with David Estes Online

Goodreads Fan Group:
http://www.goodreads.com/group/show/70863-david-estes-fans-and-ya-book-lovers-unite

Facebook:
http://www.facebook.com/pages/David-Estes/130852990343920

Author's blog:
http://davidestesbooks.blogspot.com

Smashwords:
http://www.smashwords.com/profile/view/davidestes100

Goodreads author page:
http://www.goodreads.com/davidestesbooks

Twitter:
https://twitter.com/#!/davidestesbooks

# About the Author

David Estes was born in El Paso, Texas but moved to Pittsburgh, Pennsylvania when he was very young. He grew up in Pittsburgh and then went to Penn State for college. Eventually he moved to Sydney, Australia where he met his wife and soul mate, Adele, who he's now been happily married to for more than two years.

A reader all his life, David began writing novels for the children's and YA markets in 2010, and has completed 14 novels, 12 of which have been published. In June of 2012, David became a fulltime writer and is now travelling the world with Adele while he writes books, and she writes and takes photographs.

David gleans inspiration from all sorts of crazy places, like watching random people do entertaining things, dreams (which he jots copious notes about immediately after waking up), and even from thin air sometimes!

David's a writer with OCD, a love of dancing and singing (but only when no one is looking or listening), a mad-skilled ping-pong player, an obsessive Goodreads group member, and prefers writing at the swimming pool to writing at a table. He loves responding to e-mails, Facebook messages, Tweets, blog comments, and Goodreads comments from his readers, all of whom he considers to be his friends.

# A SNEAK PEEK
# WATER & STORM COUNTRY
# BOOK 3 OF THE COUNTRY SAGA

Available anywhere e-books are sold June 7, 2013!

# One

Standing on the deck watching the sunrise, I can't hold back my smile. The air is crisp, a little colder than usual for this time of yar, numbing the tip of my nose, filling each breath with the distinct smell of salt and brine. While endless yellow clouds patrol the ocean, the half-sun splashes purples, pinks and oranges on the ever reddening morning sky.

To the starboard side I can see the shoreline, sandy at first, and then green, rolled out like a welcome mat. Above the land, the yellow clouds darken to black.

In the waters surrounding the ship, I see the familiar dark triangles of sharp-tooths breaking the surface, patrolling the ocean, hoping for an execution or a natural death to give them the chance to taste human flesh yet again.

But even the constant presence of the sharp-tooths can't wipe away my grin. Not today.

The ship lurches beneath me, riding the crest of yet another big rolling wave. But I don't stumble, don't lose my balance, don't so much as sway from the ship's movements or the tumultuous wind that whips my shirt in a frenzy around me.

Steady.

Balanced.

A seaman, through and through.

And smiling, bigger than the ocean, relishing the salt spray splashing my face as a wave crashes against the hull, living for the feel of the power rolling and throbbing beneath my feet, laughing when a flock of white-winged big-chins dive bomb the water, each emerging with a nice-sized fish clamped tightly between their beaks.

This is the life. The life of a Soaker. A typical morning in water country.

My life, all about to change.

"Huck," a deep voice rumbles from behind. Not a murmur, not a greeting: a command.

Startled, I turn quickly, my smile vanishing in an instant. "Father?" I say.

"Admiral Jones," he says, but I don't understand. Admiral Jones is what his shipmen call him.

"Sir?" I say.

"Son," he says, taking two steps forward to reach my side. "Today you become a man." His words are the truth but I know he doesn't mean them. Not after what happened. Not after what always happens.

Today's the start of my fourteenth yar, the yar I cast off my childish ways and become a real seaman, not just the son of one. "I'm ready," I say, wondering if it's true. I desperately want to look down, to look away, to escape the piercing stare of my father's crystal blue eyes, but I don't—

—because men don't look away for anyone;

—men aren't scared of anything;

—men don't cry.

My father's creed, one I've heard a million and a half times.

And men don't fail their fathers, like I have so many times before.

Resting a hand on my shoulder, my father—Admiral Jones—says, "Are you? Ready?"

Uh…I think? Maybe? "Aye," I say, keeping my gaze on his but feeling his disappointment tremble through me.

"Hmm," Father says, chewing on his lip. "I suppose we'll find out, won't we?"

I hold my breath because the way he's looking at me, so full of doubt, so uncertain, with one eyebrow raised, his nostrils flared slightly, his expression lopsided, seems to pick me apart from the outside in, like a big-chin tearing at the flesh of a fish. If I breathe I'm afraid it will come out in a ragged shudder, and then he'll know.

He'll know I'm not a man, even if I'm fourteen now.

I feel my face warm while I hold my breath for ten seconds, twenny, as he continues to stare at me, his eyes probing, closing in on the truth.

Just when I start to feel a little lightheaded, he looks away, turns, stomps off, his boots hammering the wooden deck like a funeral drum. I let my breath out as slowly as I can, closing my eyes. "I *am* a man," I whisper under my breath, trying to convince myself. "I won't fail you. Not anymore." If only I had the guts to say it loud enough for him to hear.

"Walk with me, Son," my father says without turning around.

"Aye, aye, Father," I say.

"Admiral Jones," he replies, and I finally understand. By blood he's still my father, but by rights he's the admiral, and I'm one of his men, subject to all the same rules as anyone else.

"Admiral Jones," I correct, wondering why saying it this time doesn't feel nearly as good as it always did when I practiced in my cabin.

I hustle to catch up, trying to stride the way he does across the deck. Long steps, chin up, eyes sweeping the ship, taking everything in. As we walk aft, toward the rear of the ship, two of my father's lieutenants are swashbuckling to the left, or starboard side. Their swords ring out loud and shrill and practiced as they parry and slash and block. It's a morning ritual for these two, Cain and Hobbs, one I've watched with a boyish interest many times before.

When we approach, they stop, planting their blades point-first into the deck. They each raise a flat hand to their foreheads in a rigid salute. "At ease, lieutenants," my father says.

They relax their arms but continue to stand at attention. "Mornin', Admiral…Huck," Cain says, his blue uniform turning dark with sweat stains beneath his armpits. He flashes me a smile.

"Mornin', Cain," I say, smiling back.

"*Lieutenant* Cain," my father corrects sharply. I look up at him and he's giving me those dark eyes again, sparkling blue under the morning sun but shrouded in shadow from the brim of his admiral's cap.

"Lieutenant Cain," I mumble, feeling stupid. How can I be a man if I can't even talk right?

"Mornin', Huck," Hobbs says with a sneer. Unlike Cain, he's never liked me.

I frown at his half-smirk. "Mornin'," I say under my breath.

"*Lieutenant,*" my father says again.

Stupid, stupid. "Lieutenant," I say.

"So you're a man today," Cain says, slapping me on the back with a firm hand. It hurts a little but I've never felt better.

"I am," I say, beaming.

"That remains to be seen," my father says, wiping the grin off my face with his words. How do I prove myself to him after what happened two years ago? My mother's face flashes through my mind: her quick smile, her green eyes, her long blonde hair. The way she'd read to me at night. Tales of great battles against the Stormers, our independence won and lost and won again. Many years ago.

Her face again, not smiling this time: awash with terror, twisted and stricken and looking up at me, pleading—her eyes always pleading...

"Huck!" my father barks.

I snap out of the memory, shake my head. Hobbs is snickering while Cain looks at me under a furrowed brow. Father's lips are unreadable beneath his thick salt-and-pepper beard. "Wha—what?" I stammer.

"Lieutenant Hobbs asked you a question," my father says.

I glance at Hobbs, who looks smug, his hands on his hips. "Aye?" I say. Catching myself, I add, "Lieutenant."

"Have you been practicing your sword work?" he asks.

Not the question I expected. For a moment I let the warmth of pride fill my heart, because I have. Been practicing, that is. Every spare moment I've been practicing with the wooden blade my father gave me when I turned seven. Fighting the other young boys on the ship, parrying with masts, battling heavy bags of potatoes and rice. Swinging and swinging my practice sword until it's become a part of me, an extension of my arm and hand.

337

I stick my chest out and say, "Aye."

"Show us," Hobbs says, a gleam in his dark brown eyes.

I look at him sideways, wondering what he's up to, but not wanting to disappoint my father yet again, I start to pull my wooden sword from where it hangs loosely from my belt.

"No," Hobbs says. "Not with that. With this." He reaches down and picks up a sword, shorter than his, but shiny and sharp and *real*. And the hilt…

—it has the Admiral's markings on it, a woman, beautiful and shapely, her hair long and falling in front of her shoulders to cover her naked breasts. And beneath: the skin of her stomach gives way to a long tail with scaly fins, like a fish. A merwoman. Identical to the figurehead at the bow of the ship. The ship's namesake. *The Merman's Daughter.*

The sword is my birthright, the sword I will wear until my father dies and I inherit his long blade. With a slight bow, Hobbs holds it in front of him reverently, offering it to me. Through his long blonde bangs, which hang over his eyes, I see him wink at me as I take it.

Something's up. Hobbs never winks.

In my grasp, the sword seems to gain weight and I almost drop it, awkwardly bringing my offhand up to balance it. I hear Hobbs snort, but I ignore him, because this is my time, my day.

My right.

Slowly, I raise the sword to eye level, watching in awe as it seems to catch every ray of red sunlight, sending them shooting in all directions.

My right. My sword.

"Why don't you give it a try?" Hobbs says, and I sense something in his voice—a challenge.

"Hobbs," Cain says sharply, sounding sterner than I've ever heard him.

"Uhh, aye," I say, looking between them, wondering why Hobbs looks so mischievous and Cain so angry.

I move a safe distance away, raise my sword to attack position, my feet planted firmly as I've been taught. I start to swing, but stop when Hobbs laughs. "I mean against a real opponent," he says.

I look back, my prideful chest deflating. "Sir?" I say. I can't possibly fight him. He's a man, and I'm….not, regardless of my age and who my father is.

I can feel a crowd gathering, their boots shuffling on the deck. I whirl around, taking them in, the eyes—so many eyes—staring, waiting, watching. To see what I'll do. A test. This is exactly the kind of thing my father would do.

My chance—

To prove myself—

To him.

Maybe my last chance. My mother's face, open-mouthed and screaming. Pleading and pleading.

I grit my teeth, shake my head, nod firmly at Hobbs. Raise my sword with two hands in his direction.

He laughs, deep and loud. "Me? You thought you were going to fight me? Please, kid, don't insult me. You'll fight someone closer to your own size." At the same time as I feel angry heat swallow my neck—because he called me *kid* on the day I become a man—I breathe out a silent sigh of relief. Perhaps I have a chance after all.

I look around, seeing a couple of the guys I practice with, Jobe and Ben, looking almost as scared as I feel, afraid they're about to be asked into the circle with me to prove their manhood in front of an audience. "Who?" I say, my voice quivering around the single word.

"We don't want to give you more than you can handle for your first real fight," Hobbs says, walking a lazy circle around me. Meaning...*what?*

"You'll fight one of the bilge rats," he says, the edge of his lip turning up.

"What?" I say, more sharply than I intended. What the hell is going on? "But I can't possibly..."

"You can and you will," my father interjects. "Remember what I taught you, Son."

I frown, remembering his lessons well. The bilge rats are nothing more than swine, less than human, here to serve us and be trodden under our feet. Nary better than animals, they are. When I asked him where the bilge come from, he said, "From nowhere," like they just popped out of the ground or were fished from the ocean or dropped from the sky. He wouldn't say any more than that and I knew better than to ask.

I nod. If this is what I must do to become a man, I'll do it.

"Bring him in!" Hobbs hollers and I sense movement on the port side of the ship. The crowd parts and a skinny, brown boy stumbles toward me, being half-dragged by a strong man I recognize as one of the oarsmen. The bilge rat's eyes are wide and scared, darting around him, like at any moment someone might hit him. I've seen the boy before but have never spoken to him. Usually he's on his knees, scrubbing the decks, his head hanging in defeat and resignation.

Less than human.

The big oarsman shoves him forward and he trips, nearly falls into me, but I catch his arm firmly, hold him up. He stares at the sword in my other hand, his jaw tight. For a moment I look at him—really look at him—like I never have before. For this one time, he's not just an animal, not just an object to be ignored, like my father always taught me. He looks so human, his skin browner than mine, aye, but not so different than me after all.

He jerks away from my grip and a piece of his dirty, tattered shirt comes away in my fist. I stare at it for a moment and then let it drop to my feet. Hobbs hands the boy an old sword, even shorter than mine and blunt and rusty around the edges. Unblinking, the boy takes it, swallowing a heavy wad of spittle that slides down his throat in a visible lump.

How can I fight someone like him?

I have to.

But how? He's so weak-looking, so scared…

I have no choice.

"Fight," Hobbs says, backing away, smiling bigger than ever.

I raise my sword, which has fallen loosely to my side. The bilge rat continues looking at his rusty blade, as if it's a snake, but then suddenly grips it tightly, his brown knuckles turning white. He lifts his chin and our eyes meet, and I see…

—hurt

—and anger

—and fear, too, but not as much as before.

His mouth opens and he screams, right at me, a cry of war.

I take a step back just before he charges, cheers rising up around me like sails on a summer wind.

# Two
# Sadie

The wind rushes over me and around me and *through* me, blasting my dark hair against my back, flattening my black robe against my chest.

I lengthen my strides, the dark skin of my legs flashing from beneath my robe with each step. Muscles tight, heartbeat heavy, mind alive, I race across the storm country plains, determined to surprise my mother with the speed of my arrival back at the camp.

Lonely dark-trunked leafless trees force me to change my direction from time to time, their bare scraggly branches creaking and swaying in the wind like dancing skeletons.

I can already see the circle of tents in the distance, smoke wafting in lazy curls from their midst, evidence of the morning cook fires. Although I left when it was still black out, the sky is mixed now, streaked with shards of red slicing between the ever-present dark clouds.

With the camp in sight, I call on every bit of strength I have left, what I've been saving for my final sprint. I go faster and faster and faster still, unable to stop a smile from bending my lips.

I close in on the tents, sweat pouring from my skin as excitement fills me.

That's when I hear the scream.

Carried on the wind, the cry is ragged and throat-burning.

I stab one of my dark boots in the ground, skid to a stop, breathing heavy, swiveling my head around to locate the bearer of the yell. My breath catches when I see it: a ship, moving swiftly along the coast, the wind at its back filling its white sails, propelling it forward as it cuts through the waves.

A boisterous cheer rises up from the ship, and I exhale, forcing out a breath before sucking another one in. The Soakers are here!

Instinctively, my gaze draws away from the ship, following the coastline, easily picking out the other white triangles cutting into the base of the scarlet horizon. More ships—at least a dozen. The entire Soaker fleet.

I've got to warn the camp.

I take off, pushing my legs to fly, fly fly, muttering encouragement under my breath. Before I reach the camp, however, a cry goes up from one of the lookouts, Hazard, a huge man with the blackest skin I've ever seen, even blacker than a cloudy, starless night. He yells once, a warning, and soon the camp is full of noise. Commands to rush to arms, to secure the children, to ready the horses are spouted from the mouth of the war leader, who I can just make out between the tents.

His name is Gard, and if Hazard is huge, then he's a giant, as tall and as wide as the tents. He's already on his horse, Thunder, which is the largest in the herd, the only one strong enough to carry our war leader's weight. Gard and Thunder turn away as one to the south, where the other horses are tied.

I dart between the first two tents I come to, slip inside the camp, and narrowly avoid getting trampled by a dozen men and women warriors charging to follow Gard. The Riders. Trained from birth to be warriors, to defend my people from the Soakers, they ride the Escariot, the black horses that have served my people in peace and war for every generation since the Great Rock landed on earth.

Trained like me, by fire and the sword.

"Sadie!" I hear someone yell.

I turn, see my father beckoning to me, his face neutral but serious. Hesitating, my eyes flick to where the warriors are disappearing behind the tents, soon to emerge as Riders, their steeds snorting and stomping in preparation for war. All I want is to watch them go, to see my mother flash past on Shadow, her face full of the stoic confidence I've seen on the rare occasions she's been called to arms.

Unbidden, my legs carry me toward my father, who graces me with a grim smile, his dark skin vibrant under the morning sunlight. His thin arms and legs look even thinner after seeing Hazard and Gard.

"Come inside," he says.

"I want to watch," I admit.

"I know," he says. "Come inside."

Of course he knows. He knows *everything*. But I follow him into our tent anyway.

Even when my father seals the flaps at the entrance, the thin-skinned walls do little to block out the rally cries of the Riders as they organize themselves.

When my father, the Man of Wisdom, turns to look at me, I say, "I'm almost sixteen, Father."

"You're not yet," he says patiently, motioning for me to sit.

I ignore the offer. "I need to see this," I say.

Father sighs, sits cross-legged, his bony knees protruding from the skirts of his thin white robe. "You do not need to see this." Who am I to argue with the wisest man in the village?

"I'm not your little girl anymore," I say, pleading now. I kneel in front of him, my hands clasped. "Just let me watch."

He grimaces, as if in pain, and I wonder how I came from him. My mother makes sense. She's strong, like me, like Gard, like the other Riders. But my father is so…weak. Not just physically either. I know he's wise and all that, but I swear he's scared of his own shadow sometimes.

"Please," I say again.

He shakes his head. "It's not your time," he says.

"When will be my time?" I say, slumping back on my heels.

"Soon enough."

Not soon enough for me. It's not like I'm asking to fight, although Mother Earth knows I want to do that too. I want to see what the Riders do, for real, not some training exercise. I want to see my mother fight, to kill, to knock back the Soakers to their Earth-forsaken ships.

I've got nothing else to say to the great Man of Wisdom sitting before me, so I don't say anything, keep my head down, study the dirt beneath my fingernails.

The cries outside the tent die down, dwindling to a whisper as the clop of the horses' hooves melt into the distance. The world goes silent, and all I can hear is my father's breathing. My heart beats in my head. Weird.

I look up and his eyes are closed, his hands out, his forearms resting on his knees. Meditating. Like I've seen him do a million times before, his lips murmuring silent prayers. In other words, doing nothing. Nothing to help anyway. Meditating won't stop the Soakers from killing the Riders, from barging into our camp and slaughtering us all like the frightened weaklings that we are, hiding in our tents.

Slowly, slowly, slowly, I rise and move toward the tent flaps, careful not to scuff my boots on the floor.

I creep past my father, and then he's behind me and my hand's on the flap, and I'm about to open it, and then—

—his hand flashes out and grabs my ankle, his grip much—much—firmer than I expected, holding me in place, hurting me a little.

"Nice try," he says, and I almost smile.

When I start to backtrack he releases me. Dramatically, I throw myself to the ground and curl up on a blanket, sighing heavily.

"There's nothing to watch anyway," he says in The Voice. Not his normal, everyday speaking voice, but the one that sounds deeper and more solid, like it comes from a place deep within his gut, almost like it's spoken by someone else who lives inside of him. A man greater than himself, full of power, barrel-chested and well-muscled—like Gard, a warrior.

The Voice.

When people hear The Voice, they listen.

Even I do. Well, usually. Because The Voice is never wrong.

I set my elbow on the ground and prop my head on the heel of my hand. "Why not?" I ask, suddenly interested in *everything* my father has to say—because he's not my father anymore. He's the Man of Wisdom.

Maybe the meditation wasn't him doing nothing after all.

His cheeks bulge, as if the words are right there, trying to force their way out. But when he blows out, it's just air, nothing more. Then he says, "Listen."

I cock my head, train my ear in the air, hear only the silence of a camp in hiding.

Silence.

Silence.

And then—

—the chatter of horses' hooves across the plains, getting louder, approaching a rumble, then becoming the distant growl of thunder.

"Now you can go," Father says in his normal voice, but I'm already on my feet, bursting from the tent opening, running for the edge of the camp while other Stormers are emerging from hiding.

I charge out of the camp and onto the plains, my footsteps drowned out by the grumble of the horses galloping toward me. Gard's in the front, leading, and he flies past me like I'm not even there. Another few Riders pass in similar fashion before I see her.

My mother, astride Shadow, her skin and robe so dark she almost looks like she's a part of her horse, a strange human-animal creature, fast and dangerous and ready.

She stops in front of me, perfect balanced, her sword in her hand.

"What happened?" I say.

She motions with her sword behind her, where, with the sun shimmering across the water, the white ships are sailing off into the distance, barely visible now.

"They're gone," I murmur.

*Water & Storm Country* by David Estes, coming June 7, 2013!

Printed in Great Britain
by Amazon.co.uk, Ltd.,
Marston Gate.